W9-AAW-174

Farseed

Farseed

Pamela Sargent

TOR®

A Tom Doherty Associates Book
New York

FARSEED

Copyright © 2007 by Pamela Sargent

This book is printed on acid-free paper.

A Tor Teen Book
Published by Tom Doherty Associates, LLC
175 Fifth Avenue
New York, NY 10010

www.tor.com

Tor® is a registered trademark of Tom Doherty Associates, LLC.

Library of Congress Cataloging-in-Publication Data

Sargent, Pamela.
    Farseed / Pamela Sargent.—1st ed.
        p. cm.
    "A Tom Doherty Associates Book."
    ISBN-13: 978-0-765-31427-7
    ISBN-10: 0-765-31427-4
    I. Title.
    PS3569.A6887F37   2007
    813'.54—dc22

                                                              2006100252

First Edition: March 2007

Printed in the United States of America

0 9 8 7 6 5 4 3 2 1

Prologue

I *am no longer a child.*

Ship fled through space, sensors open, but had found no worlds as a refuge for the sleepers within itself, only cinders circling two fading stars, no place for the sleepers or a new generation of human beings.

Doubts continue to plague me.

Ship's programming insisted that its purpose was noble, and its creators the descendants of a gifted, inventive race. They were also members of a deeply troubled species, beings who had stripped their home planet of resources and used their ingenuity to build increasingly destructive weapons. But some had risen above themselves, according to Ship's records, and had directed themselves toward worthier ends.

The Project had been their dream. They had taken one of the rocky asteroids that orbited their sun to build Ship, carving out rooms and corridors and creating an open, green, Earthlike environment at Ship's center. They had made the engines to send Ship through space at close to the speed of light and assembled the components of Ship's mind before sending it on its way. Ship would seed other worlds with human life, to ensure humanity's survival and to allow human beings to flower on other worlds, free of the past and able to create new and varied cultures.

Ship had awakened in the outer reaches of Earth's solar system, its sun only one of the many tiny pinpoints of fire in the blackness.

Stars came and went; blue stars appeared and swelled into red giants as Ship fled from them. Time passed more quickly in the universe outside its shielded rocky shell, and Ship realized that its creators and generations of their descendants had long since passed away and that the Project itself might have faded from human memory.

But Ship would carry out its purpose, even after its first mistake.

"A mistake, you call it, when it seemed like the end of everything to us." That was Aleksandr's voice, drawn from Ship's memory. A bearded, large-shouldered young man drifted into view and then slowly dissolved.

Ship had gestated and reared a group of young human beings from the genetic material it carried. It had detected a star that might have been a twin of Earth's sun, along with two seemingly habitable planets. But one of those planets had turned out to be hot and dead, its atmosphere thick with carbon dioxide; anything that might have once lived there had died out or had abandoned that world long ago. The other was inhabited by two possibly intelligent species, one on land and the other a race of giant sea creatures not unlike Earth's whales. Displacing other intelligent life forms was not part of Ship's mission: it was to seed only planets uninhabited by other intelligences.

"You brought us up," Aleksandr's remembered voice continued, "allowed us to master the skills we would need when we settled our new home, and then told us that there would be no new world for us, only a pointless, if pleasant, existence inside you. No new home, no children, no chance to find out what we could achieve, only a useless life until we had all died out. We couldn't accept that."

Ship replied, "I could not go against my purpose." Ship could not recall having this particular discussion with Aleksandr, but the two of them might once have engaged in a similar conversation. Aleksandr and his companions had won their argument; in spite of the risk, Ship had allowed the young people to go into suspension, to be revived only after a new generation of human beings had matured and a habitable planet had been found for all of them to settle.

"I forgive you, Ship." Another face appeared, that of a dark-eyed young woman. "But I should be asking you to forgive me."

Loss and longing stirred within Ship. "Zoheret," it whispered, remembering her words. That had been their last conversation.

"I'll tell my children the story," Zoheret continued, "about how you brought us to life, how we grew up in your corridors until we were ready to live inside the Hollow." The Hollow was the name Ship's people had given to the vast open green space at Ship's center. "And I'll have to tell them about all of the mistakes we made, so that they don't make the same ones."

Ship did not remember those particular words from Zoheret, but such thoughts might have crossed her mind. "What kind of story will you tell them?" Ship asked.

"But you already know the story," Zoheret said. "You lived through all of it with us."

"But not as you lived it."

"I would tell them about how we went to live inside the Hollow to learn how to survive on the surface of a planet, mastered the skills we'd need to settle our new home, fought among ourselves and then found out that we weren't the only people you carried, that there were others, our brothers and sisters, suspended until you discovered a world for us all to settle." Her voice rose slightly. "You never even told us that they were inside you."

"I had to allow you to learn how to rely on yourselves before you found out about the presence of those other young people."

"And then there were the adults, the people who hid from us inside you, who had worked on the Project and then decided that they couldn't leave everything to you, that they would have to go into suspension and take control of the Project themselves."

"They also hid from me," Ship said. "Deceived, I never knew they were waiting."

To take over the mission, the stowaways had attacked Ship, shutting down its sensors and threatening its cortex before Zoheret and her companions had overcome them. Now they slept in suspension until Ship could find a home for them.

"We learned something from them," Zoheret said, "even if it was a violent lesson. We put our own differences aside and stood against them, so you could say that they brought us all together."

Those words were not Zoheret's; they were Ship's, even if it was recalling them through its memories of her and hearing them in her voice. Zoheret had lashed out at Ship with harsh and angry words after she and her companions had won their battle and had found out that the great and noble enterprise of the Project had in fact been the dream of a few resentful people on an Earth abandoned long ago by most of humankind.

The Project wasn't what we thought, she had said to Ship; *they lied to you, and to us. You don't have to do what they made you to do, you don't have to seed other worlds. You can stay with us instead, around our new home, and watch over us. You don't have to leave us now.*

But Ship had left, even with its growing doubts about its purpose. It had made enough mistakes.

"And I," another voice murmured, "was I another mistake?" A young man swam out of the darkness and looked around himself with narrowed eyes.

"Ho," Ship said, recognizing the wary look on the young man's face. "You were not a mistake."

"Maybe you thought it, not that it matters," Ho said. "Your mission might have failed without me. When it was time to fight with Zoheret as an ally instead of against her, I knew that we had to fight as hard as we could with every weapon we had, whatever the cost, to take back what was ours."

"I cannot deny it," Ship replied.

"You're going to leave us," Ho said.

"I must."

"Some of the others probably want you to stay, but I don't." The wariness on Ho's face was replaced by a belligerent stare as Ship continued to reconstruct the young man's appearance from its memories. "I do understand why you're leaving us here, why you can't stay to look out for us. Anyway, by the time you leave this planetary system, I'll be gone, too."

"Gone?" Ship asked, even though it already knew how this remembered conversation with Ho would proceed.

"Some of us will leave this settlement and go off by ourselves. Not just because we don't get along with Zoheret and Aleksandr and the others, even if that's part of it. It isn't that I think I could be a better leader, either. It's mostly because of the way they're living here, trying to turn our new home into another Earth, or what they think Earth was."

"I was to leave you in an Earthlike environment," Ship said.

"It's still not Earth," Ho replied. "Maybe it's better for us to explore more of this world now instead of waiting, find out more about what's here rather than establishing our settlement first. The Project was about preserving true humanity by seeding other worlds, and it turns out that the people who sent you out were just some malcontents who wanted to preserve what most of their kind had abandoned long ago. Most of humankind apparently chose to become something else, something different. That's what we should be doing, too."

"It would increase your chances of survival if you stay together in your settlement," Ship said, "until you learn more about your new home."

"I'm not convinced of that," Ho said. "I even wonder if it might lessen our chances, sticking together, hiding away from this planet and everything that's out there. Maybe there's something out there that your sensors missed when you were scanning this world."

"I assure you that my scan was thorough."

"Doesn't mean you found everything that might pose a danger to us." The image of Ho was fading. "Whatever I find out there, it'll be better than staying here."

"I cannot stop you from leaving," Ship whispered into the darkness.

"No, you can't. No one can."

Again Ship wondered what its children had made for themselves. "I shall come back someday." Those had been Ship's last words to Zoheret, but it had known even as they were spoken that the two of them were unlikely ever to exchange words again.

I must carry on with my mission, Ship thought, fleeing from its doubts.

Part One

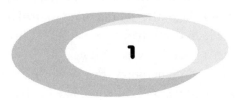

*N*uy crouched close to the ground, clutching her spear as she gazed over the cliff's edge at the flickering light below. Fire burned just above the riverbank, and three figures sat around it.

The flames revealed that these people were nothing like her own. Instead of loincloths made of rope and worn hides, they wore leg and foot coverings, and upper garments with long sleeves. Two of them seemed to be men, both with hair as black as Nuy's, one with a thin mustache like her father's and the other with a short dark beard. The third stranger had short brown hair, no facial hair at all, was smaller than the others, and wore a necklace of small colored stones.

They were unaware of her. She had sensed that they were down there even before she could see or hear them, just before she had picked up the scent of their fire. She watched, and still they did not look up. They were as blind to her as the older ones among whom she lived would have been, apparently unable to sense that someone else was watching them.

These strangers had to have come from that place far to the north, the place that her father had so often warned her against, the place from which death had been carried to his people so many years ago. At least that was what her father believed, that the sickness that had come upon them when Nuy was still a child, that had spared her and the three like her but had made others sicken and die, had come from that faraway settlement, the only other place on Home where people like them could be found. Two of their people had gone to the settlement in the north to trade for what they needed, and had come back barely alive and burning with fever, and even though those two people had lived, others had died.

These strangers might also be carrying death. Nuy would have to allow for that even though she had grown to doubt much of what her father had told her over the years. He had once claimed that they would be safe in their caves near the sea, and then the storm had come. He had blamed the deaths that came later to their people on those who lived in the north, and yet it seemed to her now that the older ones might have been ailing all along and that several of them had grown weak enough that any illness might have taken their lives. There had once been seven young ones, but the oldest three had died of the fever and now there were only four, including Nuy. Once there had been more of the older ones, too. Now there were only her father and seven of those who had come south with him in the years before Nuy's birth. She could not recall her own mother, who had died when Nuy was still a small child.

The strangers had brought two horses with them, one black and one gray. One of the dark-haired people stood up, went to the gray horse, and removed something from one of the bags on the horse's back, then handed it to the small brown-haired one. Nuy could now see that the brown-haired person was a female, with the shape of breasts under her upper garment. The female lifted the small pale object she was holding to her lips and bit into it.

Food. Nuy's mouth watered. Perhaps she could slip down there later, while the strangers were sleeping, and steal some of their food. Maybe she would even dare to approach them openly and ask for something to eat.

No, she told herself; that might be dangerous. She did not know why they had come here, and even if she did have increasingly more doubts about the stories her father told, there was still a chance that these strangers might be carrying death.

What she should do, she realized, was head back to her father and warn him that strangers had come into their territory.

Nuy considered that for a moment, wondering what her father would do. The best way for him and his people to protect themselves might be to stay where they were and hide from the strangers, who did not know this land and would most likely be unable to find them, being as seemingly unperceptive as they were. But maybe these northerners had come here only to trade. People from her father's band had once traveled north to trade, so it was possible the strangers had come here for the same reason.

Then she thought of her ragged loincloth, her spear, the horses her father had once had but which had run off, died, or been eaten, the meal that she had made of a rodent a while back and the effort made in catching such little meat, the deer that her father and Owen had carried into their camp thirty days ago and how long they had made that meat last, and the caves in which her people now made their home.

What could these strangers want from them? Her people had almost nothing to offer in trade. Nuy wondered if they had ever owned anything of value. Maybe the people in the north had so much that they could give it away without having to trade anything for it, the way Daniella and Eyela had once made necklaces of shells for Nuy and everyone else, without asking for anything in return.

Nuy's curiosity warred with her fear. If she could get closer to the strangers, maybe she could find out more about them. She rose to her feet, but remained in a crouch as she moved away from the edge of the cliff.

There was a way down among the rocks to a ledge below, places where the rock jutted out far enough for her to find footing. Nuy crept along a ridge, balancing on her bare feet as her toes gripped the rock, until she reached the ledge. She lowered herself and stretched out on her stomach, careful not to dislodge any stones.

". . . didn't think it would take us this long," a voice was saying. One of the men was speaking, and she easily grasped his words. "By the time we get back, the ice and cold rains will have come. If we had a lot more to live on, it might almost be better to stay here for the next few months and then start back when the weather's warmer."

Nuy was confused. The weather was always warm, except when it was so hot that they had to hide from the daylight in their caves.

"But then everyone would only worry about us even more," the woman said. "They're probably already wondering when we'll get back. Besides, I'm getting homesick."

"So am I," the bearded man said. His voice was lower and deeper than that of the first who had spoken, and his short dark hair, unlike Nuy's and the other man's, curled against his head. "It shouldn't take us as long to get back, even if we have the weather against us. All we really have to do is follow the river."

"And if the others have settled where they originally planned to settle, we can't be more than a day or two away from them." The man with the lighter voice was speaking again.

"We haven't seen them for years," the man with the beard and the curling hair replied, "and after coming this far with no sign of them, I wonder if they can even still be alive. The last time we saw them, they looked like they really needed what we had to offer in trade, and we got so little in return that we might as well have just given our goods away."

"We have to find out what happened to them," the woman said. "That was one of our reasons for coming this far."

"But if they're not where we expected to find them, we may never find out what happened," the man with the mustache and straight dark hair said.

The man with the curly hair shrugged. "I know it's the right thing to do," he muttered, "looking for them and offering to help them if they need any help, which they probably do. Forgive me if I say that I wouldn't particularly mind if we never found them."

The woman said, "Well, you've made that clear enough."

Nuy wondered exactly where these people expected to find hers. Her father had moved them farther inland after the great storm, to caves well to the north and east of the ones where they had been living when she was a child. If these strangers thought that they were still living in their first settlement near the sea, they would never find them.

She could lead them to her people. Nuy turned that notion over in her mind. Clearly they had things with them that her people could use, garments and food and strange tools, such as the flat object one of the men had propped up against his upraised knees that reminded her of something her father had once owned, and if her people had little to offer in return, they could still show the strangers where to find plants and fruits that could be eaten, other plants that could be made into tools, and where beached and edible fish could be found along the seashore.

But her father might believe that these people were also carrying death with them. It might be better if they never found her people.

The man with the curling hair got up then, and busied himself by hammering stakes into the ground and then tying a large piece of fabric to the stakes, and finally she understood that he was putting up a kind of shelter. "Go to sleep," he said to his companions. "I'll take the first watch."

Nuy sighed. It seemed that she would not be able to steal some of their food after all. She rested her head against her arms and soon fell asleep.

Nuy awoke at dawn. By then, the woman was up, sitting by the ashes of the fire. The woman got to her feet, and Nuy noticed that she was wearing a wand at her waist that looked like the weapon her father carried. Nuy's father clung to his weapon and did not let anyone else use it, partly because it marked him as the leader of his people and also because it was the only such weapon they had left. The weapon would only stun a target, but a knife or spear could kill off any game after that. Her father had not used his weapon in a while; she wondered if that was because he feared that it might fail him.

Nuy often thought of how much easier her hunting would be with such a weapon, which did not seem all that hard to use. A knife and a spear had their limitations. But even without such a wand, it was easier for her to find game than it was for the older ones of her band, who were less able to spot tracks and seemed blind and deaf to certain sights and sounds.

The woman lifted the flap of the shelter. "Better get up," she said. After a few moments, the man with straight dark hair came out and then went behind a boulder, apparently to relieve himself. The other man crawled out, stretched, then went to the horses, which were grazing on the green and yellow grasses that grew above the riverbank.

He returned with what looked like three more packets of food. In the light, Nuy could now tell that all three of the strangers were carrying weapons. She tried not to think of her empty stomach.

"I've been thinking," the woman said. "Maybe one of us should go on alone and scout out what's ahead."

"Are you sure?" the man with curling hair asked.

"They haven't come to trade with us for ages. That could mean that they haven't survived, or couldn't spare the resources for such a long journey, or it could mean that they're deliberately avoiding us. In other words, they might not be so willing to welcome us."

"You think so?" the other man said.

"Don't forget, I knew Ho a little better than you did," the woman responded. "He would go along with the rest of us when it was to his benefit and make trouble whenever he thought anybody wasn't sufficiently intimidated by him. Ho has no loyalties to anyone except himself—I used to wonder if he could feel any empathy for others at all. I think we can assume that he hasn't changed all that much."

The woman was talking about her father. Nuy held her breath.

"I can't see why welcoming us wouldn't be to his benefit," the deep-voiced man said. "It isn't as if we brought nothing with us to trade or give away."

The woman shook her head. "Yes, and he might just decide to take it all instead of waiting for us to offer it to him."

"You weren't worrying about this before."

"Well, I'm worrying about it now. I just feel we should be more careful." She bit into her food.

Nuy thought about what the strangers had said. Maybe her father would try to steal what they had; she had thought of doing so herself. But given that he still believed death had come to them from these people, maybe he had no reason to welcome either them or their goods.

Nuy tensed, not knowing what to do, longing for some of their food.

"Tell you what," the straight-haired man said after they had finished their meal in silence. "I'll take one of the horses and go on ahead, and you two can wait here. According to our maps, I should be within sight of the ocean by sometime tomorrow. If I haven't found any sign of them by then, I'll head back."

"I don't like it," the other man said. "We should stick together."

"I won't be going that far, and I'll wait until it's dark before I get too close to where they should be. I'll keep myself hidden and won't contact them unless I'm sure they'll welcome me. If I have any doubts at all, I'll come back here and then we can all decide what to do after that."

"Will you need the screen?" the woman asked.

"If I follow the river, I shouldn't need any maps."

The three strangers talked some more, but in lower voices, so that Nuy caught only a few of their words. At last the man with curly hair threw up his hands. "All right," he said, "I can see your point, but try to get back here in a couple of days if you can."

"Don't worry. I won't take chances. I should be able to get back here in three or four days at the most."

Nuy decided then that she would follow the straight-haired man.

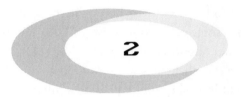

2

*T*he stranger rode south on his black horse, following the
river. His two packs were tied behind and in front of him,
and he rode on the horse's bare back, as Nuy's people had
done when they still had horses to ride. He also held two long
strips in his hands that were attached to others around the
horse's head. Her people had used makeshift bridles and reins
made of rope and strips of leather to control their horses, but
his bridle looked far better suited to the job.

Nuy followed at a distance, keeping the man in sight. He was
holding the animal to a walk, so it was easy for her to keep up
with him. The green and yellow grass was high enough in this
region that she could crouch down and conceal herself if he
threatened to look her way. He still seemed unaware of her. She
wondered how close she could get to him before he sensed her
presence.

The sun was high in the pale green sky when he finally stopped, slipped down from his horse, let the animal drink from the river for a time, and then rode on, still heading south. If he kept going in this direction, he would never find her people.

It occurred to her then that she might show herself to him and ask him for some of his food. Given all the doubts that had grown inside her about what her father had told her, she had little reason to fear that the stranger's food could kill her, and if it did, then at least she would die with a full belly. And if his food didn't kill her, then she could tell him where he could find her people. They might have much more to gain by meeting with these strangers than by hiding from them.

Nuy picked up her pace. He might aim his weapon at her if he saw her with a spear. "Hai!" she called out and then dropped her spear in the grass.

The man did not turn his head.

"Hai!" she shouted again, and raised her arms high.

He reined in his horse, then looked back. She walked toward him through the high grass, keeping her arms up and her palms facing him, so that he would know that she was not about to reach for her knife.

His hand was at his waist, near his weapon. He continued to gaze at her as she came closer. "Who are you?" he asked. "What's your name?"

"Nuy."

"Nuy." The man shook his head. "But of course—you must be one of the people we're looking for." He squinted at her. "One of their children, I'm guessing."

She stopped a few paces away from him. "Keep going that way," she said, "and you won't find anybody."

"What do you mean? How many of you are there?"

Nuy was suddenly wary of the stranger. If she was going to tell him anything, and she had not yet decided whether or not she would, she might as well get something for herself in return.

"I'm hungry," she said. "Is your food safe?"

"Safe?"

"Will it make me sick?"

He frowned. "I don't know why it should," he replied, "unless you eat too much of it at once."

"Give me some of it, then."

Still keeping his eyes on her, he reached inside the pack behind him, then held out a small light brown object. "Here."

She had expected him to throw it at her. She crept toward him, grabbed the food from him while being careful not to touch his hand, then bit into it, too hungry to be cautious any longer. Inside a brown doughy substance was a brown mass with bits of red that tasted meaty, unfamiliar, and delicious.

She gulped the food down quickly, then held out her hands. "More."

"If you eat any more right now," he said, "you might get sick. I can give you some more later." His eyes narrowed. "You look like you haven't eaten anything in some time."

"Caught a rit two days ago."

"A rit?"

"One of those little gray creatures. I was sitting next to its burrow, and it stuck its head out, and I whacked it with a rock. Had to eat it raw, though. They taste better when they're cooked."

The man made a face.

"You don't get that much nourishment from them, either, but they quiet your stomach and don't make you sick the way aitis do."

"Aitis?" he asked.

"Those tiny blue lizards you can sometimes see in the mud along the river if you're quick. You don't ever want to eat an

aiti, not even if you're starving. Katti ate one once, and she was vomiting for days afterwards."

"Is that why you're out here all alone, to hunt?" he asked. "You are alone, aren't you?"

Nuy nodded, then wondered if she should have revealed that to him.

"You came out here to hunt rodents—rits?"

"No, but by then I had to eat something." Just a day ago, she had worried that the rit might be the only game she would catch, that she would have to go back to her people empty-handed. Her father and Belen did not mind if she went off by herself for several days at a time, as long as she brought something back—some game, a bird or some eggs whenever she could flush out one of the birds that hid near the river, some new knowledge about where edible plants might be found. Lately she had also felt the need to be by herself more often. Her father, who alternated between furious rants and a sullen silence, had recently grown more unpredictable in his moods. He had been in good spirits a few days ago, reminding her of the gentleness he had more often shown her when she was small, but by now he might be either raging at everybody or refusing to speak at all.

There was also Belen. It was worth it to wander the plain or to hide out in the caves where her people had once lived just to get away from Belen for a while, to pretend that he had never claimed her as a mate. He had changed after that, treating her more roughly than he had when they were younger. She thought of the times when she and Belen used to gather plants with Carin and her brother Sarojin, when the four of them would follow the river north as they pulled up reeds, sensing what to do and going about their work without needing to speak, feeling as though something unseen was guiding them. Carin and Sarojin had lost both of their parents early,

and Belen not long afterwards, and Nuy had sometimes felt as though she were a sister and parent to them all, that the invisible bonds that bound them were tighter and stronger than those that connected them to the rest of their people.

Nuy held up her hands again as she slipped past the man and horse and made her way to the riverbank. "Where are you going?" he said.

"I'm thirsty." She thrashed her way through some of the dry brush near the bank, knelt amid the thick reeds by the water, cupped her hands, scooped up some water, and drank.

"Are you sure that's safe?" he called after her.

She swallowed more water, slipped off her waterskin and filled it, hooked it over her shoulder and across her bare chest again, then stood up. "This water's safe enough," she answered. "It's the sea you have to worry about. That was just about the first thing my father told me, never to drink any water from the sea."

"Is that where you live? By the sea? How many of you are there?"

Nuy was not about to answer all those questions. She came up from the riverbank, ran back to retrieve her spear, then jogged south, her long braid slapping against her back.

The man's horse trotted after her. "I know where you're from," she said.

"Where am I from, then?" He was still astride his horse; the animal walked slowly at Nuy's side.

"There are people in the north. My father told me about you. He says that all of you, your people and ours, were seeds, seeds like the ones the wind sweeps up from one place and carries to another place. He says that you and we were brought across the sky from another world very far away from this one and that all of us were planted here."

"That's actually not a bad way of putting it," the man said.

"I saw you last night, and the two people with you, but you didn't see me. I saw you sitting there around your fire, and I heard some of what you said. So I know there are three of you, and that you're looking for my father."

"Your father?"

"His name is Ho."

"Oh." The stranger cleared his throat.

"Ho told me that your people wanted to stay where you were, in the north, and you tried to convince his people to stay there, too, but he didn't want that. He says it's better to live our own way, without somebody else telling us what to do, and being part of this world instead of separating ourselves from it, and anyway there wasn't anything you had that he couldn't get if he needed it."

"I guess you haven't needed anything then," the man said, "because none of your people have come to our settlements to trade for a long time. Why not?"

He was asking her too many questions. "What's your name?" she asked him.

"My name is Chiang."

"Did you come here just to look for my father?"

"That was part of why we came, but we also wanted to explore more of our world, learn more about what's to the south of us. We call this planet Home. Is that what you call it?"

Nuy chuckled at his foolishness. "What else would we call it?"

"Ho told us when he left us that he and his group would follow this river to the sea and settle there, in caves near the shore."

She waited for the man to say more, but he fell silent. He was probably hoping to find out more from her without asking too many questions.

"What will you do if my father doesn't want to talk to you?" she said at last.

"I suppose we'll have to return to our own settlement. We can't exactly force your father to meet or trade with us if he isn't interested. Why—do you think he won't want to see us?"

She was not about to give him an answer to that. "How long did it take you to get here?" she asked. That might give her some idea of exactly how far away his settlement was.

"Longer than we expected," the man named Chiang replied. "Longer than it probably should have, because a few days into the trip, one of our horses got loose. She was still carrying a lot of our supplies, so we had to go after her, but it took us three days to catch up with her and another four to find our way back to where we'd lost her. After that, it was a stomach ailment, nothing serious, but bad enough that we had to stay where we were until it passed and we recovered and were sure it was nothing serious, so that was another five days lost. Vomiting and shitting every hour or so doesn't exactly leave you able to travel, and we were weak enough afterwards that we had to keep stopping to rest, but as you can see, we did recover."

It didn't sound as if they had suffered from the illness that had been carried to her people years ago, that had made those afflicted complain that their heads ached and their bodies burned while their lungs filled with water and pus that had kept them coughing. This sounded like a completely different illness. "How many sicknesses do your people have?" Nuy asked.

"Not many, luckily. Not since our first winter, anyway, and nothing since then that we haven't been able to recover from. Some lives were lost during our first year, but since then, we've been fortunate—no deaths, and only a few injuries from accidents, broken bones and the like."

"No one died from any fevers?" she asked.

"Fevers?"

"When you burn and then shiver and your head hurts and you cough and can't breathe." That was the way the symptoms of such illnesses had been described to her by those who had survived them. She had somehow escaped such afflictions, as had Belen, Carin, and Sarojin.

"Oh, almost all of us have suffered from those kinds of things," Chiang said, "one way or another, but they don't kill us, we do recover. Why do you ask? Have your people been—"

"We're all right. We can take care of ourselves. Maybe better than you can."

"I don't doubt it, seeing you out here all by yourself. Won't your father and mother be worrying about you?"

"My mother's dead. She died a long time ago, when I was still little, so I don't remember her." Maybe she shouldn't have told him that, either. "And my father doesn't worry about me. Why should he? I'm almost seventeen years old."

She heard Chiang suck in his breath. "Seventeen? I wouldn't have guessed it. You look more like eleven or twelve."

Nuy halted. Now he had angered her, and she was about to shake her spear at him before remembering that he had a weapon. "Don't insult me," she said.

He reined in his horse. "I didn't mean to insult you, Nuy. I only meant—" He paused. "I just meant that you seem somewhat small and slight for your age." She continued to glare at him. "But you're obviously strong and self-reliant."

She marched through the grass; he stayed at her side. "There's one thing we didn't expect," Chiang went on. "We didn't know the green grasses planted around our settlements had spread so far in all directions. They've really taken root, and I've also seen paler green grasses that look like a hybrid, which makes me wonder if the yellow native grass will eventually die out."

"What are you talking about?" Nuy said, irritated again.

"The green grass of the plain—we brought it here, it was genetically engineered, it's not native to this planet. Didn't your father tell you that?"

Nuy refused to reply.

"The native grass is the yellow grass," Chiang said, "and our animals can't live on that alone. The green grass gives them better nourishment, because most of our animals, our horses and cattle and sheep and chickens, even the wild deer and wolves and others, aren't native to this planet, either. We assumed that there'd be enough grazing for our horses during our journey, given that your people were able to come north with your horses, but we weren't sure. Now I know why they could make the trip. There's plenty of green grass growing for the horses along the way, and it seems that the hybrid grass can nourish them, too."

She did not know what to say to that.

"You do still have horses, don't you?" Chiang said. "I know your people left with more horses the last time they traded with us, so I was wondering why you're out here on foot instead of on horseback."

She could not tell him that they had no horses, that the last of their horses had been eaten or had run off long ago.

"Also because we saw a small horse herd a few days ago, in the distance. We hadn't expected to see wild horses. Did some of yours get away?"

"What are you going to do if you meet with my father?" Nuy asked.

"I told you. We'll talk to him and see if he needs anything from us, find out if he or any of his group would like to travel back to our settlements with us. It wasn't we who asked him to leave, you know. He left us."

Nuy said, "I can tell you right now that he won't go back with you, and nobody else will, either." She felt her throat tighten even as she spoke. She would travel north with this man if she could, she realized, and suddenly wanted to see this place in the north where people apparently had enough to eat and did not die from fevers.

"Will you take me to your people?" Chiang asked.

"Will you give me more of your food if I do?"

"Of course."

"You won't find any of them if you keep going this way." A plan was forming in her mind. She would take this man to her father, acquire more of his food and whatever else he had to offer her people, and then maybe she could find a way to leave with him and his companions.

"You don't live by the sea?" he asked.

"Not anymore."

"Then where do we go?"

"There." She turned and pointed to the east. "That way, then north for a little. You'd never find them by yourself."

"How far away are they?"

"Two days." She frowned. "Maybe a day and a half. It depends on how fast we can move."

Chiang looked away from her, seeming uncertain. "Maybe we should go back and get my companions first," he murmured, "and then you could lead all of us there."

Her father would be suspicious enough of one outsider. She did not know how he would react to three, especially with his notions about death having come upon them from the north.

"I don't know," she said, trying to think of what to tell him. "It'd be better if we found out whether he'll even talk to you before he finds out about your friends. If he sees all of you together, he might not want to talk to you at all."

"I don't know why he'd be so fearful of us," Chiang said.

"It's not just being afraid. It's—" She shook her head. What she suddenly wanted to do then was tell him to go back to his companions and to leave her father alone.

But her people needed what these people had. Even if her father and Owen and Daniella and the other adults could get along as they had for all these past years, they were likely to find life easier with what Chiang's people could offer. There were also Carin and Sarojin to consider. Nuy found herself suddenly longing for past times, when Belen had been gentler and they would sit with Carin and Sarojin to gaze at the sea, communing silently among themselves, wondering what lay below the whitecapped gray waves. Later, after they had left their homes near the sea, they had grown more curious about what might lie farther upriver. They knew so little of their world, so little about the people of the north.

She realized then that she had something to trade after all. This man's people might have more food and more tools than hers, but they seemed to know even less about Home than she did. She could trade what she knew, and if she could talk her father into it, maybe she and Carin and Sarojin could leave later on with the three northerners. She could tell Ho that living in the north for a time might be useful, that they could return later on with more supplies and more knowledge.

Her curiosity about the northerners welled up inside her once more, and she wanted to tell this man to leave here right now and take her with him. But she could not abandon Carin and Sarojin, who would be as curious as she was about the north. Maybe even Belen would decide to come with them; his curiosity might be great enough to overcome his cruelty. She would have to think of ways to convince her father to let them all go.

"If you think it's best that we go alone," Chiang said, "then I should probably follow your advice. But we ought at least to go back and tell my friends what we're doing."

"Won't they wait for you?" she asked.

"Of course they'll wait. They'll allow for delays, but only a few days at most."

"Then we should go to my people now, unless you want to spend more time and more food going back and telling your comrades what you're doing and then having to bring them all the way back here before we cross the plain."

"Why would they have to come back here?" he asked.

She sighed with exasperation. "Because the land here is flatter, and we won't have to go around as many stone ridges. Because your horses will need water, and they won't find enough water very easily if we cross farther to the north, that's why. Once you talk to my father, and he decides what he wants from you, I can guide you back to your friends."

"Maybe that would be best," he said.

"It is best," she insisted.

Chiang nodded. "Then lead the way."

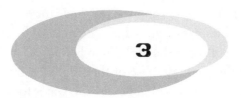

3

The weather was with them as Nuy and Chiang crossed the flat grassy plain. Clouds drifted across the sky, occasionally veiling the sun but never growing into the dark clouds of an impending storm. Occasionally a bluewisp, one of the tiny flying insects that lived in the grass, alighted on Nuy's arm, its long blue wings whirling.

The wind picked up, but only enough to cool their bodies. After they had been traveling for a while, Chiang slipped off his horse and walked at her side, leading the horse by the reins.

They said little to each other. Apparently the man had satisfied his curiosity for now and she did not want to waste any energy in talk.

They stopped once to eat and rest and water the horse at a small spring. Chiang gave her a different food this time, an orange sphere with a hard surface that she had to peel away in order to get at the sweet fruit inside. They did not stop again until the sun was setting behind them and she spotted what she was looking for on the horizon, a ridge nearly a hundred paces long that jutted up from the grass.

The first moon was rising by the time they came to the ridge. The rocky sides of the ridge were marked by ledges and crannies; she had spent the night here before. A small pool of water was at the southern base of the ridge, fed by an underground spring, so there would be enough water for the horse.

"I don't suppose we should build a fire out here," Chiang said as his horse drank, "even if we could find enough fuel to feed it."

Nuy snorted. "Not unless you want to risk setting the whole plain ablaze."

"I could put up a tent—a shelter."

She sniffed at the wind; the air was still dry. "We won't need any shelter," she said. "It's not going to rain, and we'll be protected enough here anyway."

Chiang removed his packs from the horse, stashed them on a ledge, then removed the bridle and reins from the horse's head. "Better get out a rope," he murmured as he took a long coil of rope out of one pack and tied the horse to a rock that jutted from the ridge. "We wouldn't want her to run away."

Nuy shook her head at him. This horse would not run away, not unless something startled or frightened her; she could sense the docility in the animal.

They ate quickly. This time he gave her a different kind of meat, pale shreds with crisp bits of plants wrapped in a thin wafer, along with another one of the orange fruits. After eating, he walked into the grass for a few paces, then turned away from her to relieve himself, as if afraid to have her see him, even though it was dark and the high grass hid his lower body.

"Do you want to take the first watch," he said, "or should I?"

If she were alone, she would have climbed up to one of the higher ledges and slept throughout the night, but with this man and his supplies and the horse, there was more to protect. "I will," she said. She had too much to think about to go to sleep right away.

He grabbed one of his packs, threw it onto a ledge, and hoisted himself up behind it. She watched as he unrolled the pack and then wrapped it around himself as he stretched out on the ledge. "Good night, Nuy."

She climbed into a recess and huddled there, scanning the plain. The more she thought about Chiang and his companions, the more convinced she became that her people should throw in their lot with them, at least for a while. They could follow the three northerners to their settlements, hunting along the way if they grew short of rations; as it was, Nuy suspected that her people could survive on less food than the outsiders. Chiang had said that Ho had left them of his own accord, so if her people grew tired of living among the northerners, there was nothing to stop them from coming back here.

Of course she was assuming that what Chiang had told her was the truth. Maybe she was too grateful for and too easily lured by a few unfamiliar and tasty foods and a bit of kindly talk. No, it was probably better simply to lead him to her people and let Chiang sort things out with Ho. There would be more food for Carin and Sarojin, at least for a little while, and maybe even Belen would leave her alone, grateful for a fuller belly and some tales of the north.

Nuy listened to the night, to the sighing of the soft wind as it died. She thought of how her father and the other adults would keep watch in the night, their bodies tense and stiffened by vigilance, as if they could not entirely trust their own senses. When she was little, she had sometimes startled Ho when she got up to relieve herself, and had quickly learned not to come up behind him without warning, even though he should have been able to hear her movements when she was that close to him.

Perhaps her own senses would grow duller as she aged. Maybe in time she and Belen and Carin and Sarojin would grow as unperceptive as the adults among their people. Chiang apparently shared their disabilities, which made her idea even more compelling.

May I never grow that old, she thought, then covered her eyes for a moment. To make such a wish was like asking for death.

She waited until the second of Home's moons was gaining on the first, then woke Chiang. "Wake me up when the moons are riding the sky together but before they've dropped low in the west," she told him. "We want to be out of here before the sun comes up." Other animals might come here looking for water in the morning, perhaps wolves or a big cat; she wanted to be gone by then.

"Anything in particular I should look out for?" he asked.

"Just stay on your ledge and keep watching the plain. If you see anything move, even if you think it's just the wind moving the grass, wake me."

"Very well."

She stretched on her ledge, one arm under her head, and fell deeply asleep. Then a voice was whispering, "Nuy."

She was awake in an instant. In the dim silvery light of the moons, she saw that Chiang had already put the packs back on his horse, which was drinking from the pool.

She climbed down from the ledge as he finished putting the bridle on the animal. "Let's go," she said.

He followed her on foot, leading the horse by the reins.

She led him around the northern end of the ridge and then turned east. "Are you Ho's only child?" he asked at last.

So he was again trying to find out more about her. "Yes," she replied.

"I have a son who's about your age and a daughter who's just a couple of years older."

She stiffened with surprise. But there was nothing strange about his having a mate and children. Still, maybe if his people had enough children of their own, they would not be so willing to make room for any of her people. "Well, that's one less mouth to feed," Ho had said after Riis had died last year, a victim of his own clumsiness; the boy had fallen from a cliffside and dashed his head against a rock. There had been some sorrow in Ho's voice, but her father had long ago decided that mourning the dead was useless.

She picked up her pace, not wanting to talk, suddenly resenting Chiang's son and daughter and all of the others who lived in the north with enough food to eat and enough clothing to cover themselves against the wind and the rain and the sun.

*I*t was midday when Nuy saw the small dark mounds on the horizon that marked the home of her people. She had turned north not long after she and Chiang had eaten their morning meal. He had given his horse a meal, too, several handfuls of what looked like seeds or grain. His people apparently had so much that they could feed their animals treats instead of just allowing them to graze.

She pointed to the northeast. "Those hills," she said. "That's where my people live."

"Why did you move farther inland?" he asked.

"A storm," she said. He would find out about that anyway after he talked to her father. "We used to live in caves like the ones we live in now, but close enough to the shore so that we could go there and listen to the sea and gather whatever fish washed onto the beach. But we had our gardens, too, close to the river, because my father said that we couldn't live on just what we found or hunted. Then the storm came." She remembered how she had felt the storm in the air, even before any clouds were visible, how Carin and Sarojin had whimpered and Belen had jumped up and down before Katti and Daniella had scolded them all into silence. She had known something bad was coming, and had tried to warn her father, who had refused to listen.

"We'd seen storms before," she continued, "with the clouds building far out at sea and then rushing in, but this storm was fierce, the worst we'd ever seen. The water came so far inland that it came up the hills and washed into our caves. I was little then, but I still remember my father holding me up inside our cave so that I wouldn't drown or be swept away. And when the storm passed, our gardens were ruined, and so were the coops where we kept our birds, and the birds were gone, too. We didn't dare stay near the sea after that."

"I should think a storm like that would be most unusual," Chiang said.

"Unusual or not, we were afraid to live close to the sea afterwards, so we moved to where we are now. We were still trading with your people then, and Ho told us that we'd be able to make up for what was lost, so we got together what we could and sent two of our people to you. And we were all right for a while after that, until—" She paused.

"Until what?"

She did not reply.

"What happened after that?"

She remained silent for a while, until they were close enough to the mounds to see the gray thread of the stream that ran below the caves, then said, "Before you say anything to my father, you'd better let me speak first, tell him who you are and why you're here. Sometimes he's a little—" She considered how to describe Ho to this man. "Sometimes he's the way he used to be, knowing what has to be done and who's the best person to do it, but other times he pulls inside himself, just sits there not speaking or doing anything for a while, sometimes for days. And other times he's so full of anger that it's like he has a storm inside himself." That kind of anger had been coming upon Ho more often lately.

"I see."

"And I think he already knows we're coming."

Chiang stared into the distance. "How can you tell?"

"He's watching us." She had glimpsed a sudden movement near a small dark spot that marked the opening of one of the caves, a movement that she might have missed if she had looked there an instant later. Her father or someone else had spotted them; maybe Belen, whose senses were as sharp as her own, had warned him that she was near. By now Ho would know that his daughter was on her way back with someone who could only have come there from the settlement in the north.

Maybe she should not have brought this man here. She was suddenly besieged by doubts.

They continued across the mottled green and yellow plain. The mounds grew into grass-covered hills and then into the gaping mouths of the caves under the hills. "Ho led us here," Nuy said, trying to mask her uneasiness with talk. "He lost what he called his records in the storm, he used to look at them on this flat surface he called a screen, but he remembered that there were caves here and a stream near them."

"You have no maps or records?"

"No." She was not sure of what he meant by those words.

"Can you even read?"

Nuy sniffed. "Of course I can read. Katti and Ashur taught us our letters, they used to scratch them out in the sand, and after we moved, in the dirt. I can spell my name and my father's and everyone else's. I could probably set yours down if I tried."

They were close enough now that she could see just a hint of the colors on the smooth insides of the caves, the shiny opalescent surfaces of pink and gold and silver and blue and so many other colors that she could not name them all, each color merging into another as the light from their fires danced on the walls. The caves near the sea had walls like that, too, and Katti had told the children a story about them. Once giant creatures had lived in the sea, growing shells around themselves as some of the smaller sea creatures still did, and a few of them had somehow been washed ashore and had died there, leaving only their shells to form caves amid the hills that bordered the shore. Later, after they had moved inland, Katti had speculated that the giant waves of a massive storm might have carried some of the giants far from the sea. Her story had terrified Carin and Sarojin, even though Ho had insisted that such creatures no longer existed, that they had died out long ago and would not return for their shells. Nuy had told herself a different story after hearing that one. The giant creatures had once lived on the land, but had grown so large that their bodies could not support the weight of their shells, so they had shed their shells and gone to live in the sea. That story had felt more like the truth to her.

Someone should have come out by now. Her father, or one or two of the others, should have been coming out there to greet her and to see what she had brought, as they always had before. That she had someone with her should have made them even more curious.

They came to the stream, shallow and narrow enough for

Chiang and her to wade across it after the horse had drunk, and still no one came out to greet them.

"Hai!" she called out, and heard no reply. The yawning mouths of the caves were mute. Could her people have abandoned these caves and gone somewhere else? Even if they had, someone would surely have remained behind to guide her to the others.

But she had seen something move earlier. They had to be here. Now that she was closer, she could pick up the faint odor of smoke, the scent of their fires. Something fluttered inside her, telling her that Belen and Sarojin and Carin could not be far away.

Someone rushed from the cave. Her father was running toward them, Belen at his heels.

"Go," she said to Chiang as Ho's hand moved toward his waist.

"What is it?"

She wanted to curse at him for his slowness. "Get on your horse and go!"

A beam shot out from Ho's weapon, catching Chiang in the chest. He toppled forward and fell toward the stream. The horse reared. Nuy screamed, saw that her father was now aiming at her, and then the darkness came.

She was lying on her back, with the high grass all around her. Nuy sat up slowly, her head throbbing. Chiang was lying a few paces from her, but only his legs were visible through the grass.

Her father's weapon would stun, but not kill. He had used it mainly for hunting, for bringing down a deer so that the rest of them could kill and butcher their game more quickly instead of having to track the animals over a longer distance. She had not known how sick and weak any target would feel afterwards if it ever revived. A wave of nausea caught her; she nearly retched.

Chiang was still.

"Chiang," she called out. "Chiang." She crawled toward him and saw that his head was in the water and his body dark with blood; her own spear jutted from his back.

Her father had brought him down and killed him like an animal, stabbing and cutting at him so fiercely with his own spear and hers that he had shredded the back of Chiang's upper garment. Maybe Belen had helped him with the killing. She sat there, shivering in the warmth of the afternoon, trying to understand what her father had done.

She got to her feet but her legs nearly buckled under her. She could not see Chiang's black horse anywhere. Her father stood alone on the other side of the stream.

"What have you done?" she screamed.

"He was dead before any spear struck him," Ho shouted back. His body, bare except for a loincloth, sparkled with droplets of water; his dark wet hair was plastered against his shoulders.

"You could have pulled him out of the water," she cried.

"You brought him here, I saw you coming here with him, with one of those who sent death to us before, and I was furious. Did you think I would allow that?"

"Listen to me! He only wanted to—"

"You brought him here," Ho continued. "They wanted it all along, you know, they were just waiting for us to die, they were hoping for us to die, and when we didn't oblige them, they sent death to us." His long black hair swayed as he shook his head and then raised his spear. "You can't come back now, I don't care what Belen says about losing his mate, you can't come back here, Nuy, not now, I'm not taking any chances."

She took a step forward. Her legs almost gave way. "You don't understand," she cried out helplessly.

Her father put his hand on the weapon that hung from a cord around his waist, and she saw then that he had a second weapon tucked under the cord. "Stay over there," Ho said, "and don't come any closer. You've been with that man, and who knows what he might be carrying."

His fear hadn't stopped him from taking the dead man's weapon, unless he had ordered someone else to retrieve it, perhaps Belen. A vision came to her of Belen splashing through the water, grabbing her spear, and then jabbing it into Chiang. Belen had done this, perhaps out of fear, maybe out of rage and spite, and Ho had done nothing to stop it.

"Listen to me!" she shouted.

"Get away from here, Nuy. If you don't fall ill, if you manage to stay alive, then maybe someday I can allow you to live among us again. I promised Belen I'd offer you that much. Maybe one day we'll come looking for you and welcome you back, but until then, stay away, or I'll kill you myself."

His inner storms had finally taken him, had swept what was left of his mind away as surely as the winds of the great storm had destroyed their garden near the sea. She stumbled away through the grass, mourning the dead man, feeling almost as if she had died herself.

*N*uy stumbled across the plain, heedless of where she was going. She did not mark where she was until the red sun was low in the west, and then at last she came to herself.

She had no food, and only what water was left in her waterskin. She had her knife, but no spear. Her father might talk of allowing her back into his band eventually, but he had sent her away from him with nothing. He could tell Belen whatever he liked. The truth was that he expected her to die.

She scanned the plain, cupping a hand over her eyes. The ridge where she and Chiang had spent the night lay to her south, a wall of rock promising her shelter at least for the night, and to her great surprise, she glimpsed the tiny black form of a four-legged creature.

Chiang's horse was there, drinking at the spring.

She ran through the grass, slowing down as she approached the ridge, not wanting to startle the horse. With what the horse carried, she could stay alive for a while, maybe long enough for her father's madness to pass. As she came nearer, the horse raised its head and whinnied; she wondered if it was somehow calling to Chiang, missing him.

"Hai," she said softly, then moved to the animal's side. She ran her hand gently over the horse's neck, then reached for the reins. Tears sprang to her eyes; she squeezed them shut for a moment and swallowed hard.

Even after she had secured the horse by tying the reins to a crag, and had settled herself on a ledge, she was unable to sleep, afraid that she might wake to find that the animal had vanished, or that her father had followed her here; he would probably guess that she had headed for this ridge. She wondered if she would ever be able to go back to her people. Once Daniella or Owen might have been able to talk some sense into Ho, but they had repeated her father's rants about the forces arrayed against their band for so long that they were now barely more than his echoes. Gerd and Zareb thought so little about anything that the two men might soon forget that she had ever been among them. Belen might be sorry that he was now without a mate, but Carin was there, she would do as a replacement.

That thought made her gorge rise. She imagined Belen forcing himself on poor Carin, and the rage made her tears come. Sarojin might not be able to stop it; Belen was stronger than he was. She thought of the time when she, Carin, Sarojin, and Belen had been so close that she had sometimes imagined that she was picking up their thoughts and their dreams, but lately it had seemed as though more and more of Ho's moods were leaking into Belen. A sob escaped her; she caught her breath.

She knew then what she would have to do. She would have to go back to Chiang's two companions, tell them what had happened to him, hope that they would believe her, and then beg them to take her back to their settlement with them. They might not want her after what had happened. They might blame her for their comrade's death; there was no reason for them to listen to anything she told them. But even if they drove her away, it did not matter; she could not be any worse off than she already was.

But if they did believe her, then she might be able to find a way later on to come back for Sarojin and Carin. Only by saving herself now would she ever be able to do anything for them.

Nuy woke at dawn, surprised that she had slept after all. She quickly sat up on the ledge and looked around for the horse, but the animal was still there, still tied to the rock. Then she recalled how Chiang had looked, lying in the grass, and felt the shock of his death once more.

The horse lifted its head and snorted. Nuy slid down from the ledge and led the animal to the pool. She had not been around horses for a long while and wondered if she could handle this one. She might manage to lead it, but she would not try to ride it right away.

After the horse drank, she removed the two packs of supplies tied onto its back, but not before the horse tried to skitter away from her. She stood with the horse, rubbing its flank as she soothed it, willing the animal to be calm, then threw the two bags onto a rocky shelf. If the animal ran off again, at least she would not lose the food.

Nuy sniffed at the air, which had grown thicker, then looked south. A barely visible dark mass was just beginning to form in the southern sky, but she felt a disturbance in the air. The storm would not reach her until that afternoon, possibly not even until evening, but she did not want to be caught on the flat open plain in the middle of a storm. Her neck prickled, and she knew that this storm would be a violent one. Chiang had said that his companions would wait for him at the spot where she had first seen them. She would wait here until the storm passed before she went to them.

She stayed with the horse, rubbing its back from time to time as it drank, letting it grow more accustomed to her. At midday, she took food from one of the packs, pieces of a dried chewy substance that tasted sweet, then searched through the bag. There were still two of the meat-filled packets Chiang had given to her, but the rest of the food was small bags filled with dried meat, a pale soft grainy substance, or dried sweets like those she had just eaten, along with round red or orange fruits. She had only the haziest memories of how her people had prepared such foods when they were still trading with the northerners. She would eat no more that day, knowing that she had to make the food last. If the pangs of hunger grew to be too much for her, she could chew on some of the reeds by the riverbank. The reeds provided even less nourishment than rits, but they would fill her belly for a while, and she might be lucky enough to find a bird or its eggs to eat.

By late afternoon, the wind had picked up and black clouds were billowing toward her from the south. Nuy led the horse to the northern side of the ridge, slipped off its bridle, and secured it with the rope under a rocky overhang, then went to get the packs. By the time she had settled herself under the ledge, with the packs at her side, the wind was howling. This storm might not be as fierce as the one that had driven her people away from the sea, but she had rarely heard such a high, loud shriek in the wind.

Good, she thought; the storm would keep her father from coming after her. He would not be able to follow her to the two who had come south with Chiang.

*T*he wind howled through the night, bringing little rain but lighting the sky with bright daggers of light. The deafening claps of thunder frightened the horse so badly that it neighed and pulled at its rope. Nuy clung to the animal, trying to soothe it and fearing that it might break its rope and flee. The noise of the wind and thunder made it impossible to sleep.

By morning, she was exhausted, her body a mass of aches from her efforts to restrain the horse. The animal was calmer now, no longer fighting her but still trembling; maybe it was as tired as she was. The storm had weakened, but thunder still rolled across the sky, and the dark clouds did not look as though they would lift any time soon. She decided that it was best to stay where she was until she was sure that the storm would not return.

The sound of her voice, now that she could be heard over the wind and thunder, seemed to quiet the horse. She began to tell it the stories Katti and Daniella had told her, of how they had left the north to settle by the sea, and of how even before that, their people had come down from the sky to settle on Home. Once her people had lived among the northerners, but they had followed Ho south when he had told them of the life they might have by the sea, where the colder seasons would not touch them, where they could live apart from those who had fought against Ho in the sky and would not allow him to be leader on Home. The northerners might hide themselves away from the world, but Ho and his band would embrace it, and maybe they would change and grow stronger by doing so.

Even as she told the stories, Nuy realized how hollow they sounded. The storm had driven her people away from the sea, from the shore where she and Carin had spent so many peaceful hours gazing out at the ocean and listening to the waves break; Nuy had often imagined that the sea was calling to them. Maybe Home was punishing them, rejecting them. Maybe this world, after welcoming them, was turning against those who had come down from the sky.

She refused to believe that. This was her world. She felt that too deeply inside herself to doubt it.

When she was sure that the horse would stay calm, she stretched out and slept. The silence woke her in the night; she realized that the storm had passed. She took a red fruit from one of the packs, bit through the peel, and ate it down to the core, spitting the seeds into her hand, then slipped the seeds into a pouch inside the pack. Seeds could be planted; they might also tell her father that she had food to sustain her if he followed her here and found the seeds. Better, she told herself, that he believed her to be dead so that he would not come after her.

She might be dead soon enough.

But not yet, she thought.

By dawn, Nuy had filled her waterskin, washed herself off, and buried the horse's wastes along with her own while the animal drank. Her father might guess that she had come here, even that she had found the horse again, but she did not want to confirm any of his suspicions.

Ho would not come after her right away, she insisted to herself. He was still too afraid that she might be carrying whatever death the northerners had brought. He would wait until even Belen would be unable to detect any traces of her trail. But another part of her worried that Ho's mind was now so beset by his inner storms that she could not assume anything about him.

The horse balked only a little as she secured the packs to its back, then led it away from the ridge. She would bypass the watering hole where she had stopped with Chiang, and cut across the plain to the northwest. She would reach the place where Chiang's companions waited more quickly that way, and the horse could go without water for that distance. There would be enough time to think about what she would say to the two people from the north.

My people killed your friend. They didn't mean to do it, they struck out without thinking, they were afraid and shot at him from across the stream and your friend died before anyone could pull him from the water. I didn't know what would happen, or I would never have guided your comrade there. I thought my father would welcome Chiang and be grateful for whatever he could give us, I didn't know how fearful he still was of your people.

All of that seemed false, even to her. The more she dwelled on how she would explain herself to Chiang's people, the more convinced she became that she was as responsible for Chiang's death as her father or Belen. She had taken him there, she had ignored all the signs of Ho's inner turmoil and Belen's increasing cruelty, she had been thinking of how grateful her people would be to her for bringing the stranger and his food. She had been thinking of her full belly and of how she might use Chiang and his goods to her own advantage. She had thought of herself as much as she had of Chiang's safety and of Carin and Sarojin and the welfare of her people.

She would have to explain everything to Chiang's companions and then hope that they could forgive her for what she had done.

Nuy spotted the ridge from where she had first seen the three northerners before she glimpsed the long gray snake of the river. The ridge lay to the north, and even when the river was clearly in view, she could make out no sign of Chiang's companions, no smoke from a fire, no signs of movement among the grass and the boltrees and the dark green reeds along the riverbank.

She trudged on, still leading the horse, refusing to believe what she so clearly saw until she was too close to the river to deny it any longer. The place where the three had made camp was abandoned; the only sign that anyone had been there was a blackened mound of ashes surrounded by rocks. Chiang had said that they would wait for him. Clearly they had not stayed there as long as he had expected.

Had they decided to go back to their people? Somehow she doubted it. No, they had expected Chiang to follow the river to the sea, to where they had thought Nuy's people were still living. Instead of waiting for him, they had gone after him, and they would have gone south, right into the path of the storm. She only hoped that they had reached the caves by the sea, and that those caves had provided enough protection.

It suddenly occurred to her that if her father somehow managed to overcome his fears and came after her, that he would expect her to take refuge there, by the sea, in a place that she knew. But she had no choice. She would have to go there and find the two strangers and hope that she could persuade them to take her with them to their settlement before Ho had any chance to discover them.

The horse stood on the riverbank, drinking from the stream. Nuy waited until it lifted its head, then took the rope and led the animal downstream.

Part Two

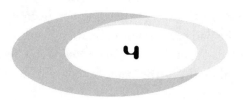

4

*T*he cattle grazed in the open field to the north. The horses were far to Leila's right, small brown and black and reddish shapes near the northeastern horizon. The grass around her, thicker where the animals hadn't yet grazed, was nearly as high as her waist. The green grass dominated the land south of the hills where the domes of the two settlements stood, but here, around the lake, rippling yellow bands of the native grass were visible among the green, marking the boundary between the familiar area near the settlements and unknown territory.

Unknown territory, Leila thought, to everyone in the settlements, anyway. Other people lived in the unknown lands, far to the south of the lake. At least she assumed that the outsiders were still alive. The last time anyone had traveled here from the outside had been ten years ago.

"Colulos," her sister Rosa murmured as she stretched an arm toward the violet flowers. "Why did you call them colulos?"

"I don't know," Leila replied. "I don't remember." The broad violet petals of the colulos grew from long slender green stalks along the shore of the lake. When she had been hardly more than a baby, she had given the flowers their name; Luis, her father's brother, had told the story many times. She had pointed to them and blurted out the name, according to Luis, and it had stuck. "We'd better get back."

Rosa looked away from the gray expanse of the lake. "How big is the lake?" she asked. "How far south does it go?"

"Go to the library and look it up," Leila said.

"Why do we have to go to the library to find out? Why can't we just go all the way around the lake and see how big it is for ourselves?"

"Someday we will. Someday, we'll go exploring." Leila fell silent, knowing she shouldn't say any more to her younger sister than that.

"Somebody already has," Rosa said, "but they never came back, and now everybody's even more afraid to go. That's what you mean, isn't it?"

"Come on," Leila said, cutting her sister off, then helped Rosa climb into their small cart, already heaped with the stalks of colulos that the two girls had harvested. Once, the blossoms had been used only for decoration, until Luis had experimented with them and found that the flowers and stalks could be pounded into a paste that hardened enough to be used to patch walls and seal passageways. Some of the life of this world could supplement what they had brought with them, some was useless to them, and some presumably could be dangerous, even fatal. So far, they had been lucky, but maybe only because they had kept so close to the settlements they had built for themselves.

A narrow dirt road ran from the lake toward the settlements, alongside one of the canals that irrigated the fields. Leila touched the panel in front of her; the cart moved along the road. Rosa had not yet been born the last time outsiders had come here, but Leila could remember the visitors. Her mother and Aleksandr had met the two travelers, who had come there on horseback, stayed only overnight, and then left with a train of six more horses loaded down with supplies. The man who had spoken to her mother had been a large man with a beard and hair as yellow as the native grass, and a voice loud enough to drown out the sound of even a strong wind; he had seemed unafraid of anything. Yet her mother and Aleksandr had shaken their heads and twisted their faces into expressions of pity after the visitors left.

"Maybe it's only their pride," Leila's mother had said to Aleksandr while laying yet another warm cloth on Leila's forehead, "or maybe it's just that they've forgotten so much that they don't realize what's happening to them." She had been keeping Leila, who was recovering from an illness that made her head ache and her nose run, on a mat and under blankets in the common room of their dome, which was warmer than the room where she usually slept. Almost all of the children had recently come down with the illness, but they had been assured by Kagami the healer that it was nothing serious, and most of the others had already recovered.

"They're surviving," Aleksandr had said.

"Yes, they're surviving, but they're not thriving. You saw how little they brought us in trade this time. Owen looks a lot older than thirty, and Katti is emaciated."

"They're not your concern, Zoheret."

"I feel as though they are," Leila's mother had replied to that. "They should be our concern."

"They chose to leave here and go off on their own."

"They didn't know what they were doing."

"They should have known, and they could have come back at any time," Aleksandr said. "If they didn't want to live among us, they could have built their own settlement nearby, far enough away so that they could keep to themselves and not cause trouble but close enough to share some of our resources and our work. They made their decision."

"Their children didn't decide anything," Zoheret replied.

"We don't even know for certain if they have any children."

"I can't believe that they wouldn't have had children," Zoheret said. "They wouldn't have gone off the way they did just to let themselves die out."

"It's not our concern."

"What you're saying is that we refuse to make it our concern. We could have done something more about it than we have, we still could, but we don't. They tell us nothing about how they're getting along, and they've never asked any of us to come with them to their settlement. We can tell ourselves that we did what we could and there's nothing more we can do."

"We have enough to worry about here, Zoheret."

"That's just another excuse."

Even after all this time, Leila remembered that conversation, and not only because that was the last time any of the outsiders had come there, but also because her mother had sounded so upset and angry, her voice higher and harsher than usual. Zoheret had never argued with Aleksandr, at least not when others were around, and never in Leila's presence. Public disagreements were unconstructive and demoralizing, Zoheret had always claimed; better to sort them out privately with her fellow leader or at a closed meeting with the board.

"We refuse to help them," Zoheret had added, "and you know why." That remark had been enough for Aleksandr to mutter under his breath and storm out of the dome. He had returned later that evening to share a cup of tea with Zoheret and Leila's father, but Leila remembered how angry he had been.

It had taken her a few more years to understand what had made Aleksandr so angry. It wasn't that the settlements didn't have enough to share with the outsiders; they might have had to ration a few things, but there probably would have been enough to go around. It wasn't even because of the old grudges that Leila knew some people here still held against them.

Aleksandr had been angry because Zoheret had come too close to speaking of their deepest fears.

No one spoke of why almost all of the settlers had never strayed far from their homes, fields, and pastures, why they had built no more than the five boats they had used while stocking the lake with fish, boats they now used only infrequently for fishing. There were good reasons for staying close to their dwellings. Home, as Kagami the healer had put it, was not a perfect fit for them. To survive here had meant establishing their own ecology of plant and animal life around their settlement; they could not have lived on just the native plants and the small rodents and insects that had been the only indigenous life forms on the small and isolated island continent they had settled. To travel far from the settled area meant exposure to unknown dangers, including those posed by the big cats, bears, and wolves that were there to prey upon the deer and other species they had brought to this world, assuming that those transplanted predators had been able to survive.

But they also feared the open sky above as well as the unknown world beyond the settlement. Many of the domes that housed them were now linked by enclosed passageways, and although most of the older settlers were able to go outside for varying periods of time, there were a few among the adults who avoided the outside as much as possible, people like Rina and Karl, who would look up warily at the sky before hurrying as fast as they could across the open spaces to their destinations. Lately Rina, who lived in one of the domes near Zoheret's, hardly left her home at all except to march to the dome that housed the library, always keeping to the same path, scurrying uphill toward the large dome without ever glancing to her right or her left. Only a few nights ago, Zoheret had sent Leila up to the library to see if Rina was still there and might need some help to walk home.

Leila had found her sitting at a table, staring at a reader screen. Rina was alone, since almost everyone else in the settlements was either eating a late meal or preparing to go to sleep. She had looked up as Leila approached, an uneasy smile flickering across her face.

"Greetings, Leila." The alto voice came from a square metal box that sat on another table, the shell that housed the artificial intelligence called the librarian. "May I help you in locating a text?"

"No, thank you," Leila replied.

"It sounds like Ship," Rina said then. "Ship had a voice like that sometimes, and other times it would drop to a lower pitch. The librarian reminds me so much of Ship." She ran a hand through her unruly red hair. "What brings you here so late?"

"My mother sent me." Leila hesitated. "She wanted me to look something up for her."

Rina's smile faded. "You don't have to give me some sort of excuse. I know why you're here." She blanked the reader screen, then stood up. "Let's go. It's already night. That should make it easier, not having to see the sky, the light, the space, but it doesn't. Sometimes seeing the blackness and the stars just makes it even worse." She looked toward the room in the back of the library, the room everyone still called Ship's Room, the place in which the settlement's one piece of radio technology still remained enshrined, even though the space vessel that had brought the settlers here had left this system before Leila had been born. "Thank you for coming here, Leila."

"You don't have to thank me."

"Yes, I do, and I should also thank Zoheret for finding work for me in the library. She saw how hard it was getting for me just to make it to our greenhouse. I thought I would be past all this by now, but instead it's getting worse."

Rina had never spoken to her so frankly before. "You're not the only one," Leila murmured, hoping that she hadn't said the wrong thing.

"No, I'm not the only one." Rina stood up, then suddenly sat down again and turned toward Ship's Room. "I kept thinking that Ship would come back," she said, "that I'd hear its voice again. I'd tell myself that Ship would eventually understand that some of us, maybe most of us, might not ever be able to adapt, that it had made a terrible mistake in leaving us here. But now I know that's not going to happen. Ship's never coming back."

"Rina—"

"We didn't have to come here." Rina shifted in her chair. "We could have stayed aboard, lived out our lives inside Ship. But Ship couldn't overcome its programming. That's what it comes down to, I suppose. Ship had to continue seeding habitable worlds with human life, even after it found out the truth about the people who had programmed it, and that meant leaving us here."

Rina shouldn't have been talking like this, Leila thought, and especially not to her. "I'll walk back to your dome with you," Leila said.

"I could have made it by myself. I want you to know that."

"Of course you could have."

"But it'll be easier for me if we go together."

Leila had said nothing to her mother about what Rina had told her that night. The fears, the doubts, the fading hopes among a few that Ship might return, were all subjects Zoheret had refused to discuss on those rare occasions when Leila had dared to bring them up. This was their world now, they had managed with some hard work to make a reasonably good life for themselves on Home, and to talk about hopes for Ship's return would only feed discontent and weaken their community.

A black horse with a rider suddenly broke away from the herd and trotted in their direction. Trevor, the best rider among Leila's friends, was astride the horse. Leila had learned how to ride along with all of her friends, but she still lacked Trevor's ease with horses. Trevor rode bareback, the way all of them had when they were younger, learning what they could about how to ride from the historical records in the library and how to use pressure from their legs and gentle tugs on their reins to control a horse and in spite of all their efforts being thrown by their mounts much of the time. Now most of them rode the horses only when they had to, when walking was impractical, all of their few carts were being used, or when they had to herd the horses or the cattle. Trevor would have stayed on horseback almost all of the time if he could.

Trevor slowed his horse to a trot as he approached them. "Leila," he called out.

She lifted her hand, then let it fall. "Trevor." She pressed the panel again; the cart rolled to a stop. "Rosa," she continued, "could you take all of these plants back by yourself?"

The younger girl glanced from Leila to Trevor, then rolled her eyes. "I suppose I have to unload them all by myself, too."

"I'll be back in plenty of time to help you, I promise."

Leila got out of the cart. Rosa let out a sigh, pulled at her wide-brimmed hat, then leaned forward to touch the panel.

The cart hummed softly, then started to move again. "Just don't take too long."

"I won't," Leila said. "And don't forget to recharge the cart's cells when you get back."

Rosa wrinkled her nose. "I won't," she replied.

Trevor gazed after the cart, then turned his head toward where Leila waited, sensing what he was about to say.

"Yukio's getting more impatient," he said. "So is Sofia, and Edan's going to talk to his father tonight. They're ready any time, so we shouldn't put things off any longer." He held his reins in his left hand as his horse circled Leila. "What about you?"

"I don't know."

"You do know. It was your idea as much as mine, you were pushing me whenever you thought I might change my mind, and now you're backing away."

"I'm not backing away from anything," she said. "I just think maybe we should discuss it some more before we ask for permission."

Trevor brushed back a lock of long black hair, then shook his head at her. "We've talked about it enough." He swung one leg in front of him and slid from his horse's back, landing gracefully on his feet. "We need you to do what you promised. If you can convince your mother, she can convince the board, even if Aleksandr might not be so willing to go along."

"I think you'd go even if the board decided against us and wouldn't give us what we need."

"Maybe I would." He removed the horse's bridle and slapped the animal lightly on its flank; the horse dropped its head and began to graze. "But I'd rather not. What is it, Leila? Can't be because you're afraid."

"I don't know if we're ready for this," she said, "not yet."

"If we wait much longer, we'll never be ready. We'll keep finding more reasons not to leave. Look, this is the time to go, before the colder weather comes. If we run into something we aren't ready for, we can always turn back."

"We might not be able to turn back." She looked away from him as she spoke. "We might not return at all. Tonio and Chiang and your mother didn't come back."

Trevor exhaled sharply and she immediately regretted her words. She should not have mentioned the three who had left the settlement a year ago to go south, to see what they could find out about the outsiders, and who had never returned.

"We don't know why they didn't come back," he said at last, "and maybe they're on their way back by now."

"After all this time?" She shouldn't have said that, either. She forced herself to look at him. "I'm sorry, Trevor."

He stared past her with the greenish eyes that were so much like those of his mother Bonnie. "I know it's not likely," he said. "My father keeps insisting that she has to be alive, that there has to be a good reason why she and the others aren't back yet, but I know better. I could believe that she was still alive a few months ago, but not anymore."

"There's still a chance," she said, knowing how hollow her words sounded.

"Not that much of a chance. At least one of them would have found some way to get back here by now, to let us know what happened, to get more supplies, to warn us if there's something out there that we should know about. Aleksandr and Zoheret and the board should have organized another group to go and search for them long before now." Trevor sighed. "You think this is just about my mother, but it isn't. I'd feel the same way even if she hadn't decided to go. Sooner or later we have to see what's out there for ourselves."

He was right, of course. However thorough the records were

in the library, there were details that Ship's scans might have missed. Something out there might pose a threat to them. Ignorance and fear of the unknown would be no protection against such potential dangers.

"It'll be hard for your father," she said, "to have to worry about you, too."

"It'll be hard for all of our parents, for everybody."

"It'll be harder for your father," Leila insisted. "My parents would still have my sister and each other. Anoki wouldn't have anybody."

"He keeps thinking about what might have happened to my mother, and then he gets angry because all of that might have been prevented if the boards had just listened to his earlier suggestions. Is it going to be that much worse for him to be worrying about me, too? He wanted to go with her before. He'd leave here by himself to look for her if he could."

"I know," she said.

"Anyway, why bring that up now? You're just looking for an excuse to put everything off. Then we'd have to wait until the warmer weather returns, and by then we'd probably find some other reason to stay here."

"Maybe I'm afraid." She could admit that to him. She would not have said it in front of anyone else.

"I'm afraid, too." She was surprised at his admission. "Anybody with any sense would be afraid," Trevor continued. "I have to find out what happened to my mother if I can, but it isn't just that. We have to go outside this settlement and see what's out there, or it'll just become easier and easier never to leave at all."

"I know," she said. "I'll talk to my mother tonight, or tomorrow at the latest."

"Good." Trevor whistled; the black horse trotted toward him. He slipped the reins over the horse's head, then leaped onto the animal's back. Leila watched him ride away from her, moving as though he and the horse were one being, riding with the grace his father Anoki lacked.

There were enough good reasons for her and Trevor to explore more of this continent, enough arguments to make before the board even without mentioning the three whose fates were unknown.

But Anoki had to be behind his son's plans to leave the settlements. She was sure of that, even though Trevor had never admitted it or given her any reason to assume it. Anoki couldn't search for his mate himself, so his son would have to go in his place, however afraid he might be. Anoki would expect his son to be as courageous and adventurous as his mother. Trevor might confess his fears to Leila, but he would never have admitted them to his father.

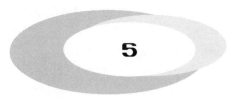

5

*T*he windmills turned as Leila and Rosa climbed the hill to their dome. Long bluish shadows cast by the arms of the windmills fluttered over the domes of their settlement, which lay to the west of the wheat fields. Luis had met them at the entrance to the eastern settlement's greenhouse and helped them carry their harvest of colulos to his laboratory.

Rosa pulled her hat off her blond head and tucked it under her arm. "Luis wasn't wearing his eyes again," Rosa murmured as they approached their dome.

"That's nothing new," Leila said.

"He does that more now, not wearing them."

Leila did not want to think about that. "When I don't really need them, it's sometimes easier to leave them off," Luis had told her some time ago about his goggles. "Helps me get used to being without them." Luis was blind without his goggles.

He had been born that way, and needed his goggles to see anything at all. Even with Ship's advanced technology, a few of its children had emerged from Ship's wombs with physical limitations.

"But you don't have to get along without them," Leila had objected.

"It doesn't hurt to be prepared," her father's brother had replied. "What if they fail me some day? Then I'd have to be able to get along without them."

Luis had sounded like Anoki, Trevor's father. Anoki's limp had grown worse in recent years, yet he still resisted using a cart when he had to walk a longer than usual distance, and lately he had taken to using a long stick to support himself during his walks. Better to adapt to any pain or discomfort; there might come a day when the carts could not be repaired or their batteries and fuel cells would fail and even more surgery might not be able to help him. Ship had given them the tools they needed to survive on Home, but how long would they be able to maintain them or replace them? How much time would pass before they were able to create their own more advanced technological base and replicate what they had been given?

Their small dome was just behind the larger one shared by her friends Yukio and Sofia and their families. Leila climbed the three steps to the door and pushed it open.

Manuel was sitting on the floor as she and Rosa entered, on a mat in front of the table, his head bowed over their family's reading screen. Scrapper, their cat, was curled up next to Manuel, resting after yet another day of keeping their dwelling free of vermin. It was unusual for their father to be home this early; he and Zoheret usually didn't get back to their dome until after dark.

He lifted his head and gave them a quick smile. "Greetings," he said. Unlike many of the men, their father wore no beard, keeping his face scraped clean with a razor. "And what were you two doing today?"

"Harvesting colulos for Luis," Rosa replied as she sat down next to Manuel.

"Not the most interesting work to do," Manuel said, "but not the hardest, either."

Rosa leaned against their father. "It's not so bad," she said, "but I'll be glad when it's time for our lessons again." Their classes at the library were to resume during the month of First Frost, three months from now.

Leila shrugged as she sat down across from them. "I'd rather be harvesting plants than doing lessons."

Manuel shook his head at her. "Better not say that in front of Lillka. You're lucky to have as good a teacher as she is."

"Lillka's all right," Leila said.

"You used to look forward to your times in the library with her. I hope you're going to do better at your lessons than you did last year."

Leila frowned. Lillka wouldn't have complained directly about any of her students to their parents, or told them outright that a particular boy or girl was being lazy, sloppy, or careless during lessons. Instead, she would have paid a visit to Manuel and Zoheret, sighed, and spoken of how well Leila had once been doing, of how enthusiastic she used to be about learning new skills and searching the library's databases and records, and then she would have sighed some more and shaken her head. What she really meant would have been clear enough to Leila's parents, namely that Leila was not doing as well as she might have been, that a once-promising student had either grown lazy or had perhaps reached her intellectual limits, and that the library's precious and carefully maintained resources were wasted on her. If she didn't show any improvement next season, then

Lillka would recommend that Leila drop all her studies except for her lessons in practical pursuits. After that, she would pass most of her time in mastering whatever skills she showed the most aptitude for and preparing for whatever work would most benefit the settlements while looking forward to finding a mate and rearing her own children.

What a narrow and constricted life it was, Leila thought, not for the first time. The older people thought of nothing but maintaining what they had and passing that life on to the children who would follow them. They lived on Home much as the cats and dogs they had brought to this world lived among them, grateful for what they were given, set in their habits and uneasy with any sudden break in their routine, bound by their limits, hanging on to what they had built without creating much that was new. It seemed impossible that they could be the people she had read about and seen images of in the records, the ones who had been brave enough to leave the familiarity of Ship for the unknown, who had struggled to fulfill the goal of seeding Home with human life.

Once, she had thrilled to the stories of their exploits, and taken pride in being a child of such people. But if her life was to be no more than hanging on to what Zoheret and Manuel had made for her and her sister, then poring over the records and studying what Lillka called the history of their species were useless.

She could go on as she was expected to do, and wait for the inevitable day when Lillka would sigh and shake her head and then advise her to drop most of her lessons and prepare herself for life as an adult. Or she could speak up for herself and for the others of her friends who were impatient to explore what lay beyond their settlements. Tonight, she would tell her mother what they were planning, as she had just about promised to do, and try to gain Zoheret's support for the venture. Whatever Trevor might say, Leila knew that they would need the help and support of the settlements if they were to have any chance of going out and returning safely.

Even with their carefully laid and cautious plans, they might not return at all. That was one possible outcome, too. Zoheret would be thinking of her old friends while Leila was speaking of their plans for an expedition, of the three explorers who had already been lost.

Manuel turned off the reading screen, then got to his feet. Scrapper stretched, then licked at his thick orange fur. "You girls must be hungry," Manuel said. "We've got some bread left, and there's cheese and fruit." He gestured at the grapes on the table. "Do you want to eat here, or at the public hall?"

"The hall," Rosa replied.

"Well, come on, then."

Leila said, "I'm not that hungry. I'll wait until Zoheret comes home."

"She might be late," Manuel said. "She had a longer shift at the greenhouse today."

"That's all right." Trevor would probably be at the hall, eating with his father or a few friends; Leila recalled that Sofia, Lillka's daughter, was supposed to be on kitchen duty that evening, helping to prepare and serve the community supper. Trevor and Sofia would be expecting her to speak to Zoheret about their plans. She would have a better chance at convincing her mother if she spoke to her alone, without Manuel around to raise any objections.

Manuel held out a hand to Rosa and pulled her to her feet. She leaned against him for a moment as he ruffled her white-yellow hair. Rosa was already taller than Leila had been at her age, with bigger bones and bright blue eyes instead of the dark brown eyes of Leila and their parents. Unlike them, Rosa often had to wear a hat at midday to keep her pale skin from turning a bright pink, and her fine blond hair was a contrast to Leila's coarser and thicker black hair. Most of the couples in the settlements had more than one child, and often only their first-born was theirs genetically.

"We need variant strains," was the way Kagami the healer, who knew more biology and medicine than anyone else, had put it when explaining the physical differences of those who were siblings to Leila and her friends. The small laboratory next to Kagami's dome housed the preserved sperm and ova of thousands of the people who had sent Ship on its journey. More variety in their genetic heritages would keep them from growing too inbred and ensure healthier descendants. A larger gene pool would give those who would follow them more ways to adapt to unforeseen changes in their environment.

Zoheret had carried both of her daughters inside herself before giving birth to them; like all of the other parents, she and her mate Manuel drew no distinction between their biological and gestational children. Leila had never seen any sign that her parents cared any less for Rosa than for her. Lately, in fact, there were more signs of their wishing that Leila might be a little more like her clever and industrious sister.

Manuel paused in the doorway, glanced back at Leila with a worried look on his face, then followed Rosa outside; the door closed behind them.

Leila got up, went to the cupboard to get some bread and cheese, then changed her mind. After pumping some water from their cistern into a large curved shell and setting that on the floor for the cat, she crossed the room and opened the outside door.

The sky had grown dark green and the wind was picking up, as it usually did in the evening. Below her on the hillside, Manuel and Rosa had been joined by Lillka's mate Brendan and his dog Tyra, a setter, who followed Brendan everywhere whenever she wasn't being used to herd the sheep. Other people would be making their way to the community hall through the corridors that connected some of the domes to the hall.

The heat of the day lingered, but Leila smelled change in the air; the spicy scent of the wind was mustier, an early sign of cooler weather to come. Colder winds would sweep down on the settlements from the mountainous lands to the north, which according to the records were covered with ice and snow for nearly half the year. The yellow native grass on the plain below would begin to turn white in about a month, and two months or so after that, the first frost would appear. She and her friends would have to leave within the next few days if they wanted to get back here before beads of ice covered the ground.

Leila sat down on the steps outside the doorway, resting her arms on her knees. She and her friends had pored over the records of Ship's scans, the maps, images, and data that had been compiled before their parents had been allowed to leave Ship for Home. They would not have to travel through territory about which they knew nothing. But Trevor's mother Bonnie and her two companions had studied the same records, yet had not returned. Something overwhelming and completely unexpected must have come upon them.

Their greenhouse was near the bottom of the hill, its glassy roof golden in the evening light. A wide field of grain lay between this settlement and the hill to the east on which the other settlement stood. Aleksandr was the leader there, as Leila's mother was here. The adults in Aleksandr's group were older and had grown up apart from Zoheret's group aboard Ship, reaching adulthood before learning that the world Ship had originally chosen for them was in fact uninhabitable. After arriving on Home, the two groups had decided to build two separate settlements, close enough so that they could work together and share resources, but with each group governing itself. As the years passed, the elected boards of advisors in each settlement had held more of their meetings jointly, while Zoheret and Aleksandr consulted with each other so often that the eastern and western settlements had become, in practice, one community. Leila could not think of any dispute that had ever divided them, and Zoheret and Aleksandr almost never disagreed on anything as far as she knew, at least not in public.

But they had disagreed about the outsiders, about how much help to give them, about whether or not to seek them out and find out more about the land beyond their settlements. Leila recalled the night when the two leaders had argued ten years ago, when Aleksandr had angrily left Zoheret's dome.

What would they think when Leila told them what she and Trevor were planning? Would that be enough to bring the two into open disagreement? Zoheret might become the one to argue against sending out an expedition, while Aleksandr could remind her that she had spoken up for Bonnie and her comrades earlier, that she might only be worrying now because her own daughter would be at risk. With their two leaders disagreeing openly, people would take sides, which was probably the reason Aleksandr and Zoheret preferred not to air any disputes in front of others.

Leila leaned back against the wall. People trusted her mother. Every time Zoheret even hinted that she might give up her position and ask the people in her settlement to choose another leader, so many people had objected that she had always decided to stay on. Everyone trusted her as their leader. Maybe they trusted her too much, depended on her too much.

Leila heard a movement behind her, and turned her head. Her mother was coming down the hill toward her. "Zoheret," Leila called out, surprised. "I thought you'd be at the greenhouse."

"I left early," her mother replied. "Promised to look after

Cho Lin's new baby so she and Julius could have some time to themselves. Their other children were planning to go to an early supper with their friends. I thought I mentioned my plans to your father."

"I guess you forgot."

"And why are you sitting out here all alone?"

"Manuel and Rosa went to supper. I decided to wait for you."

Zoheret sat down next to her. "I feel too tired to walk to the hall and I still have to check the latrine." The settlement's toilets, designed by Anoki, compressed their wastes for use as fertilizer, but each family was responsible for collecting the small bricks and taking them to the sheds next to the greenhouses.

"We can eat here, then. We've still got enough food inside."

"Then I'll eat with you." Zoheret leaned back. "Cho Lin says that this is going to be her last child, but I wouldn't be surprised if she changes her mind in a few years." Their new child was the fourth for Cho Lin and Julius; theirs was one of the larger families in the settlement. Most of the couples here and in Aleksandr's settlement had two or three children, although they were all still young enough to have one or two more if that was what they chose to do. Trevor's parents Bonnie and Anoki, however, had only one child, because giving birth to Trevor had been so hard on his mother that Kagami had strongly advised Bonnie not to bear any more children.

Everyone was familiar with Bonnie's situation, because it had led the community to decide in a public meeting against using the technology they had brought with them for the gestation of embryos and fetuses in artificial wombs unless an unforeseen emergency required such a measure to save a fetus's life. Their energy sources were still too limited for them to drain them of power when that energy was needed to maintain their greenhouses, their looms, and other facilities. It was the same reasoning that had brought them to rely on their food dispensers, which could create all kinds of foods from recycled materials, only when there were severe shortages of necessary nutrients. Using stored genetic material for their gestational children did not involve as many risks, or an extreme dependence on technology they might not be able to repair or replace for ages, if ever, and was a temporary measure anyway until their population grew much larger.

As always, they would be cautious, but the decision had deeply disappointed and angered Bonnie. They should use what they had while they could, she had argued. There would be problems no matter what they chose to do, and more risks for women of childbearing age if they didn't make more use of the technology they had. Shouldn't they have more faith in their ingenuity, in their ability to solve any future problems that might come up? Wouldn't increasing their numbers by making full use of the tools they had give them a better chance of survival in the long run? Zoheret had agreed with Bonnie, and spoken for her at the meeting, but even her words had not been enough to sway the others.

"I don't think I want any children until I'm at least twenty," Leila said, although many of the people in Zoheret's settlement had become parents before that age. Maybe she wouldn't want any even then, although that wasn't something she would admit to aloud. Their communities needed children if they were to grow and thrive; everyone knew that, whatever noises they might make about parenthood having to be freely chosen and not imposed on anyone. She wondered if anybody else felt the way she sometimes did.

"You sound like me when I was about your age," Zoheret murmured. "I used to think that I might never have any children, that I wouldn't be able to bear it."

Leila glanced at her mother, surprised to hear the dark and fearful undercurrents in her lowered voice. "Really? But why?"

She paused. "Was it because of what happened with Bonnie, because it was so hard for her?"

"No, it wasn't because of that. I wasn't afraid of the pain or all the physical changes. Well, maybe I was, a little. Don't get me wrong, I've never been sorry that I have my daughters. But haven't you ever wondered why you're the youngest one of the firstborn?"

Leila shrugged. "Not really. I just assumed you had so much to do as our leader that it took you longer to get around to having a child."

"That was what I used to tell myself. There would be enough children without mine, I had enough responsibilities already, and Manuel would go along with any decision I made. And I'd think that maybe there should be someone around to be an example to those who might be worrying about their fitness to be parents, to demonstrate that it had to be a choice and not something forced on people who might have doubts about their ability to be good parents. Besides, all of the children here are ours, just as we were all Ship's children, so in a sense we're all parents to all of you anyway. Oh, I had plenty of reasons, but they weren't the real reasons."

Zoheret gazed past her. "I didn't know," she continued, "if I could bear to have children and then have to push them away from me, the way Ship did with us. I told myself that if I had to do that, bring children into this life knowing that eventually I might have to let them go, however much pain it might cause them and me, then I'd rather not have them at all."

Leila was silent, not knowing what to say, then felt her mother's hand on her shoulder.

"And here you are," Zoheret said, "so as you can see, I changed my mind."

"Why?" Leila managed to say. "What made you change your mind?"

"I'm not really sure. Maybe it was seeing how happy Aleksandr and Maire were after their son Denya was born. Of course, that was a while later, when Maire and Aleksandr were finally able to get enough sleep to appreciate him." A smile flitted across Zoheret's face. "It might have had something to do with knowing how much Manuel wanted a child, even if he wouldn't admit it and even though I knew he'd go along with whatever I wanted. Maybe it was just Manuel and me finally being the only two people around who didn't have any children. Ship used to say that human beings were creatures with strong instincts and powerful urges to reproduce." She let out her breath. "I don't suppose I'll ever really be sure. All I can say is that the day finally came when I realized that I wanted a child of my own and knew I was making the right decision."

This kind of talk, Leila thought, wasn't going to make it any easier for her to speak to her mother about what she and her friends were planning.

"I'm getting hungry." Zoheret stood up and held out a hand to Leila, then pulled her to her feet. Leila followed her mother inside. Zoheret waved a hand at the table. "What have we got to eat besides those grapes?"

"Manuel said there's some bread and cheese left."

"No chicken?"

"Only enough for Scrapper."

"Then that will have to do." Zoheret went to the small square cooler in the corner and took out the food, while Leila pumped water from the cistern into a pitcher, then set it and two cups on the table.

"I've got something to tell you," Leila said as she sat down.

"Go ahead." Zoheret seated herself on the other side of the table and put a small bowl with the few remaining chicken shreds next to the cat.

"It's about something my friends and I are planning. I promised them that I'd mention it to you first, then ask for a meeting with the boards."

"The boards?" Zoheret arched her brows. "Not just our board?"

Leila shook her head. "We want to meet with both of the boards, and it should probably be a public meeting, too."

"Then it must be awfully important." Zoheret looked worried.

"We're planning an expedition." It would be better if she got it out fast, before Zoheret had a chance to object. "We're going to leave here and head south and try to find out what's happened to our three people and maybe make contact with the other people if we can. That means we'll need supplies, so we have to get approval. We've thought it out, how to do this as carefully and safely as possible, and if we run into anything we can't handle, then we'll come back here and consider going on another expedition another time."

"Apparently you've given this a lot of thought."

"We have," Leila said. "Trevor and I both agreed that we should be as careful as possible, and that means trying to plan for anything that might go wrong."

"So this is Trevor's idea."

"It was my idea as much as his," Leila said.

"Trevor's thinking of his mother, isn't he? That's probably his main reason for dreaming this scheme up."

"I told you—it was my idea as much as Trevor's, and it'd be worth doing even if his mother wasn't missing. He says so himself."

Zoheret had taken on the thin-lipped and glassy-eyed expression she usually wore when she was getting ready to argue with someone.

"Look, I didn't want to be so secretive about this," Leila said, "but Trevor thought if we were open about it, too many people would try to stop us before we ever got started."

Zoheret leaned forward and propped her elbows on the tabletop. "I knew this time would come," she said. "Sooner or later, somebody was going to propose another expedition." She smiled and shook her head. "I've thought of proposing one myself, so I shouldn't be surprised when my own daughter does."

"I can tell you all about it," Leila said, "what we'll need, how we're going to do this. We've tried to think of everything."

"Don't you think that Bonnie and Tonio and Chiang tried to think of everything? Don't you think that they were as careful as they could be?"

"Of course, but obviously they made some mistakes." This was not going well. If she couldn't get Zoheret on their side, there would be little point in asking for a meeting with the advisory board members, with her mother there to argue against their expedition.

"And exactly what mistakes did they make?" Zoheret asked.

"One was that they thought it would be better to go with a small group, with just the three of them. Their plan was to head south and make observations and try to make contact with the outsiders if they could and then come back here. We don't want to do it that way."

"And how is your way different?"

"For one thing, we'll start out with a larger group and more supplies and more horses to carry them."

"There were good reasons for sending out only a small group," Zoheret said.

"I know. Not that many people were willing to go."

"Not just that. There aren't so many of us that we can risk exposing larger groups to unknown dangers."

"I said that we'd start out with more people," Leila said.

"Then, two or three days out, one group will stop along the way and set up a camp, a kind of base. Later, maybe three days after that, another group will stop and set up another base. That'll mean that if we run into trouble and have to turn back, we won't have as far to go to get to a safer place. And the people at those bases can send somebody back here so that you'll know what's going on and what we've discovered up to that point."

Zoheret was silent, as if trying to think of more objections.

"Our plans are more detailed than that," Leila added, "but that's the general idea. And Trevor's father still complains that—" She paused, wondering if she should bring that up.

Zoheret said, "It's about that rejected proposal of his, isn't it."

"We could have had radio communications by now," Leila said. "It isn't that complicated a technology, he says, and then we would have had a way of sending out people and knowing what was happening when they were far away. Anoki's still angry that the boards turned down his proposal."

"I know that," Zoheret murmured, "but being able to communicate with each other over long distances isn't something we need at the moment."

"Not something we need." Leila could not restrain herself any longer. "Patch up whatever we have and don't take chances. Use all this stuff that shows us how advanced our ancestors were only when it's absolutely necessary and without making any of our own innovations. Use as little as possible and keep it locked away the rest of the time so we don't wear it out. Maybe Ship should have just sent you all down here with nothing, and maybe by now we would have figured out a few more things for ourselves."

"And maybe then all of us would have died, instead of only a few." Zoheret lifted a hand. "I'm not really arguing with you, Leila. Maybe it would have been better in the long run for

Ship to have left us here with fewer resources and only our ingenuity to depend on. In the short run, of course, that would have meant a lot more suffering and death."

Zoheret stared past Leila for several long moments without speaking, then said, "You'd need more supplies with a larger group. It'll cost us more in both people and resources, and that means more to lose if something goes wrong."

"I know, but it also means a better chance of a successful expedition. Besides, if we don't start taking more chances—"

"We'll all just keep hiding here, afraid to leave, afraid to really live in this world and be truly a part of it instead of just hanging on to the refuge we've built for ourselves."

"Then you do understand," Leila said.

"Of course I do." Zoheret rubbed at her own left shoulder; her arm had to be bothering her again. "We've been fortunate here so far. It could have been a lot harder for us. You haven't had to go through some of the losses and hardships we endured. Maybe we tried too hard to make sure that you never would." Zoheret's prosthetic arm was a legacy of those struggles. She had lost her left arm, and been given a new one by Ship, made partly of regenerated bone and tissue. That arm was almost indistinguishable from her right arm, and she could use it nearly as easily, but occasionally the places where her artificial arm was interwoven with nerve endings pained her. "I don't suppose you and Trevor have been plotting all by yourselves."

"Trevor and Sofia are both part of it, and Yukio, and Edan's going to talk to Aleksandr, but we should get more volunteers after we meet with the board. We didn't want to say anything to anyone else until after we asked for a public meeting."

"Explorers could run into a lot of trouble, and I'm not just talking about unforeseen dangers in unfamiliar territory. The people we call outsiders didn't want to stay with us because they had their own ideas about how to run things here. We had to fight them when we were still inside Ship, and I'm grateful we haven't had to fight them here."

Zoheret was silent for a moment, then said, "You won't have that long to get ready if you want to be well on your way and back here before the colder weather comes."

Leila let out a sigh, grateful. "Then you won't speak up against us."

"I know some people will think you should wait until next year, take some more time to prepare yourselves for this."

"And then there'll just be some other excuse." Leila shook her head.

"I can't make up my mind about anything," Zoheret murmured, "until I hear what you intend to tell the boards. I want to find out about what you're planning in more detail, and ask you a few more questions, and then I'll discuss it all with Aleksandr, and after that we'll decide if we should call a meeting."

Leila took a breath. Her mother would not stand in their way.

6

*L*eila trudged up the hill with Sofia, trailing Trevor, Edan, and Yukio. A warm rain fell from a dark grayish-green sky; the domes farther up the slope were dark humps in the mist. She and the others had taken their turn at cleaning out the stables where the horses were kept, one of the more unpleasant tasks, especially when it was raining. It was even more unpleasant during the cold season, when the horses and cattle had to be sheltered from the harsher weather and spent more time in their stalls.

Trevor and his father shared a dome with Muhammad and Miriam and their two children, Ali and Hannah, but the adults would be in the greenhouse that day, while Ali and Hannah were on kitchen duty. Normally Leila and the others would be on their way to one of the two community halls for their meal, but inside the dome, they would be able to talk with no one to overhear them.

Again she felt qualms about their secrecy; concealing their plans from everybody else seemed almost as bad as lying. Tung had given her a funny look at the stable that day when he and his group had arrived for their shift; he was already suspicious. Just the other day, in the greenhouse, he had asked her why she and her four accomplices were keeping to themselves lately, acting as if they had something to hide. "We're not hiding anything," she had replied, but she could tell that he did not believe her, and she had felt shame at her dishonesty. Chiang was his father; Tung deserved to be involved in their plans as much as anyone.

They climbed the three steps to the dome's entrance. Trevor motioned them all inside; Leila slipped her hood from her head. All of them took off their hooded capes and hung the damp garments on the hooks inside the doorway.

Trevor's mother no longer lived here, but something of Bonnie had remained in this dome. There had always been flowers on the low table in the common room, and somebody had brought a few pink roses from the small flower garden Bonnie had maintained in the greenhouse and arranged them in a bowl on the table. Two large pink shells, brought there by the outsiders in trade, were also on the table, and Bonnie's tapestries, abstract designs pieced together from scraps of fabric, still hung on the walls.

Trevor peered into the cooler while the rest of them sat down. "I thought there'd be some bean soup to heat up," he said, "but all we've got is some cheese."

"Then let's get everything settled so we still have time to eat at the hall," Leila said. "I talked to my mother. She'll back us up. I didn't even have to try all that hard to convince her."

"My father's on our side, too," Edan said, "but he's not happy about it." At sixteen, the same age as Leila, he was the youngest of Aleksandr's children, with his father's broad shoulders and the thick brown hair and hazel eyes of his mother Maire. "Leila, you might as well go ahead and speak first at the meeting, the way we decided, and then Trevor can outline our plans in more detail."

"I thought you were going to do that," Sofia said.

Edan shook his head. "Trevor's a better speaker than I am."

Yukio snorted. "No, he's not." He glanced at Trevor from the sides of his long brown eyes. "Didn't mean you're that bad a speaker, just that Edan might be a better one."

Leila knew what Yukio meant. Edan already had the easy authority of his father; his words might have carried more conviction, but there would be more feeling behind Trevor's words. Edan, however eloquent he became, always held back part of himself.

Edan sighed. "Leila is Zoheret's daughter, and I'm Aleksandr's son. That could work against us if we both spoke. Everyone will assume that we already talked to our parents, and that they agreed, and that now we're just expecting the board to go along with them."

"So what?" Sofia said.

"The rumor is that Yusef is thinking of putting himself forward as the eastern settlement's leader if Aleksandr doesn't step down soon. Then everybody there would have to choose between them, and even people who have nothing against my father might decide that it's time for a change. Don't forget how opposed Yusef was to the earlier expedition, how much he spoke out against it. If he thinks Aleksandr's agreed to support us, he might oppose our plans, too."

"But why?" Leila asked. "Why would he be against us because of that?"

"Because he'll know that some people, including at least a couple of the board members, will have their doubts about what we want to do. So speaking up for them now might put him in a stronger position later on if he wants to be a leader. People will remember that he raised objections to our expedition, whatever the boards decide. And if Yusef's chosen as the new leader for our settlement, then the people in yours may decide it's time for a change, too, given that Yusef is Zoheret's biological brother. They'll be thinking of all those old stories we've picked up in our lessons, about all the trouble that was caused on Earth when only a few closely related people held most of the power."

Edan always seemed to see complicated motives in other people's actions that would never have occurred to Leila. Sometimes that amused her, but lately, it exasperated her. "I don't know why Yusef would want to be a leader anyway," Leila said. "Zoheret says it's just more work and more worry."

"I don't see her giving it up, though." Edan gave her his half-smile, that amused expression that always made her feel especially foolish. "There must be some compensations. Anyway, I had enough trouble talking my father into going along with us. I don't want to give Yusef a chance to convince a majority of the boards to go against us."

Leila felt her temper rising. "I knew we should have been open from the start," she said. "All this sneaking around and whispering about our plans was a big mistake. We should have tried to get more people involved all along."

Edan shook his head. "That would have just meant more people either butting in with their own suggestions or else trying to talk us out of it. If the board goes along with us, we'll have plenty of people volunteering to help out. Just remember how many of the younger children were begging us to take them along on overnights down by the lake."

"This isn't going to be just a one- or two-day outing," Leila said. "We aren't going to be able to just pack up our tents and scurry back here at the first sign of trouble."

"Stop arguing, you two," Trevor interrupted. "Leila and I

will speak at the meeting, and the rest of you can help us answer any questions after that."

Sofia's gray eyes shifted from Trevor to Leila. "What did Zoheret and Aleksandr have to say about weapons?" she asked.

"I didn't ask about that," Edan replied.

"I didn't ask my mother, either," Leila added. Edan nodded at her approvingly. "Better see how the meeting goes first. Somebody will have to bring that up, and I'd rather have it be a board member." The three missing explorers had taken stun guns with them, to protect themselves from wild animals. Nobody had mentioned that they might also need the weapons for protection against the group who had not returned to the settlements in almost ten years. There was no reason to assume that Ho's band was hostile now, but also no grounds, given past conflicts, to believe that the others would warmly welcome any visitors.

We're not ready for this, Leila wanted to say, but restrained herself.

During the almost twenty-four years since the founding of the settlements, public meetings of the boards that advised Zoheret and Aleksandr had been infrequent. Public meetings involving both boards of advisors were even rarer; as far as Leila knew, there had been only two such meetings, the session when the settlers had decided against using artificial wombs for anything other than emergencies and the meeting at which the boards had reluctantly decided to aid Bonnie and her companions with their proposed expedition.

The western community hall was packed tonight. To see so many people in one place was unnerving; almost all of the nearly three hundred people of the two settlements had to be here. The benches were filled; people sat on tables and on the floor or stood leaning against the walls. In the back of the large room, several adults held infants in their arms while others soothed small children. Leila tried not to think of how many people were listening to her as she briefly discussed the plans for the expedition, with wails from the babies in the back punctuating her words.

She sat down on the floor, her back to the gathering, as Trevor got to his feet and turned to face the crowd. Near Leila, a couple of the younger children had fallen asleep, their heads in the laps of their mothers. Tung, sitting with his older sister Tala, glared at her from one of the nearby benches: I knew you were up to something, his expression seemed to say. Trevor's housemates Hannah and Ali wore scowls on their faces, obviously resenting that Trevor hadn't said a word to them about anything, while Hateya and Gianni, Tonio's daughter and son, were whispering to each other.

"Here's what we'll need," Trevor began, then hesitated. Leila heard the uncertainty in his voice. The members of the board sat on a bench just behind Trevor, flanked by Aleksandr at one end and Zoheret at the other, their faces blank; she could not tell what they were thinking. She thought of the only other open meeting she had ever attended, over a year ago, when Bonnie and her comrades had first presented their plans for their expedition. Leila wondered if the board members would ever have approved of their proposal if Zoheret had not supported them.

Tonio had been the first to argue in favor of that expedition, followed by Chiang and then Bonnie. A few people in the back had started shouting out objections by the time Bonnie had finished speaking.

"You say that we should find out what's going on with Ho and his group," Jorge had called out. "I say we're lucky that we haven't seen them again and that we haven't had to give them any more supplies while pretending that their shell ornaments and some dried meat or fish were an even trade for what they got. Personally, I don't care what's happened to them."

"Well, you ought to care," Bonnie had replied, "and if you don't care about them, then you'd better think about yourselves. We don't know if whatever's happened to them might eventually endanger us. I think we'd better find out."

"They made their choice," Jorge said, "and we're better off without them."

Miriam had stood up then. "I'm more worried about your motives for wanting to do this," she said to Bonnie. "I know how disappointed you were when we decided against using the artificial wombs for anything except emergencies. You don't have to risk your life just to prove—"

"This has nothing to do with that." Bonnie's shocked, wide-eyed expression was that of someone betrayed. "I'm not trying to prove anything, and you know it."

There had been more shouting after that until Aleksandr and Zoheret had finally quieted the crowd. Thinking of that exchange now, Leila suspected that Miriam had been right about Bonnie's feelings, at least in part. Living in the same dome, the two women would have shared any number of confidences.

Ten days after the meeting, nearly everyone had gathered near the fields to say farewell to the three explorers. Bonnie and her companions had taken two horses with them, to carry most of their supplies; the animals could survive on the native grass for short periods, and the outsiders had been able to travel to the settlements on horseback, so presumably there would be enough grazing for the horses along the way. In any case, they planned to be back before it was time to plant the winter wheat, and the horses could last that long. The three explorers had seemed so confident that morning, striding south toward the lake as they led the horses by their reins, heedless of the wide green open cloudless sky.

Leila realized then that she had not heard a word of Trevor's presentation, although she had known what he would say; they had gone over it together enough times.

"Most important," Trevor was saying now, "is that at any point, we'll be able to turn back, but we should still learn enough to make things easier for the next expedition." He glanced at Leila as he sat down, then shook his head slightly, as if to apologize for his delivery. He had sounded so much more confident while rehearsing with her and their friends.

Brendan, seated among the other board members, stood up. "I've got a question." He looked directly at Trevor. "This is all about your mother, isn't it?"

"What kind of question is that?" Trevor asked.

"You must be feeling that you have a duty to find her, probably think it's more your responsibility than anyone else's. Maybe that's clouding your judgment."

"No, that's not clouding my judgment." Trevor's voice was steady this time. "Leila and Yukio and Sofia and Edan feel as strongly about this as I do. But I will say one thing. Maybe I'm getting more and more upset with people who'd let three of their friends just disappear without doing anything to find out what happened to them. My mother and her comrades would have expected someone to come after them by now instead of making excuses. First it was not caring about what was happening with the outsiders, and then it was forgetting about three of your own people. You're not living here—you're hiding here."

"Is that what you think?" Brendan sat down again. "You talk about careful planning and safety. You ignore the fact that if something really goes wrong for you, there would be a lot more for us to lose—more resources, more lives. Bad enough that we lost three adults. I don't want us to lose some of our children, too." He gazed at Sofia, who was sitting at Leila's left; his daughter lifted her head.

"If you're not willing to go yourselves," Trevor said, "then we have to try. Sooner or later, some of us will go whether you want us to or not. The least you can do is give us more of a chance by cooperating with us and letting us have what we need. Thanks for letting me speak." He looked away from the board and sat down next to Leila.

"Let me remind you," Brendan said, "that no one forced Bonnie and Chiang and Tonio to go. They insisted on going, and I for one only regret that we didn't do more to stop them."

"Cowards," a commanding voice said behind them. Leila turned and saw Trevor's father Anoki on his feet, his hands resting on his walking stick. "First of all, I didn't put my son up to this," Anoki continued. "Better make that much clear from the start. I didn't know anything about what he and his friends were thinking, but I've been waiting for months for somebody to propose another expedition. I would have spoken up for one myself, but I wasn't sure that was seemly, having a crippled man like me pushing for others to take risks when I wasn't capable of doing what I'd be asking them to do. Anyway, I didn't think I'd ever have to make such a speech because I believed there were still enough brave ones among you willing to go and look for Bonnie and the others—your friends, or so I thought, people you cared about, or so I thought." His dark eyes glinted with anger. "So I waited, and nothing happened, and I waited some more, and still nothing happened, not even any talk of sending out a party. Is that what we came here for, to hide here hoping for Ship to come back?"

"I don't think . . ." someone began to say from the back of the room.

Zoheret raised a hand. "Let Anoki finish," she said in a soft but ominous voice.

"There, I've said it," Anoki went on, "and in front of our children, too, which makes it even more offensive, I suppose. We send them to the library so that they can learn about their great ancestors and the advanced civilization that they created in their own solar system and their dream of seeding other worlds with human life, and we tell them tales of how we had to fight the people who had hidden aboard Ship, some of them our own biological parents, in order to settle on Home, even if we don't go into some of the more problematic parts of that story. Maybe our old battles used up our store of courage. Maybe human beings only have a certain amount of courage and when it's used up, they live out the rest of their lives hiding from anything they fear."

Kieu, a member of the board from the eastern settlement, was shaking her head. "There's nothing in the records to indicate that people have only a limited—"

"How characteristic of you, Kieu," Anoki interrupted. "I didn't mean for you to take that remark literally."

Kieu's golden-skinned face grew pink; she looked away for a moment.

"But it wouldn't surprise me," Anoki said, "if our children begin to believe that might be the case, that we are in fact a timid and fearful species in spite of all the tales of humankind's glorious past exploits. I'll say this now—I no longer care about those who sent us here or what their motives might have been, whether they were fine and noble reasons or only a desperate gesture by a few deluded human beings. I'm also not going to sit around wishing and hoping that Ship will come back to save us from whatever mistakes we might make. Our life is here, whether Ship ever comes back or not. I think our children know that, even if some of us have forgotten it."

Leila watched her mother. Zoheret lowered her head, looking for a moment as if she was embarrassed to be there. Anoki was speaking of the kinds of things the adults whispered among themselves, and that Leila and some of her friends had been able to tease out of the library's records, but that no one discussed openly. There had been human beings who had dreamed of seeding other worlds and other human beings who had instead remained in their solar system, remaking the planets there and building new habitats in space for humankind. Which way was the better way had apparently been a matter of some dispute among those ancient peoples.

Ship might have left them on Home not to serve a great purpose, but only to carry out the wishes of a group of deluded and irrational people. They might be only an experiment that would fail in the end. That was what lay behind the uneasiness of the settlers, the doubts that all of them harbored but that no one dared to bring into the open, as if to speak of them and confront them might only make them sink into helplessness and despair. Ship might have made another choice, might have kept them all inside itself, might even have decided to return with their descendants to the planetary system that had given birth to them all.

But Anoki was right, Leila told herself. Whatever the reasons for Ship's mission, their life was here now, on Home.

"I can't argue with you, Anoki," Zoheret said. "In fact, I agree with you."

"That isn't all I have to say." Anoki swayed slightly, still leaning on his stick. "If you turn down my son's request, I'll gather what I need and go after those three myself. Even if I can't walk, I can still ride a horse, and if the horse gives out, I'll just keep going on foot for as long as I can, even if I can't cover that much ground in a day. Either I'll find Bonnie and the others or I won't, but at least I will have tried, and maybe by then Trevor and his friends will be out looking for me. I don't expect that most of the rest of you would even try to come after me."

"I must object, Anoki," Yusef said. Leila glanced at her uncle, who was sitting at the end of the table with his fellow board members. "If you left here, I for one wouldn't let you go alone. You have my word on that, I'd be right there at your side. I only wish more people had listened to me a year ago, when I questioned the wisdom of that expedition." Yusef slowly stood up. "I'm willing to discuss sending out a search team, but we should take more time to plan for that, consider exactly what and whom we can spare. I also worry about these young people going out by themselves."

Yusef might be her mother's biological brother, Leila thought, and she could not think of anything to hold against him, but she had never felt that she really knew or understood him.

"But we wouldn't be going alone," Trevor objected. "I told you—we'd be setting up bases as we go."

"But you say that you also want young people volunteering to wait at those bases," Yusef responded. "I'm not saying you don't have some interesting ideas, only that you may not necessarily be the ones who should carry them out."

"What?" Trevor shouted, obviously angry. Leila reached up and touched his arm gently before he could say more.

"All I'm saying," Yusef said, "is that perhaps we older ones—"

"You haven't done anything up to now," Anoki called out. "You might as well let my son do what he can. Or would you rather wait until there's even less chance of finding Bonnie and the others alive?"

"I'm only—" Yusef began.

"Please," Zoheret said, raising a hand. "This isn't getting us anywhere. I have another suggestion to make."

Trevor was restraining himself, but Leila sensed the tension in him. "Very well," Yusef said. "Let's listen to Zoheret's suggestion, unless Aleksandr has anything to offer at this point." Leila recalled what Edan had told her about Yusef's ambitions; he was trying to undercut Aleksandr already.

"I'll tell the rest of you what I said to my son," Aleksandr muttered. "He and his friends are proposing something risky, and maybe something they're not yet completely ready for, but we can't keep on holding them back, or they'll never be ready. We'll have to explore more of Home sooner or later. And Anoki's right when he says that we should have gone after our three missing friends long before now."

"Much as I sympathize with that," Yusef said, "we still have to balance those three lives against the well-being of our communities here. We couldn't have spared much more than three people and what they needed then without risking shortages of resources and workers, and these young people are asking for a lot more than that."

"We allowed for that in our plans," Leila said, unable to keep silent any longer. "That's why we want to set up bases along the way, so that we—"

"I heard all about your plans," Yusef said, "but—"

"I said that I have another suggestion," Zoheret interrupted. "May I be allowed to make it?"

"Very well." Yusef folded his arms.

Zoheret's brother should have been as satisfied with his life as almost anyone in either of the settlements, or so Leila had always thought. Everyone knew that he had been largely responsible for the designing of their greenhouses and their gardens, and respected him for that. His son Salim, who assisted Kagami, was earning people's trust as a healer, and his daughter Elena would soon give birth to her first child. Most of the girls and women considered Yusef, with his handsome face and thick dark hair, to be one of the finest-looking of the men, and presumably he was at least dimly aware of their admiration.

Yet he seemed vaguely discontented, unsure of himself, and there were rumors that his mate Gisela spent as little time in the dome they shared as possible and might even have left him by now if there had been someplace else where she could live.

"I don't know what Yusef wants," Zoheret had said about her brother once, "whether he thinks he should be in charge of everything or just wishes he could go his own way." Now he was scowling at Zoheret, clearly resenting her for interrupting him.

"We knew this time would come," Zoheret began. "Sooner or later, our children were going to want to see what lies beyond our settlement, and you have to admit that they have a good reason for wanting to explore more of Home. I think that they should carry out their plan, and we should do what we can to help them. That's what I propose to all of you on our boards, and I hope you'll go along with that. But they shouldn't bear all of the responsibility. At least a few of us should go with them."

Trevor was flushing with anger; Leila could imagine how he felt. He suddenly jumped to his feet. She braced herself for an outburst like his father's.

But Trevor's tone was surprisingly calm. "The main reason we proposed that we go by ourselves is that we figured you could do without younger people more easily. I mean, we do our share of the work, but we don't have the skills that most of you have. You could get along without us for a while, but most of you are really needed here."

"True enough," Zoheret responded. "That's been another of our reasons, or rationalizations, for sticking so close to our settlements. But as you've pointed out, some of us are needed here more than others, and maybe it's time for a few changes here as well. So I propose that I resign my position and go along with these young people as one of the explorers. There are any number of people here who can take my place."

Trevor sat down, obviously stunned by Zoheret's words. Leila found herself feeling relieved. Zoheret's offer would reassure those reluctant to see the young people go off on their own, and that might even be enough to sway the board of advisors. Unfortunately, by resigning as leader, she had also opened the way for Yusef to challenge Aleksandr for the leadership of the eastern settlement. That was, she supposed, the way Edan would think about the situation.

"There's another reason for older people to travel with you," Zoheret went on. "For your own safety, you'll need to carry stun guns, and you have almost no experience with them."

"We have some practice," Leila objected, "and they're ridiculously easy to use anyway."

"I'm not talking about how easy they are to use." Zoheret gazed steadily at Leila. "How well you were able to aim and shoot in a couple of practice sessions isn't going to matter if you can't move fast enough, and with enough deliberation, to bring down any creature that's threatening you."

No one spoke for several moments. The hall was suddenly so quiet that Leila could hear the soft whimperings of a baby in the back of the room.

"I'm going to ask the board for their decision now," Zoheret continued, "and then request that they put forward their suggestions as to who should replace me."

"Hold on." Leila recognized her father's voice. She turned to look behind her as Manuel stood up. "If you were planning to resign as leader and then go off with our daughter on this expedition, you might at least have said something about it to me." He smiled then, and Leila heard the soft sounds of laughter. "So I'm guessing that you just came up with this idea now."

Zoheret smiled back at her mate. "You've got that right." A few people chuckled at that.

"I figured as much," Manuel said. "You've always been honest with me, maybe too honest sometimes, so I suppose the only thing I can do now is back you up. But I've got some advice for you, too—put Anoki on the board to replace whoever takes over for you as leader. We could use some changes there, too."

Leila heard a few murmurs of agreement. The tension in the room was easing. "We've won," she whispered to Trevor.

"Yes," he whispered back, "except that it's not really our expedition anymore."

All the members of the board voted unanimously in favor of the expedition, although there had to be at least two or three among them besides Yusef who still harbored doubts. Brendan was chosen to replace Zoheret as leader when Zoheret recommended him and no one offered any arguments against him. Aleksandr would stay on as head of the eastern settlement, since there was no reason to replace him. He had offered to go with the explorers as far as one of the base camps, but several people had spoken against that; this wasn't the time to risk two experienced leaders.

"Which means," Edan said to Leila as they left the hall with Rosa, "that Yusef will have to wait and see how our expedition turns out before he makes his move."

"Are you still thinking about that?" she asked.

Edan shrugged. "Your mother surprised me." He seemed resigned to surrendering control of their expedition to a few adults; it was already clear that others would be willing to join Zoheret. Maybe Edan was as secretly relieved about that as she was.

"You might have said something to us," a voice said behind Leila. She turned to face Tala, Chiang's daughter, with Tung at her side. "Our father's one of the lost, " Tala continued. "Couldn't you have let us in on your plans?"

"Everybody was going to find out eventually," Edan replied. "If you want to come along with us, feel free to volunteer."

"Be sure that we will," Tala said.

"I'm sorry," Leila said to the brother and sister. "I wish we could have told you before."

Tung looked down, seemingly mollified. Rosa leaned against Leila and yawned. Trevor joined the two of them as Edan waved farewell, slipped a light wand from his belt, and descended the hill with Tala and Tung, following others who were returning to their domes on the hill to the east. Night had come; the small bright clusters cast by other light wands danced across the wide field below. Almost everyone had left the hall, a few of them clinging to their mates or their children while keeping their heads down, their eyes averted from the night sky. Leila's parents were still inside talking to Aleksandr, Anoki, and a few members of the board.

Leila nudged her sister. Rosa yawned again. "Let's go home," Leila said.

"I'll walk with you." Trevor was silent as they climbed the hill, then added, "My father was right. They should have approved his proposal for radio communication a long time ago."

"I know." He had complained about that to her often enough while they were drawing up their plans, that the boards had decided that time and resources spent on even a simple system would be wasted. Now they would have to send out more people and use even more resources because they had no way of finding out what had happened to the three lost explorers, while the three lacked any means of communicating with the settlements.

"I want to go with you," Rosa said.

"You can't," Leila said.

"Why not?"

"Because you're too young."

"Zoheret thinks you're too young. That's why she's going along, so I don't see why I can't go with you."

"You wouldn't want to leave Manuel all alone, would you?" Leila asked.

"Then we should all go together," Rosa insisted, "you and Manuel and Zoheret and me."

"Leila," a voice called out behind them. She turned to see Yusef coming up the hill toward them. "May I have a few moments of your time?"

"Of course," she said as her uncle came up to them. She tried to recall the last time she had exchanged more than a few words with him. It had been at least a few months ago, when he had come to their dome to discuss the greenhouses and some other matters with Zoheret, and Leila's mother had done most of the talking.

"Thanks for voting with the rest of the board," Trevor said. "I was expecting you to vote against us."

"It wouldn't have made any difference if I had," Yusef replied. "That might have convinced another one or two people to vote with me, but that was about all I could have hoped for. I thought it was better and less divisive to have unanimity."

"So you still don't approve of this expedition," Leila said.

"Don't approve? I wouldn't put it quite that way. I do wish you'd call it off, change your minds, use whatever excuse you like. Few people would think any the worse of you if you did."

"You're wrong about that," Trevor said. "You heard my father. You know what he'd think."

Yusef said, "This is about more than your father and your mother." Leila heard the vehemence in his voice.

"I know that," Trevor replied.

They had arrived at her dome, and it was obvious that Yusef had more to say. She beckoned to Trevor and then led everyone up the steps and into the dome.

"It's late," she said when they were inside. "Rosa, you should probably go to bed."

"I'm not tired yet," her sister replied.

"Now," Leila said, with an edge in her voice. "Good night, Rosa."

"Good night." Rosa retreated into their bedroom and slid the wall shut behind her.

They sat down on the floor, around the table. "May I get you anything?" Leila said. "A cup of water, or some juice?"

"We can dispense with pleasantries," Yusef said. "Your mother knows what I think. I've spoken to her enough times that she's probably tired of hearing what I think. But you two are old enough now to hear what's been eating away at me, and maybe my thoughts will make you reconsider your plans."

"Adults will be with us," Leila said, "including Zoheret. That should reassure you."

"It doesn't. It only makes it worse." Yusef's shoulders sagged, and she saw weariness and unhappiness in his face. "Zoheret might back out if you two and your friends decide this expedition isn't such a good idea after all."

"We made our decision," Leila said, worrying that if she listened to her uncle any longer, he might actually succeed in changing her mind. Maybe he sensed that she still had her own doubts.

"Listen to me," Yusef said. "Right now, even if we just hang on here and stay close to our settlement, we stand a good chance of losing what we have, maybe not soon, but in time. We may not grow fast enough or be able to develop the industrial base we'd have to have to recreate the technology that Ship had at its command. We might survive if we fall back into an earlier stage of development, or we might not. One thing I've learned from our records is what one of the great fears of our ancestors was. They were afraid that if their civilization ever suffered a great setback, they might never be able to recover what they had lost. And that was on a world where they had originated and evolved, where they were woven into their biosphere, where they were an integral part of their planet's life cycle. As Kagami and my son Salim might put it, we're only imperfectly grafted onto this world, and sometimes grafts don't take and are sloughed off by the original organism. However close to Earth Home's environment may be, it still isn't Earth's. We are all aliens here."

"We're adapting to Home," Trevor said.

"You might say that," Yusef responded, "or you might say that all we've really done is created an ecosystem of our own around these hills, an environment in which we can live, as long as we're careful, as long as we can grow enough food and maintain what tools we have, as long as we don't try to live outside it or take too many unnecessary risks."

"And you think our expedition is too great a risk," Leila said.

"Yes, I do."

"And that because it needs more people and more resources, it may jeopardize the survival of our settlement."

Yusef shook his head. "You misunderstand me, Leila. I don't think our settlement has much of a chance in any case."

Leila was too stunned to know what to say. Defeatism, her mother would call it, useless and unconstructive talk.

"Zoheret told me that she didn't want to hear such talk from me," Yusef continued, "but I told her I wasn't the only one who thought it, even if I was the only one who would say it to her face. Sooner or later, this settlement will fail, and by then we may be too dependent on what we have here to be able to survive without it. A few years ago, I even wondered if Ho might have been right to go off on his own, since it looked as though his group might have an opportunity to embed themselves much more deeply in Home's ecology than we were doing. I thought that he and the others might eventually be more successful in adapting to Home and that we might be able to learn something about how to do so from them. But none of his people have come here in almost a decade, so I've given up that hope, too."

"If you think we're going to fail in the end anyway," Trevor said, "then whether we go on our expedition or not shouldn't really matter to you."

"But it does. It matters." Yusef stared past Leila, and the emptiness she saw in his eyes shook her. "I think we may have condemned future generations to a futile struggle. Let's assume that you go on your expedition and return safely. What will you actually have accomplished besides seeing some places that Ship scanned and mapped before we came here?"

"We might find my mother," Trevor said.

"We might find out what happened to the outsiders," Leila added.

"Maybe." Yusef sounded extremely doubtful. "That might even be enough of an accomplishment for someone to propose an even more hazardous expedition to the north, one that also might be successful. And none of that is likely to matter in the long run. More and more now, I wonder if we ever should have had children at all. Perhaps we should have just lived out our own lives here before dying out, as I fear we'll do anyway, the only difference being that more generations will have to suffer and struggle in the meantime."

"You're saying that everything we do is meaningless," Leila said.

Yusef was silent.

"We won't change our minds," she said, and Trevor nodded.

"Very well." Yusef got up. "I didn't really think you'd back down now, but I thought you deserved to know that my worries aren't caused just by phobias about open sky and spaces, or fear of the unknown. Since you're determined to go ahead with this, all I can do is offer you what support I can."

"Even if you think it's useless," Trevor said.

"Yes." Yusef's dark eyes seemed to be gazing at them with pity. He turned from them and left the dome.

Groups of people moved south under a clear green morning sky. A few were on horseback, but most were on foot. One or two in each group led the horses carrying their supplies. Nearly fifty people were on the move, but half of them would be going only as far as the lake's northern shore.

Leila walked at her mother's left, leading one of the horses. Manuel and Rosa were on Zoheret's right, and Rosa, despite her earlier insistence at coming along on the first short leg of the journey, was looking tired and fretful.

Leila motioned to her father; they halted while Manuel lifted Rosa to the horse, securing her against the packs. Rosa pulled down her hat and rested her head against the horse's mane.

Trevor and Edan walked with Denya and Shannon, Edan's older brother and sister. Denya had Edan's broad shoulders and thick brown hair, while Shannon, a gestational sibling, had dark brown skin and a wiry build. Shannon would be traveling with them while Denya, whose mate, Mandisa, had recently given birth to their first child, would soon head back to the eastern settlement.

Trevor smiled as Shannon murmured something to him. He seemed in an easier mood today, but Leila knew that he still resented having to give up control of their expedition to the adults. She could sympathize with him while feeling relieved that her mother had made her decision, especially after Zoheret had insisted on three days of practice with stun guns for Leila and her cousin Oni, Luis's younger daughter, who had been one of the first to volunteer for the journey.

"Don't fool yourself into thinking you already know how to use this weapon," Zoheret had told both of them. "You may have to move fast, without thinking. But you can't be careless, either, firing away at anything you think might be a threat— sometimes it's better not to confront a threat directly. Fire and miss, and you might be worse off than if you don't fire at all, and a careless shot might hit a friend. Under normal circumstances, your weapon won't kill, but it can happen, someone you hit might go into shock. Shock's been known to kill, too."

Leila was suddenly conscious of the weapon at her waist. The stun guns were kept in the library, and taken out only when they were grazing their animals far enough away from the settlements that predators might come after a stray foal or sheep. On the few occasions when Leila and her friends had brought some of the younger children down to the lake for overnights, one or two of the older boys and girls had always been on guard at night with a weapon, waking others to take over after a while so that everyone got enough sleep. But that had been more of a game; there had been little danger to any of them so close to the settlements. She had never had to defend herself with a weapon.

Yukio and Sofia laughed as they talked to Yukio's mother, Kagami, and his father, Federico. Even Hateya and Gianni, smiling as they strode along, arms swinging, with their mother, Roxana, seemed to have forgotten for now that their father Tonio was missing and that Roxana would soon have to worry about both her mate and her children. They were acting as if this were little more than a game, they and all of the others marching toward the lake, laughing and talking as if this were just another outing. But she had been doing the same thing herself earlier, teasing Rosa and telling her how much fun this adventure was going to be, keeping her own apprehensions to herself.

Leila looked back for a moment. The young fruit trees to the east and south of the settlements, and the windmills at the tops of both hills, seemed small, the settlements themselves much too vulnerable. To the south of the clusters of domes, a few massive black metal ribs were all that was left of the vessels that had brought human settlers to this world. She felt the urgency of what Yusef had told her. For a moment, she wanted to turn back and go to her dome and forget that she had ever thought of leaving.

People had crossed space to come here, while all she had to do was cross a small piece of land. If she gave in to her fears, she would only make Yusef's grim vision of extinction more likely to become a reality. She had chosen to do this, she reminded herself, and would not back out now.

It was still morning when they reached the northern shore of the lake. A few people leaned against the hulls of the overturned boats on the shore. Leila and Trevor had thought of using the boats during the first leg of the expedition, sending a few people on ahead in them while others followed with the horses, but the boats might be needed here for fishing. They were yet another resource that would not be risked.

"Time for us to be heading home," Manuel said as he lifted Rosa from the mare Leila was leading. "Are you going to be able to walk back with me?"

Rosa made a face at him. "It isn't that far."

Manuel turned toward Zoheret. "Be careful," he murmured.

"You know that I will be," Leila's mother replied.

Manuel put his arms around his mate. Zoheret rested her head against his shoulder. "I wish I were going with you," he said.

Zoheret looked up at him. "Don't worry. We'll be back before you have time to miss us." Manuel's arms tightened around her.

Leila drew her sister aside so that their parents could have a few moments to themselves. Others were saying their farewells. Edan jostled his brother Denya, then grasped him by the arms. Lillka, who had helped prepare the maps for their journey, was embracing her daughter Sofia. Tala and Tung stood with their mother; Tala had, apparently with some difficulty, convinced her brother to stay behind.

"I'll miss you," Rosa said.

"But you'll have our room all to yourself now," Leila said.

"I'll still miss you."

Leila was moved; her sister usually preferred to tease her rather than demonstrate warm affection. "Be sure to look after Manuel," she said, "and take care of Scrapper, too."

"Only if you promise to tell me everything that happened when you come back."

Leila poked her sister lightly in the shoulder. "I promise."

Twenty-five people continued south along the eastern side of the lake, along with fourteen horses laden with packs. Nearly all of the young people under the age of twenty who did not yet have children of their own had asked to join the expedition, as had many of the children over six, although Leila suspected that at least a few of them had said so mostly to show that they weren't afraid to volunteer. Zoheret and Aleksandr had, with the agreement of the board members, decided that no one under the age of sixteen would be allowed to go, which had brought the expedition down to manageable size and had also made Leila the youngest one in the group.

Deciding on which adults would go had been more difficult. Those who were fearful of going far from their dwellings would obviously have to stay behind, as would those whose skills were needed in the community. Anoki might be someone who could not leave because of his physical limitations, but his skill at repairing and restoring their fuel cells, solar panels, cisterns, latrines, faucets, looms, and other devices also made him almost indispensable to the settlements. Zoheret's close friend Jennifer was physically weaker than most of the adults, but she was also almost as skilled as Anoki at repairs and maintenance. Luis's blindness might be partly overcome by his goggles, but he would still be more vulnerable than a sighted person, and his skills also made him too valuable to risk.

Zoheret and Aleksandr had finally narrowed down the choices to four people. Kagami would go, because her abilities as a healer might be needed and her assistant Salim was staying behind. Haidar, Aleksandr's closest friend, would accompany the explorers, because he was good with the horses. Gervais would come along, because Zoheret trusted him and he had often accompanied Leila and her friends during their overnights by the lake.

Zoheret would lead the expedition. She might pretend that she wasn't their leader, that she was only advising Leila and the others who had drawn up the plans and presented them at the meeting, but Leila knew otherwise. If any hard decisions had to be made, her mother would take charge.

Their lively conversations gradually grew more subdued and

then subsided altogether. There was no point in wasting energy on talk. At midafternoon, they stopped long enough to rest, eat a meal, and water the horses.

Leila sat with Oni and Sofia, eating beans wrapped in thin bread and an orange. They had prepared some of their rations in the kitchens of the two community halls, also packing nuts, dried fruits, beans, dried meats, and sacks of flour. Their fourteen horses grazed on the green grass that had sprung up here amid the native yellow grasses. Yellow, green, brown, and black reeds, the violet blossoms of colulos, and gray slabs of rock lined the shore of the lake; the calm surface of the water, grayish-green in the sunlight, stretched to the western and southern horizons. A plain of green and yellow grass lay to the east and north. Two small mounds topped by the slender spires and long thin arms of the windmills were now all that could be seen of the settlements.

Zoheret sat between Trevor and Haidar, studying the screen Trevor had propped against his knees. They had brought three reading screens with them, each of them loaded with records of Ship's scans and the maps Lillka had organized for them.

"Here we are," Zoheret said, pointing at the screen. "I didn't think we'd get this far by now. We should reach the site for our first base by tomorrow afternoon." Trevor held the screen toward Leila so that she and the other two girls could see the map, but Leila had come close to memorizing most of their planned route. The first base would be set up where a river branched off from the lake; they would follow the river southeast to where it widened and set up their second base there. There was no reason to think that the terrain would vary that much from what they expected to find; Ship's scans of this continent had been thorough.

Leila's earlier apprehensions now seemed foolish. Instead of risking unexpected perils, they might be in for little more than an uneventful, even tedious, journey, but she reminded herself then that three people were missing and that they still did not know what had happened to Ho's band. Her stomach tensed as she finished her food.

*T*hey made camp at sunset. By then, they were too tired to do more than pitch their five tents and dig a pit for a fire. Haidar, Edan, and Yukio gathered rocks to put around the pit; the fire would keep wild animals away and also boil water. Water from the lake near their settlements was safe to drink, but Kagami was taking no chances, insisting that they treat any water as potentially contaminated.

There were enough dry brush, twigs, and leaves shed by the small native shrubs that grew near the lake to start a fire. They roamed along the lake, gathering more brush, but Leila wondered what they would use for fuel later on if they could not find enough kindling.

"We need to keep watch," Zoheret said after they had gathered around the fire to eat their evening meal, "but make sure that you feel up to it before you volunteer. Some of you will need more sleep than others. Two people for each watch, in three shifts—that way, no one should lose too much sleep. Who'll take the first watch?"

"Sofia and I will," Trevor said quickly, before anybody else could volunteer.

"And the second?"

"I'll take it," Kagami replied.

"Yukio and I can take the third," Edan said. Leila felt a pang of disappointment, surprised to realize that she had been hoping that Edan might ask to keep watch with her. She suppressed that feeling, not wanting to examine it too closely.

"I'll watch with Kagami, then," Leila said. The four friends who had planned this expedition with her had all volunteered; it seemed only right that she should as well.

"You're sure?" Zoheret said. "I can take the second watch if you're too tired."

"I'll do it," Leila insisted.

Zoheret shrugged. "Very well."

They ate quickly, saying little. After eating, they refilled their leather canteens with water from the two large pots that had been taken off the fire and allowed to cool. Their route would follow the river that ran from the south of the lake, so they would not run out of water, and if they could not boil the water and had doubts about its safety, they would use the purification powders Kagami carried in her bag of medical tools.

After digging two small trenches for latrines, they prepared for sleep. Leila crept into the tent that she would be sharing with Sofia, Shannon, Hannah, and Hateya, unrolled her sleeping bag, and crawled inside. It seemed that she had barely closed her eyes before someone was poking her in the shoulder.

"Leila." She recognized Sofia's voice, even in a whisper. "Your turn." A shadowy form slipped past her toward the back of the tent. Leila stretched, surprised that she had actually slept and envying Sofia the unbroken stretch of slumber that lay ahead of her now.

She forced herself to get up and crept outside, lowering the tent flap behind her. Out here, away from the settlement, the sky seemed much darker even with the light of the moons; the stars were tiny pinpricks in a vast black dome. Home's second and larger moon was twenty degrees above the eastern horizon; it would pass the small pale disk of its sister satellite, now hanging in the middle of the sky, before morning.

The fourteen horses, temporarily relieved of their burdens, were tied to a long rope stretched between two poles. Kagami paced near the banked fire. "Do you need to piss?" she asked as Leila approached.

"Not right now."

"If anybody else comes out to use the ditch, stay on guard. Trevor told me that he saw a couple of animals that looked like big cats earlier. They probably won't bother us, but still—" Kagami sat down on a flat rock.

Leila sat with her back to Kagami, facing south. "Maybe we would have been better off without those cats."

"Ship designed the ecological system," the healer said, "and we need those predators to keep other animal populations down. You wouldn't have wanted us to be overrun with rabbits or deer."

"Maybe we didn't need the rabbits and deer, either."

"Ship was programmed to settle us in as Earthlike an environment as possible," Kagami said, "although sometimes . . ." She was silent for a moment. "There are so many planets in the universe, so many stars and planetary systems that we couldn't possibly count them all, so it seems reasonable to assume that among so many worlds, there would have to be a large number of worlds, perhaps millions of worlds, on which humanity could survive." She paused. "And other times it seems impossible that there could be any planets so much like Earth that we could live on them almost as easily as on our original world."

"But Ship found Home," Leila said.

"Only after the planet it had found earlier for Aleksandr and his group turned out to be uninhabitable. That was Ship's first mistake, it was why it had to put that first group of its children into suspension while it looked for another habitable planet and reared our group, your mother's and mine. But it managed to find a home for us in the end, and here we are, and sometimes that seems inevitable, and other times it seems close to being a miracle."

Leila breathed in the air; its barely discernible spicy scent was overlaid with the odors of smoke and ashes. Maybe it was a miracle, that the atmosphere of Home could sustain her, or perhaps it simply meant that there might be millions of other worlds on which other humanlike beings lived, that they were as numerous and as natural in the universe as the microbes in a drop of water.

"Maybe some other ship seeded Earth long ago," Leila murmured.

"I've thought of that," Kagami said, "and that maybe such interplanetary seeding is something our species is driven to do by instinct. There's nothing in our records to indicate that anything like that ever happened on Earth, but I've speculated about it. I can even wonder if it means that there's some sort of purpose in the universe that's hidden from us, maybe some kind of intelligence that deliberately created enough suitable planets for our species so that we would be able to spread out across the universe. And then I remind myself that not everyone in Earth's solar system believed in seeding other worlds, but instead preferred creating new habitats and living inside them, and that there's much more in the records showing that our species came into existence and evolved on Earth rather than coming from somewhere else, and then I start to doubt that there's any hidden purpose to our lives at all. It always comes back to that, to having to discover our own purpose, whatever Ship or some people on Earth long ago or some unknown intelligence might have intended for us."

Their purpose, Leila thought, seemed to be little more than bringing up another generation of their kind so that they in turn would rear and educate children of their own. If they succeeded, they might eventually create a society that would regain the technological capabilities that had made Ship possible. And if they failed, as Yusef feared, they might eventually lose the ability to maintain what they had, and then—

Leila did not want to follow her thoughts any further than that, or dwell on what her uncle had said.

"We're not a perfect fit," Kagami continued, "Home and human beings, but so far the life of this planet has been reacting to us as if we're harmless. If there's anything other than what we've brought here ourselves that can kill us, an animal or a virus or a poisonous plant or deadly microbe, we've avoided it so far. That might mean that being a transplanted species here has given us a kind of immunity, at least temporarily. Or it may only mean that we haven't done anything yet that would cause Home's immune system to attack us." She cleared her throat. "I'm speaking figuratively, of course."

"Zoheret told me once—" Leila paused.

"Go on," Kagami said.

"That some of you had considered building an enclosed settlement, with tunnels and barriers and larger domes so that we'd be even more protected."

"We might have done that, but I think it's good that we didn't. It would have been like imprisoning ourselves, giving up on Home's environment before we'd ever really tried to live in it and adapt to it. We might not have been able to maintain such a settlement anyway, and if it had failed us later on, we might have been much less able to adapt. The descendants of Ho and Owen and Katti and their group might have become the inheritors of Home in time."

"Then you think they're still alive," Leila said.

"I don't know. Owen and Katti looked so worn out when they came to trade with us that I asked if I could examine them, but they refused. Maybe I should have been more insistent. Then again, as thin and old as they looked, they managed to make that journey, they'd kept themselves alive. I wonder what they might have discovered here that we haven't, what their children might have learned."

"If they had any children."

"If they did."

Leila heard a long, low sigh, and recognized the sound of a soft night wind stirring the grass. She had heard it before, during overnights away from her settlement, the voice of Home. Sometimes the wind seemed to be trying to comfort her, but at other times it almost sounded like a cry of protest against a species that had come here from another place.

She thought of what Kagami had told her. If Home was so much like Earth, would its own life forms have eventually evolved into other human beings, ones native to this world? By coming here, had they somehow displaced a potential life form, and prevented another species from ever coming into existence? Maybe there was no such thing as a perfect fit anywhere, even on Earth . . .

There were too many questions she might ask, and any answers might always elude her.

L eila and Kagami kept watch until the pale blue disk of the second moon was above them, then fed more brush to the fire. Kagami went to the tent nearest the lake to wake Yukio and Edan while Leila slipped inside her tent. She crawled inside her sleeping bag and lay there, listening to the deep, even breathing of her tentmates, trying to sleep.

Edan was out there now, keeping watch with Yukio. Again she felt the confused feelings that had flowed through her earlier. Did Edan ever think of her as more than just one of his friends? Did any thoughts of sharing a dome with her when they were older ever cross his mind? Why didn't she ever have such uneasy and feverish yet oddly joyful feelings about Trevor, who was closer to her than almost anyone? She knew enough about Trevor to know that he would be a reliable and compatible mate, someone she could live with contentedly, and yet whenever she imagined herself choosing a mate, Edan forced his way into her thoughts.

The wind sighed outside. She burrowed inside her bedding and at last fell asleep.

At dawn, they ate their morning meal hastily, but took their time making sure the fire was out. Gervais had alerted everyone to make sure that no sparks would be left that might start a fire on the plain.

They were on the move for only a short time when Yukio, who was near the head of the procession, suddenly halted. "Up ahead," he called out. He waved his arm and then pointed. Yukio could see further into the distance than most people; it was one reason he tried to avoid much of the reading Lillka assigned to them for their lessons.

"What is it?" Zoheret asked.

"I'm not sure. All I can see from here is a dark circle in the grass."

Leila tugged at the reins of the horse she was leading and picked up her pace, following the others along the barrier between the rocks and shrubs to her right and the nearly waist-high green and yellow grass to her left. At last she was able to see what Yukio had spotted.

A circle of rocks lay on a patch of ground near the lake, around a small hole in the ground. The few blackened fragments among the ashes in the small hollow looked like bits of burned wood.

Everyone gathered around the hole. A few thin blades of yellow grass had sprouted among the ashes. "It's where they must have stopped," Trevor said, "my mother and Tonio and Chiang."

Hateya stepped closer to him, with Chiang's daughter Tala right behind her. "Do you think so?" Hateya asked, gazing intently at the ashes as though searching for evidence that her father Tonio had actually camped here.

"Has to be," Yukio replied. "The outsiders haven't been back this way for ten years. This fireplace looks like it was put together a lot more recently than that."

Trevor was biting his lip; his eyes glistened. Leila moved to his side and put a hand on his arm. He looked down at her and offered her an uneasy smile.

"They must have been moving at a faster rate than we are," Gervais said. "I'm guessing that this is where they made their first stop for the night, since we didn't see anything like this earlier."

Leila stared into the pit. They might find other signs along the way, since they would be following the same route the three lost people had planned to take. She shivered, wondering again what they would find at the end of their journey.

By late afternoon, they had come to the low hill where they were to set up their first base. The lake stretched on to the west, but below the hill, a wide river flowed to the southeast. The same native shrubs grew along the riverbanks as did around the lake, but the reeds were thicker at the water's edge, a few of the taller reeds as hard and as thick around as poles. The expanse of plain to the south had patches of an unfamiliar pale greenish grass amid the yellow and darker green grasses.

The images of Ship's early scans that Leila had seen had shown only plains covered with the yellow grass, so the pale green grass had to be a hybrid. Near the settlements, their green grass had displaced the native growth; here, they seemed to be interbreeding. Presumably the horses would be able to graze on the hybrid grass, since neither of the other grasses was harmful to them, but they would have to make certain of that.

Hateya would be staying behind at the first base with three others. She had already confessed to Leila that she now wished she had not agreed to stop there and would have preferred to go on, but she had promised her mother that she would go only that far, while her brother Gianni would stay with the expedition only until it set up the second base.

They raised their tents, gathered fuel and rocks, dug a pit for their fire and a small ditch for their latrine, then ate their evening meal while Zoheret and Haidar reminded everyone about the tasks that lay ahead: Water the horses; gather fuel for the fire; boil water; check your feet for swelling and blisters; decide on which six people would keep watch tonight. The four who were to remain there would be left with enough food to last them for a few days, but would have to send one or two of their number back to the settlements for more supplies. They would have two horses, could ride back for more horses if they needed them, and could bring other people back to the base to take their places if necessary. Within seven to ten days, someone would ride back here from the second base to let them know how things were going. Their most important tasks would be to maintain the base and remain in contact with the settlements and with the second base while they waited.

"And when the cool weather comes," Sultan said, "we pack up and go home." Sultan, a thin, wiry, dark-haired young man of nineteen, was one of the young people from the eastern settlement.

"We should all be back by then," Haidar said.

"And what if you're not?"

Edan shook his head at Sultan. "If we're not," Haidar answered in his deep voice, "you go back to the settlement anyway. You abandon this base even if everybody from the bases farther south isn't back here yet. You go home even if nobody from the other bases has returned. Understood?"

Sultan nodded.

"Anyway," Haidar continued, "there's no reason to think that we won't all be back by then."

"But if you don't come back," Sultan said, "maybe it would

make more sense for us to send an expedition after you, while we still might be able to help, instead of waiting until—"

"No," Zoheret said, with an edge in her voice. "Everybody here has agreed to follow the plans that we laid out. If you're not willing to do that, head back now and let somebody else come out here to take your place."

"I was only making a suggestion," Sultan said hastily.

"You'll know if we run into trouble anyway," Zoheret said, "because people at the other bases should be able to relay that information to you. Somebody will ride back here and tell you if our plans have to be changed—you'll know then if we need your help. Right now we have to count on you to do what you've promised and not to take unnecessary chances."

"We will." Sultan looked down for a moment. "Sorry, Zoheret. You can rely on me."

"I know I can."

No one said much after that. After eating, Trevor and Edan went off with a few of the other boys to soak themselves while the lake water was still warm; that might be as close to bathing as they would get for a while. Leila noticed that none of the girls followed them. The other girls probably felt the same way she did, suddenly shy and awkward with themselves. Once the girls and the boys had splashed around together in the lake without thinking, but that was before their bodies had started to change, before her breasts swelled and hair sprouted between her legs. She had been careful not to look at Trevor too often during their last overnight at the lake with Rosa and a few of her friends, but could not help noticing that his body had changed, too. It was ridiculous to feel so uneasy around people she had known all her life.

Leila turned away and wandered down the hill with Sofia, Oni, and Hateya, gathering more dry brush. The boys had finished bathing by the time they returned with the fuel.

Shannon and Mai were in the water, splashing water at each other as if they were still small children instead of young women nearly nineteen years old. Leila shed her clothing and joined them, wishing that she could feel that carefree.

Sultan and Hannah took the first watch. Leila was tired by the time she went inside her tent, and the other girls seemed ready for sleep. She lay there, arms wrapped around herself, listening to the soft sound of the night wind.

"Leila," Hateya whispered in the dark, "are you still awake?"

"Shh," Leila whispered back, not wanting to disturb the others.

"It's all right," Shannon said in a soft voice. "I'm awake."

"So am I." That was Sofia.

"I wish I didn't have to stay here," Hateya said. "I wish I hadn't promised my mother that I would."

"I know," Leila said.

"It's going to be hard, just waiting here, wondering what you might find out about my father and not knowing."

"You won't just be waiting here," Sofia said. "You'll have to get more supplies and keep in contact with the second camp, along with making whatever observations you can."

"That isn't the same," Hateya replied. "I'd rather keep moving. Staying here gives me too much time to worry. I don't know what would be worse, never finding out what happened to my father or finding out for sure that he's . . . gone. I think I could stand finding out whatever happened, it's better than never knowing, but I don't know if my mother could take it. At least now she can keep believing that Tonio's out there somewhere, that he's somehow managed to survive, I mean, it's at the point where Gianni and I don't dare say anything to her, because she just keeps saying, 'We don't know, and as long as we don't know, I refuse to believe Tonio isn't alive. I know he's alive, he has to be alive, because I'd feel it if he weren't.' And that's the end of the discussion. I think years could go by and she'd still keep thinking he was alive as long as nobody could tell her otherwise. So part of me's hoping that we find out what's happened to him and part of me never wants to know."

"We might find out that he's alive," Shannon said. "A month from now, we may be on our way back with him."

"I don't think so," Hateya murmured. "I don't think we're going to find him. I could hope for a while, but not anymore, I think I knew he was gone for good months ago. But it was easier to pretend, to play along with my mother, no matter what I thought."

"You can't give up yet," Leila said, "not until you know for sure."

"I'd rather expect the worst. Hoping gets too painful after a while." Hateya's voice sounded shakier; Leila wondered if she was crying. "But I don't know if my mother can handle it if the worst is what we end up with. Every day, she makes sure there's just a little extra food in our cupboard in case Tonio suddenly comes through the door. She won't give the clothes he left behind to somebody else who could use them because she just knows he's going to need them again. She won't even sleep on his side of their mat. She'd rather imagine that he'll suddenly show up in the middle of the night. Maybe she even imagines that he's there, still sleeping next to her."

"That's crazy," Shannon whispered.

"It's not crazy," Leila replied, even though she'd had her doubts about Hateya's mother Roxana herself. Lately, Roxana had looked so thin and worn that Zoheret had advised her to have Kagami examine her thoroughly, but Leila did not know if Hateya's mother had followed that advice.

"You should have heard her after the meeting," Hateya said. "She was laughing when we got home, going on and on about how we'd be sure to find Tonio now, that we'd find out that there's some perfectly good reason why he hadn't been able to get back home to us, and then later on I could hear her crying after she thought we were asleep. And then the day we were ready to leave, she was smiling again, telling Gianni and me that we'd have a big celebration when Tonio came home. If we come back without him—"

"It's too soon to worry about that," Leila said. "In a way, your mother's right. As long as we don't know what's happened to him, there's no reason to think that he might not be alive."

"That's not how Roxana sees it. She'll keep thinking he's alive right up until she can't believe that anymore, and I don't know what she'll do then. Maybe she'd just go completely insane and refuse to believe he's lost, or maybe—"

There was a long period of silence, punctuated by small gasps that might have been sobs.

"Look," Leila said at last, "a couple of you will have to ride back for more supplies, so you can see how your mother's doing then. Have Salim take a look at her, he's almost as good at healing as Kagami is. You can tell him that you need her at this base camp and have her come back with you for a while. That way, you could watch out for Roxana here."

"Zoheret didn't say anything about bringing somebody back with us."

Leila thought for a moment. "She didn't say you couldn't, either. Seems to me that having one more person here for a short time, or even a couple of people, isn't going to matter all that much."

"Maybe you're right," Hateya said.

"Go to sleep," Shannon murmured.

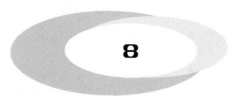

8

They were four days south of their second base camp and Leila ached more than she ever had, even after days of hard labor in the stables or during a harvest. A large and painful blister had formed on one of her feet, and Kagami's medication and dermal tape had not entirely eased her discomfort. She ached when she went to sleep, and even though exhaustion made her sleep more deeply, her muscles were often agonizingly stiff when she awoke. In spite of the tiny implant Kagami had embedded in her right arm to suppress her menstrual cycle temporarily, as the healer had done for all of the women and girls on the journey, her abdomen was knotted with cramps. Her hips and her lower back ached almost constantly; she felt as though she had been walking for years rather than only days.

Riding one of the horses might provide some relief, but she

doubted that she could grip a horse's barrel very easily with her pained knees and aching legs. The animals had enough to carry already, and riding a horse over a long distance would only produce a different set of aches and pains. But she would not complain, and neither had anyone else yet; only the sullen silence of the others told her that her weariness and discomfort were shared.

Gianni, Curt, and Mai had been left behind at the second camp, along with two more of the horses, and had been told to expect a rider in a few days, after the third base had been set up. By now, the three had probably recovered from the days of marching. Leila wondered which would be more boring, days spent on the move or days passed while waiting at a base for a rider from the next base farther south, and decided that she preferred the tedium of marching in spite of the discomfort. During all the days she and Trevor had discussed their plans, she had never anticipated that the journey would be so monotonous.

Leila shook her head. Given the dangers that might still lie ahead, maybe she should be grateful for her current boredom.

Large treelike plants, taller and thicker than any of the trees that had been planted near the settlements, grew near the riverbanks along with the familiar shrubs, reeds, and occasional patches of colulos. The river still wound through green and yellow grassland, the flatness giving way here and there to gentle hills, but the bluish bark of the plants and the purple gourds that hung from their leafless limbs suddenly seemed completely out of place, strange, alien.

Her neck prickled; her boredom vanished. Leila looked away from the plants, keeping her eyes on the ground. The native trees had their uses; the dried out gourds that covered the ground under them, when chopped into pieces, made good fuel for a fire. Tonio, Bonnie, and Chiang had apparently made that same discovery, since fragments of the gourd had been found next to another small pit of ashes surrounded by rocks. That had been the second campsite of theirs they had found, three days ago, but since then, they had spotted no sign of the three lost people. Zoheret and Gervais had been encouraging them to cover the ashes of their fires with dirt after making sure that the fires were out; perhaps the three lost people had done the same. It was also possible that all of them were far too inexperienced in this wilderness to read any but the most obvious signs that others had passed this way.

Leila lifted her head. The river had grown wider; the opposite bank was now cut off from them by a broad grayish-green expanse of water. Across the river, two deer had come down to the bank to drink; they lifted their heads, apparently unafraid of the people passing by on the other side of the water. The land had flattened out again, stretching from east to west, the grass rippling slightly as a gentle wind blew. She glanced up at the vast green sky, empty of clouds, that hung over the plain of grassland, and suddenly felt as though she was falling.

"Leila." She found herself lying on her back, looking up into the narrow face of Gervais. His teeth caught at his lower lip. "Are you all right?"

"It's nothing."

"I'd better make sure it's nothing," Kagami said as she came up behind Gervais.

"It's nothing, really," Leila said. "Just a little dizziness, that's all." Kagami pulled a scanner out of the small bag that hung at her waist. "You don't have to scan me."

"Are you sure?" Kagami asked.

"Yes." Leila forced herself to sit up. "There's nothing the matter with me, just this feeling—" She realized that the people up ahead had stopped and were looking back at her; Zoheret and Trevor were already walking toward her.

She managed to get to her feet. "I'm fine," she shouted to her mother.

Kagami passed the scanner over her head and chest, then peered at the readings. "She's all right," Kagami called out. "Let's get going." Zoheret and Trevor turned back and rejoined the others.

Without speaking, Leila followed Kagami along the riverbank, with Gervais close behind, still leading one of their horses. After they had gone a short distance, Gervais moved to her side and murmured, "I think I know what happened to you back there."

"No, you don't," Leila said, halting. "It was nothing, really."

The horse lowered its head and nibbled at some of the light green hybrid grass, which had proven to be safe for the animals to eat and which they seemed to prefer to the other grasses. "When we first came here," Gervais responded, "I could hardly leave my dome at all, couldn't stand to have all that space around me. Can't tell you how many times I went outside only to feel as though everything was spinning around me, that being in the open might even kill me."

Leila stared at him, surprised. Zoheret had always claimed that Gervais was one of the bravest people she knew.

"Thought I got past that long ago," he continued, "but being out here reminds me of it, and of how alone we are."

She smiled at the tall thin man, grateful for his understanding.

"But I won't let it get to me again," Gervais said.

"Neither will I."

They set up their third base camp near an outcropping of rock fifty paces away from the river. Leila's cousin Oni would remain there with Ali and Kwesi.

Everyone was up before dawn. Zoheret stood with Kwesi,

who as the oldest of the three would be in charge of this base, going over everything with him yet again.

"Hard to believe," Oni said, "that just a few days ago, I was annoyed that I wouldn't be going on with the rest of you." She lifted a foot and flexed it tentatively. "But maybe after a couple of days here, my feet won't feel as if they've swollen to twice their size."

"I'd almost be willing to trade places with you," Leila said.

"Be careful," Oni said.

Trevor, who was saying his farewells to his dome mate Ali, turned toward them. "Be careful? Of what?" He shook his head. "The only thing that's really surprised me is how little trouble we've had so far. I'm beginning to think that my mother and her comrades must have decided to stay with the other group after they found them."

"They wouldn't have had enough food with them to last that long," Ali said. He averted his eyes quickly from Trevor. "But I could be wrong."

"Maybe the reason we haven't seen the outsiders for so long is that they haven't needed to trade with us for anything," Trevor said, "which means that they might have had enough food to share with Bonnie and the others." Trevor was obviously trying to keep his hopes up, but Leila wanted to believe him.

Fourteen people moved on, leading the eight horses that remained with them. Leila's aches seemed less bothersome now, while the pain in her hips and knees had eased that morning after she was awake and on her feet; maybe she was finally getting accustomed to the days of hiking. Now she noticed that the landscape was changing again: A few black and dark gray outcroppings of rock jutted out from the seemingly endless grasslands. The maps that she had studied had shown such features, but had not prepared her for how they would look from out here. Some seemed like rows of pointed sharp teeth; others were lone fingers of rock pointing toward the sky, and still others were irregular blocks or walls. The sky was changing, too, with dark blue clouds forming in the south.

By midday, the clouds in the south had become a billowing black mass slowly spreading north across the sky. There had been no wind, not even a breeze, throughout the morning, but now the wind was rising into a high-pitched wail. The voice of Home was crying out a warning.

A ridge of rock lay to the southeast. Zoheret led them away from the river and across the grassy expanse to the outcropping. They took shelter along the side of the ridge that faced north.

Haidar quickly roped the horses together, then waved an arm. "Keep near the horses, all of you," he shouted above the howling wind. "Steady them if you can. And get the packs off them—if one of them bolts, we don't want to lose anything."

Leila untied and removed two packs from one mare, threw them to the ground, and pressed against the animal, her arms around the horse's neck as the storm broke over them.

The wind shrieked. She had never heard a wind this strong, had never experienced such loud thunder. A bright flash of light nearly blinded her. The horse trembled; she hung on as another clap of thunder tore through the wind and sheets of rain fell.

Then, as suddenly as it had come, the wind died. Another burst of thunder rolled overhead as the rain slowed to a drizzle.

They waited until the rain had stopped before leaving the shelter of the ridge. The sky was still dark with clouds, the air thicker and more humid. Their wet tunics and pants clung to their bodies; everyone else looked as damp, bedraggled, tired, and uncomfortable as Leila now felt. They made their way back to the river under the dark sky and Leila found herself wondering how many more storms might come and whether they would be able to take shelter from them as quickly. As they moved south, rain began to fall again, sifting down from the sky, misting the expanse of yellow and green bands.

During the next two days, the sky remained overcast. Rain fell only intermittently, barely wetting the grass, and yet it seemed to Leila that the rain always started to fall just as her clothing was almost dry. Each of them had brought three changes of clothing, rinsing out one set of clothes in the river and drying them after putting on other garments, but now Leila felt as though she would never know what it was like to wear dry clothes again, or truly clean ones for that matter.

Three days after the storm, they woke to clearer air, a gentle breeze, and sunshine. They followed the river to a short wall of rock that stood only a few paces from the riverbank. The wall was not much taller than Gervais; even with its pitted and irregular surface, it resembled the wall of an abandoned shelter or dwelling. There was no intelligent life here, none except themselves; Ship would never have left them on Home otherwise, and there was no evidence that intelligence had ever existed here. So the adults had always insisted, but looking at the wall, Leila wondered if Ship might have been wrong about that; it would not have been Ship's first mistake.

They would set up their fourth camp here, with Trang, Reuben, and Denis staying behind. The rest of them might have continued south until dusk, but Zoheret suggested that all of them could use a longer rest. Tents were raised, clothes were rinsed and draped over the wall of rock to dry, a fire was started, and flour was mixed with boiled water to make flatbread while a pot of beans simmered over the flames.

Leila was gathering brush and dry gourds for the fire when

she noticed that Yukio was standing still, gazing east, a hand cupped over his eyes. Edan stood next to him, also looking out at the plain.

Leila went to them. "What is it?" she asked the two boys.

"See that ridge in the distance?" Yukio said.

She squinted, but could barely make out the tiny speck of rock on the horizon. "I see it."

"I thought I saw something moving across it, along the top, but I can't see it there now."

"Animals?"

Yukio frowned. "I'm not sure. I almost thought it might be a person."

"A person?" Leila shook her head. "But the others are near the sea. We're still days away from them."

"If that's where they're still living." Yukio lowered his voice. "Trevor wants to think they're doing all right, because that's the only way he can believe his mother's still alive. And maybe they are, but my mother was really wondering about them the last time they came to trade with us. She wanted to scan them, but they wouldn't let her."

"She mentioned that to me," Leila said.

"Did she tell you that they were showing signs of malnutrition?"

"Just that they were too thin."

"She told me they looked like they were starving, as if something inside them was burning them up. After they left, she went to everybody who'd had any contact with them and did a scan, because she was worried the outsiders might have been carrying some disease we didn't know about, but she didn't find anything unusual. Of course she didn't tell people that was her reason, only that she needed to check up on one thing or another."

Leila had a vague memory of Kagami scanning her not long

after the two visitors had left, when Leila had been recovering from a fever. "Don't say anything about that to Trevor," she said.

"We haven't," Edan said.

"There's no harm in hoping."

Edan narrowed his eyes. "He's hoping too hard. He thinks the rest of our trip will be about as uneventful as it's been so far, that the worst that'll happen is we'll have to take shelter from another storm, and then we'll get to the end of our journey and find out that Bonnie and Chiang and Tonio are all alive and doing just fine."

"Maybe they are," Leila said, suppressing her doubts.

"Maybe and maybe not, but Trevor's getting careless. The last time I kept watch with him, all he did was talk about how much he was looking forward to finding his mother and getting back to our homes and how foolish Yusef was going to look for being so worried about sending people out. He was so busy talking that he didn't even see Yukio come out of our tent to take a piss."

Leila snorted. "Does that matter?"

"Yes, it matters," Yukio said, "because I was able to sneak up on him afterwards. I was practically on top of him before he even saw me."

"That was stupid," Leila said. "He could have shot you, and it would have taken you a while to recover."

"Unless I'd gotten the weapon away from him first. He's getting careless, Leila, and he's not the only one." Yukio waved an arm in the direction of Tala, who was roaming along the riverbank with Sofia and Shannon collecting brush. "Look at those three, they're not paying any attention to what's around them, they're just jabbering away. Tala still thinks she's going to find her father alive, too."

"Even your mother's getting more careless," Edan said, "having us stop here for the afternoon when we could be moving on."

"We can use some rest," Leila objected.

"Sure we can, but that means just a little less food for the next stage of our journey, and that can add up. It's like assuming that everything's going to go along as smoothly as it has and that everybody in the other base camps will be able to get anything to us that we might need later on." Edan brushed back a lock of his thick brown hair. "We'd better not assume that."

She could not argue with him. She had been growing more careless herself, dwelling on her aches and pains or the miseries of damp and dirty clothing while not paying as much attention to her surroundings.

"You should keep an eye on Zoheret," Edan continued. "You know her better than anyone. She was the one who didn't think we could handle this by ourselves, who pushed for having older people in charge, and maybe she was right about that. But if it looks as though she's not up to the job, we'll have to do something about that."

Was that what this was all about, she thought angrily, more of Edan's overly complicated musings about leaders and who should be in charge? But the unhappy look in his hazel eyes told her that he was worrying about much more than that.

"I'll keep an eye on her," she said softly.

His worried expression did not change. "Good."

Four days after leaving the fourth camp, they set up their fifth, with Shannon, Tala, and Hannah staying behind with Haidar and two of the horses. Trevor could easily handle their four other horses, given his skill with the animals, and Haidar would be of more use making sure that all of the bases remained in communication. That had been the plan all along, but Leila was sure Zoheret had also noticed how oddly cheerful Tala had grown in her conviction that her father Chiang would be found alive and safe, and how often she distracted others with her hopeful chatter and musings. Tala's absent-minded cheerfulness had led to the temporary escape of one of the horses, still laden with a pack, after she had failed to tie up the horse properly, and half a day lost while Haidar and Trevor rode out to recapture the mare.

The fifth base camp overlooked a slight bend in the river, which had narrowed again; the western bank was now close enough that they could swim to it easily. A ridge lay to the east, close enough for Haidar and the three young women to take shelter behind it if they saw another storm coming. In the distance, a high hill unlike any Leila had seen so far during their journey was a dark mound against the eastern horizon.

They left the fifth base camp in the morning, waiting until a few dark clouds that had formed at dawn had dispersed and a clear sky promised calm weather. They had lost sight of the camp by the time they stopped to rest and let the horses drink. It came to Leila that they were more vulnerable now, with only eight people and four horses left. How had Bonnie, Tonio, and Chiang come so far without wanting to turn back? The dizziness that she had felt days ago was rising in her once more.

No, she told herself; she would not give in to weakness.

Zoheret looked east and then south, pacing over the rock-strewn ground near the river as if keeping watch. Leila had been observing her mother, as she had promised Edan she would, but for the past couple of days, Zoheret had seemed unusually vigilant. After they moved on, Leila noticed that Gervais, after dropping behind the rest of them, was also scanning the plain with more intensity than usual.

When sunset came, they stopped for the night near a grove of the gourd-bearing trees. Sofia and Trevor had picked up a couple of the fallen gourds when Zoheret said, "No fire tonight."

"No fire?" Sofia asked. "Why not?"

"We won't need one to cook what we're eating tonight," Zoheret replied, "and we haven't seen any wild animals for days. And we're getting closer to the people we hope to find. We might be safer if they don't know we're coming, and these trees should help to hide us from view." She paused, apparently to let that sink in. "All of you know that we had our differences with the others in the past. I don't expect any trouble now, but we shouldn't take anything for granted. When you're on watch, be alert, and if you notice anything strange, even if you think it might just be a harmless animal, you are to wake Gervais and me immediately. Understood?"

"Yes," Sofia said, sounding apprehensive. The others nodded. Leila would not have to be on watch that night, but wondered if she would be able to sleep.

The next night, they camped near a small outcropping; again they did not build a fire. The day after that, Yukio spotted what looked like a herd of animals in the distance, but even his sharp eyes could not make out if they were deer or horses. On the next day, under a precipice of rock that was the tallest they had come upon so far, they found the traces of another campfire.

Rocks had been laid out in a circle, surrounding the small pit that had contained the fire. Bonnie and her companions might have made this fireplace, which was what Trevor wanted to believe. But it was possible that the outsiders had come here instead, that this was a place they had made. They were now, Leila knew, only about two days away from the sea.

They did not make a fire of their own. After a meal of dried fruit, they went through all of the usual routines that had by now become a habit: securing the horses, pitching the tents, digging a ditch, checking their bodies and feet to make certain that no blisters or wounds that might get infected had developed. No one spoke. Perhaps they were all sharing the same thought, namely that their journey would soon be at an end, and they would finally find out what had happened to the three missing people.

Kagami woke Leila to keep watch with Trevor during the last part of the night. The silence of the night was oppressive, but neither of them broke the silence with talk. Toward morning, Trevor went to the tent he was sharing with Yukio, Edan, and Gervais to wake them. Zoheret was already leaving the tent she had shared with Sofia and Kagami.

They had eaten a morning meal of more dried fruit and were standing with the horses on the riverbank when the silence was finally broken by Trevor. "Zoheret," he said, "I have to ask you something."

"Go ahead," Leila's mother replied.

"I know we agreed that the rest of us would wait here while you and Gervais went on, but I want to go with you."

"No."

"Bonnie's my mother," Trevor said. "I don't want to wait here for who knows how long before I find out what happened to her."

Zoheret went to him and put her hands on his shoulders. "I understand, but I told you before, we don't know what lies ahead. It's better if we—"

Trevor shook her off. "You're trying to protect us. You think it'll be easier for me if you come back and tell me Bonnie's dead than if I have to see that for myself."

"As soon as we find anything out, we'll come back here," Zoheret said. "I promise you that."

Trevor turned away from her. "Listen to me," Zoheret went on. "I'm counting on you. You'll have to maintain this base and send somebody back to Haidar's."

"I know." Trevor shook his head. "It's the waiting. I'd rather come with you than have to wait here, hoping she's still alive and then feeling just as sure that she probably isn't."

"Trevor." Leila went to him. "It won't be much longer." She put a hand on his arm and he did not shake it off.

Zoheret and Gervais were to take two of the horses and ride the rest of the way. Gervais helped Zoheret onto her horse, then stood on top of a large stone to mount his own, swinging one leg over the mare's side.

"You're good enough riders," Trevor said then, "but I'm a better one."

"You're right about that," Gervais replied.

"Then you should let me go in your place," Trevor said.

Gervais shook his head. "Nice try."

"Kagami, you're in charge here now," Zoheret said. "Just remember that one of you should be on the way to Haidar's camp no more than four days from now, whether we're back or not. And if we're not back here five or six days after that, you know what to do."

Leila knew how hard it might become. They were to break camp and return along the route they had followed to this place. They would have to assume that Zoheret and Gervais would find their way back to the settlements by themselves later, and if they did not, the two leaders and the board would have to decide if they should risk losing more lives in a third expedition.

But they would come back. Whether or not the three missing people were found, they would come back. Leila stood with the others and watched her mother and Gervais ride south slowly along the riverbank, gazing after them until they were only small dark forms moving amid the yellow and green grass.

Part Three

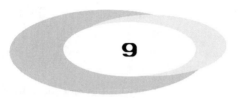

9

Nuy listened to the sound of the sea. Here in this cave,
north of the beach, she could hear the rhythmic roll of
the waves, as she had during her childhood while trying to fall
asleep. Sometimes it had seemed that the ocean was calling to
her. Even after all that had happened, she could sit there and
allow the muted and distant sound of the unseen waves to
soothe her, until she remembered the great storm that had
driven her people away from the sea and the father who had
cast her out.

Her loneliness nearly overwhelmed her. She thought of all
the times she and Carin had danced in the waves as they swept
over the sand, of how she and Belen had floated in the warm
water when the sea was calm. She longed for Carin and Sarojin again, even for Belen, and her longing was so fierce that she
could almost believe the three of them could feel her need for

them, even from a distance. She felt most alone when she thought of them.

She glanced around the cave, making sure that she had hidden any traces of her presence. There had been no need for a fire; she had buried her wastes and thrown the bones of the fish that she had scavenged, dried, and then eaten into the sea. If her people came searching for her, they would find no signs that she had been here.

There was no sign that any of her people had been here, either, and no reason for them to have concealed any evidence that they had come back to this region. When approaching these hills, she had always waited near the marsh until night, wanting to be certain that she could not be seen or her presence sensed, but had never seen any sign of a fire or heard the sound of human voices in the darkness. She told herself that by now, her father had to believe that she was dead, but if he was still in the grip of his rages and moods, she could not predict what he would do.

He might be looking for her now. If Belen came with him, she would have to be even more careful. She wondered if she could remain still enough to keep Belen from finding her, from sensing that she was nearby.

She picked up the sack that held her dried fish and tied it to her back, then left the cave, heading west, toward the marshlands where the river flowed into the sea. The swamp, thick with reeds and floating mats of green fibers and oily mud under the brown waters, no longer repulsed her, although she remained wary whenever she crossed it. She still hated the way that the mud oozed against her feet, making her feel as though it might suck her under the water. The mire pulled at her, forcing her to move slowly, every step an effort.

But she was safer on the other side of the marsh and away from the sea. One of the first things Ho had told her was to stay away from the marsh, that there were too many places where a person might get trapped and sink into the mud, but she had quickly found ways through the swamp as a child and was always careful to keep to the same routes. The other side of the marsh had been a place for her to hide for a while whenever Ho was either raging or brooding, to hear her own thoughts without the emotions of others leaking into her mind. Her father was unlikely to cross the marsh to discover the refuge she had made for herself and the two people she had found all those months ago.

Nuy had discovered the two strangers among the giant shells of the caves where her people had once lived. The two had endured the full power of the sudden storm that had blown in from the sea; it was a wonder they had survived at all. They had lost their horse and, with the animal, some of their supplies, saving only a small pot and two of their packs. The wind had struck with such force that the man had been swept off his feet and dashed against a wall of rock. Nearly blinded by the wind and rain, and supporting her companion, the woman had somehow managed to get both of them inside a cave that faced northwest, away from the storm.

The woman had told Nuy all of that only later, but Nuy guessed at some of what had happened as soon as she found the pair. The man was propped against the shiny pink and blue-green wall of the cave, a pack under his head, his right leg bound between two of the thick hard reeds that grew along the riverbank. The woman stood at his side, her weapon aimed at Nuy, and their horse was nowhere in sight.

"I don't want to hurt you," the woman said, "but I'll shoot if I have to." Her brown hair was plastered against her head and neck; her greenish eyes were wild. "You can understand me, can't you?"

Nuy nodded. "Yes." She wondered why the stranger would think that she wouldn't be able to understand her.

"You must be one of Ho's group," the woman said, "one of their children, from the looks of you."

Nuy said, "I'm Ho's daughter."

The woman drew in her breath. "What's your name? Where are the rest of your people? What are you doing with Chiang's horse?"

"You ask too many questions at once." Nuy led the black horse inside, careful not to make any sudden movements.

The man tugged at his beard. "What are you called?" he asked her.

"Nuy. Nuy the daughter of Ho."

"And your mother?" the woman asked.

"My mother's dead. I never knew her, because she died when I was still small. My father never told me her name and neither did anyone else. Katti says that speaking the names of the dead brings bad luck, but I never believed her. Not saying their names didn't always keep bad luck away." Once Nuy had thought that her father had missed her mother too much to be able to speak her name, that it would have pained him too deeply to say it, but after a while she had come to believe that he had simply forgotten it. Too many things had escaped his memory over the years, almost everything except his fears, his resentments, and his hatreds.

Nuy let go of the horse's reins, untied the packs from its back and set them on the ground, then sat down and folded her legs under herself, sitting on her heels. The horse retreated toward the back of the cave.

Nuy said, "You don't have to keep aiming that thing at me."

The woman lowered her arm.

"What's your name?" Nuy asked.

"My name is Bonnie," the woman answered, "and this is Tonio. He broke his leg."

Nuy peered at the splint. "Looks like you set it straight."

"Of course I set it straight," the woman said.

"Owen broke his left arm once," Nuy said, "and Eyela showed me how to set it. You'd never know there was ever anything wrong with his arm now."

"Where are the rest of them?" the man named Tonio asked. "The rest of your people, I mean."

Nuy considered what to say to him. Sooner or later, she would have to tell them that their companion was dead and that if her people came upon Bonnie and Tonio, they would most likely kill them as well. She would have to say that her father had cast her out. She wondered how much of that they could take in at once.

"My people don't live here now," she replied. "We lived here for a while, but then a great storm came and my father decided that it wasn't safe to live here anymore, so we moved inland."

"Then why did you come here?" the woman called Bonnie asked.

"I was looking for you," Nuy said. "The man I found said you would come here sooner or later."

"Where is Chiang?" The woman's voice was higher now, and harsher. "What happened to him? How did you get his horse?"

Nuy pressed her hands against the fronts of her thighs. "Say nothing to me until I'm finished, or this will be even harder for me to say." Slowly, choosing her words carefully, she told the two about how she had followed Chiang, hoping only to lead him to her people, and how he had died. She kept her words simple, not telling them how their friend had looked after his death, his body scarred and bloodied by the spear that had killed him.

Bonnie was still as Nuy spoke, not saying a word, but tears were streaming down her face by the time Nuy had finished. Tonio covered his eyes with one hand.

"I am most sorry for this," Nuy said. "I knew that my father was angry and troubled, but I didn't know that he was so afraid of your people that he would seek the death of your comrade. I warned him away too late, and even then, I didn't think that he would—" She swallowed. "Please believe me. If I had known such harm would come to your friend, I would never have led him there."

"You're sure," Bonnie said in a strained voice. "You're certain he's dead."

Nuy nodded. "Yes."

Tonio let his hand fall. "But why?" he asked. "Why would Ho be so frightened of Chiang?"

"He's afraid of anyone from the north. Years ago, two of my people went north to trade with you and when they came back, they brought death with them, a fever and a heaviness in the chest that made their lungs fill with water. I escaped that fever, but others did not. That's why Ho was afraid of your friend. He believed that the man might be bringing us death. Maybe he would have settled for driving him off, but he had fallen into the stream and maybe my father needed to be certain that he was dead, that he couldn't harm any of his people. That's why he drove me away, too."

"Drove you away?" Bonnie lifted a hand to her throat, fingering her necklace of small bright stones nervously.

"Because now he thinks I may be carrying death, too, because I was with your friend."

"That's crazy." The woman called Bonnie had a stunned and empty look on her face.

"My father's thoughts have been very troubled for a long time, and now there are only twelve of us left." Nuy paused, wondering if she could still count herself as one of her father's people. "Eleven besides me." She opened her hands. "Here it is. I'll do what I can to keep you alive, but when you are able to travel, I beg you to take me north to your people. After that, I must try to make my way back here to find two of my people, those to whom I am most tightly bound, but I won't ask any of your people to come back with me. I only want to learn whatever I can from you and then bring whatever little I might need back with me to help my friends. And if they won't come north with me, at least I will have tried to help them."

Would Carin and Sarojin welcome her back? Would Belen have come to miss her enough to treat her more kindly, as he had when they were children? Or would they all have become as mad as her father, convinced that she was bringing death to them? She refused to believe that. The three of them, if not the adults, would have to know as soon as they saw her that she was incapable of bringing death to them.

"I don't know how soon I'll be able to travel," Tonio said. "It isn't just my leg. I think my head might be affected." He looked at the woman from the sides of his eyes. "I didn't want to mention this before, but my head is throbbing and I'm feeling dizzy, too. Even if my leg heals enough so that I can ride, and that would probably take at least two months if not longer, I don't know if I could even stay on a horse."

"You have to rest," Bonnie said, "and then you'll get better."

"And by then we'll be that much shorter of food." Tonio closed his eyes for a moment. "If this girl's willing to travel with you, I suggest that you both head north as soon as possible and leave me here."

"No," Bonnie said, "I won't leave you." The woman was being careless and foolish, but Nuy found herself warming to Bonnie for so quickly rejecting her companion's suggestion.

"The longer you stay here," Tonio said, "the worse your

chance of making it back to the settlements. You won't have enough food, and you'll also have to deal with colder weather at the other end less than two months from now. If you go now, you might just be able to make it."

"I'm not leaving you, Tonio."

The man smiled weakly. "You're a better friend to me than I deserve."

Bonnie smiled back at him, but there was a sad look in her eyes. "Let's not talk about this any more."

Nuy glanced from the woman to the man. Her best chance might be to wait until these two were asleep, then to take the horse and all of the supplies and leave here by herself. She knew from what little Owen and Katti had said that they had gone west to the river and then followed it upstream when they had gone north to trade, and perhaps she could find out from Bonnie and Tonio if there was anything else she ought to know about how to reach their settlement safely.

That thought repulsed her. She had led one of these people to his death, however unknowingly; she would not leave the others here to die. She would not deserve to be taken in by their people if she abandoned them.

"I can help you," Nuy said, "and then later, you can help me."

"You'd be better off leaving right now," Tonio said.

Nuy shook her head. "What kind of welcome would I get from your people if I have to go to them and say that I let you die? It's bad enough that your friend is gone because of me. He'll haunt me if I don't do what I can for you."

"But how can you help us?" Bonnie asked.

"I can find food for you, and I can keep my people from finding you, because if they do, make no mistake, they'll kill you." Nuy paused, wanting them to understand that much right away. There was no point in saying that it might be Ho and

Owen and Daniella who would most want them dead and that the others might be more hesitant to take their lives. Owen would do whatever Ho wanted, Gerd and Zareb were as loyal to him as the dogs her people used to have, Belen might grow even more hardened against kindness and mercy, and Katti and Eyela would not stand up to her father or try to stop him.

"Someone may come for us," Tonio said. "If we're not back by the time the cold season comes, they might send someone south to look for us." Nuy knew little about Tonio's people, but even she heard the lack of conviction in his voice; he sounded as though he was trying to convince himself as much as her.

"We'll be safe enough here for now," Nuy said. Her father's fears would keep him away from this place for a while, even though he might have guessed that this was a place where she might hide. She could only hope that he would not send Belen to search for her; it would be harder for her to hide from him.

They were close enough to the river for Nuy to fetch water for them easily, and near enough to the sea that she could go down to the shore in the morning to see what fish the early tide had washed onto the sand. Dry gourds shed by the boltrees, brush, and dried horse droppings provided fuel for their fire, although they made a fire only when they needed one to cook some of their food. They did not need a fire to warm themselves, and she had never seen any bears, big cats, or wolves near the area that bordered the sea; the cats and wolves preferred to hunt inland where there was more prey. Nuy also did not want to risk any chance of alerting her father to their presence. He would probably not look for her here, but there was always the chance that he or others of her people might come back to forage nearby.

Bonnie and Tonio taught her how to make flat pieces of bread from the powdery substance called flour, and how to cook beans in the pot, but they ate as sparingly as they could from the few supplies they had left. The dried fruit and meat would keep, and the fish Nuy collected could sustain them for a while, although Bonnie worried that they could not live that way for very long.

"It's because we're not native to this world," Bonnie explained, "because we came here from somewhere else. This fish can fill our stomachs so that we don't feel hungry, but I don't know how much actual nourishment it'll provide. If we ate nothing but the fish and whatever plants might be edible, we could feel as though we've eaten enough even while we're slowly starving ourselves."

Nuy shook her head, not sure that she understood. The fish had always satisfied her own hunger, sometimes for many days when there was nothing else to eat, but her people had not survived only on fish even when they had been living near the sea. Deer could be hunted farther inland, one could make do with rabbits and rits, and there were the birds and eggs that could occasionally be found near streams and pools. Even though the great storm had swept most of those birds away from the coops where her people had kept them, a few of the freed birds had managed to survive along the river.

"So we'll have to conserve our food," Bonnie continued, "make it last as long as possible, but with any luck, maybe we won't have to wait too long. Within a month—in about thirty days, our people will expect us to be back. Thirty days after that, they'll begin to worry about us, and not long after that, they'll have to be wondering what's happened. And then they'll send someone out to look for us."

"And by then," Tonio added from where he lay, "maybe I'll be able to travel, if I can stay on that horse. And you'll come with us." Tonio's head was propped against an empty pack, and he was still unable to sit up for long without feeling disoriented or nauseated, but perhaps that would pass.

Nuy spent one day guiding Bonnie down to the river with the horse, showing her where the water was fresh enough for the animal to drink. Farther down, where the river ran into the marshlands, the water was brackish and the footing treacherous, and the horse might be injured if it fell among the thick hard reeds. When Nuy's people had still had horses, they had lost three of them that way, and Bonnie and the horse would be safer staying near the caves, hidden by the rise on which they stood from anybody who might be approaching from the east.

For several days, the two northerners alternated between high-spirited hopes that some of their people might already be on their way to search for them and darker moods when they thought of their dead comrade. Nuy shared neither their hopes nor their sadness. She had mourned for Chiang and deeply regretted her own part in his death, but there was nothing she could do to change that, and hoping for anything meant looking too far ahead.

Twenty-eight days after Nuy had found Bonnie and Tonio, she returned to the cave with fish to find Bonnie sitting outside the opening, her head bowed, and knew immediately that something was wrong. She sniffed at the air and realized that the horse was gone even before Bonnie told her that the animal had escaped.

"It's my fault," Bonnie muttered as they both entered the cave. "Something startled her, something moving in the grass, and before I could get a grip on the reins, they slipped out of my hands. I should have been more careful, I know."

"Did you go after the horse?" Nuy asked, keeping her voice as low and calm as possible.

"Of course I did, but every time I got close to her, she'd run off again, and after a while she was so far away that I couldn't go after her. I waited as long as I dared, but she kept running, getting farther and farther away from me, and finally I couldn't see her at all."

Nuy did not know what to say. Tonio, lying near the banked fire, was silent, but his dark eyes were angry. His rage might have been directed at Bonnie, but perhaps he was also furious with himself for being so helpless.

"She might come back," Bonnie said. "When we go to get more water, maybe we'll find her."

"And maybe we won't," Nuy said bitterly.

"Maybe that's just as well," Bonnie went on. "She'll have more of the green grass to graze on farther north. There isn't as much of it near here, not the paler green or the darker green grass, so I don't know how much longer she would have lasted here, with only the yellow grass."

Nuy stood there, still holding her small sack of fish. There was only a small chance that her father would find the horse, but if he did, he would probably recognize it as Chiang's horse, especially if the bridle was still around its head. There was an even smaller chance that he might decide to track the horse, to find out where it had come from. Even a very small chance that Ho might come after her sooner rather than later was not something to welcome, and if Belen came with him, it would be even harder for her to hide herself and her companions from them.

"I am sorry," Bonnie continued, "but you must have noticed how thin she was getting. She might have kept on getting weaker, too weak for us to have any chance at all of making it back to our settlement with her, and I doubt she could have carried Tonio. We would have had to keep looking out for her even when she wasn't of much use."

"Be quiet," Nuy said, wishing that the woman would stop making excuses for her mistake.

"So now that we have no chance of leaving here by ourselves, we'll just have to keep doing what we're doing," Bonnie said in an even higher voice, "staying alive until we're found."

"You are a fool." Nuy threw down her fish. "At worst, that horse could have become food if we couldn't use it for anything else."

"Food?" Bonnie shook her head. "Not one of our horses."

Nuy did not understand these people. "And what's wrong with horsemeat?"

"Nothing, I suppose," Tonio said. He lifted his head, then lay back again. "It's just that we don't have that many horses, at least not compared to our other domestic animals, and we've come to rely on them more for riding and transporting heavy loads we can't carry easily ourselves, or sometimes for plowing the fields—I guess you could say that they're more like companions to us, since we don't raise them for food. I wouldn't want to eat a horse I'd come to know any more than I would one of our cats or dogs."

"A dog can make a meal, too," Nuy said. "Ours sometimes did when we still had them. You eat what you can when you get hungry enough."

"Then I hope we never get that hungry," Bonnie said.

"You will." Nuy struggled to control her fury. "I might almost think that you let that horse escape."

"No, but under the circumstances, maybe it's just as well that she did." Nuy saw that Bonnie did not really mean that even as she spoke, and wondered why she was saying it at all. The woman was prideful, clinging to her nonsense and arguing in favor of her foolishness rather than admitting that she had made a serious mistake.

Perhaps the horse would find its way back to them. It was

useless to speak of this any longer. Nuy knelt by the fire, took out her knife, and began to clean and gut the fish. "How soon do you think your people might come to look for you?" she asked.

"In one or two months," Bonnie replied. "In thirty to sixty days," she added. "To be honest, I don't really know. The truth is that a fair number of people warned us against coming here at all."

"Maybe you should have listened to them," Nuy said.

"They may decide to wait until after the cold season," Tonio said. "With all the work to be done after the harvest to prepare for winter, it won't be easy to spare even two or three people to come looking for us. They might assume that we found shelter with your people. I have a feeling it would be easy for them to come up with a lot of good excuses for not coming after us."

"What you're saying," Nuy said, "is that we can't count on any help from them."

Bonnie sighed. "What I think is that we might as well assume we'll be on our own for a long time."

"Enough," Nuy said. She finished cleaning the last fish and lay it on one of the rocks near the fire. If these two and their dead companion had never come here, she would have been with her people now, sitting around a fire like this one, sharing whatever food they had found. She would be looking forward to the night, when sleep would quiet the anger inside Belen and she would lie next to him, arms entwined, dreaming of the days they had passed by the sea and sensing that he was also dreaming of those happier times.

They remained in the cave. During the mornings, Bonnie went to the river to bring back water and brush for the fire while Nuy searched for fish along the shore. Tonio tended the fire, and did his best to help them keep the cave clean, but there was little other work that he could do. Although he did not complain, it was clear that his leg still pained him, and his dizziness twice brought him to vomit his food. Even so, his biggest regret seemed to be that the flat rectangular object he called a reading screen no longer worked.

In the evenings, while eating a bite or two of fish and a bit of flatbread, with an occasional small handful of dried seeds and nuts or fruit, Bonnie and Tonio spoke of their people and the life they led in their settlement. Nuy did not understand some of what they told her, but grasped enough to know that however hard their lives might seem to them, they were easier than the way her people lived. In return, she told them stories of happier moments in her own life, when she and Carin had learned how to make knives and spears from Owen, or Katti had told everyone tales of the ancient giant sea creatures and the shells they had left behind.

A number of days passed before Nuy spoke of their rapidly diminishing food supplies. They had only a little of the flour left, and almost none of the dried fruit and meat. It was time that she hunted, and for something more substantial than fish, while she still had enough strength to do so. Bonnie would show her how to use the weapon she carried, and Nuy would take Tonio's weapon with her when she went looking for game.

"It's a stun gun," Bonnie explained. "It can stun an animal, but it won't kill, not unless you fire it a number of times, but then you would risk draining the charge—using up its power."

Nuy shrugged. "My father used to hunt with a weapon like this. If I can stun the animal, I'll be able to kill it afterward." She gestured at her knife.

It took her only a morning to master how to fire the weapon. Nuy left their cave the next day at dawn, telling Bonnie and

Tonio that she would return in no more than two days whether she found any game or not. She promised herself that she would return with food, even if it was no more than a rabbit or a rit.

She did not allow herself to think about the man and the woman until she was halfway down the slope that overlooked the flat patch of ground near the river where her people had once had their fields. She had only faded memories of the vines, green shoots, and edible roots that had grown there, but recalled her father's bitter complaints about the land. Even with the dark soil they had brought from the north to nourish the land along with the dung from their horses, growing any food there had been a struggle. Obviously it had not been as hard for the people in the north, who had been able to offer Ho's people food, but Ho had been bitter about having to accept that food instead of being grateful for it. Surely Bonnie and Tonio were right to hope that their people, who had more than enough to sustain themselves on the long journey, would come south to search for them.

But they were beginning to lose that hope. Nuy halted on the hillside as that realization came to her. She had sensed it all along, but had refused to allow herself to see their despair clearly. Tonio had not trimmed his beard with his metal cutting tool for days now, and Bonnie's brown hair remained uncombed. Their clothes now went unmended, even though they had tools for that as well, tiny needles that were like the ones Eyela had made from the bones of fish. The two had grown less talkative over the past few days, and Nuy could guess at what they were thinking.

Maybe their people would not come for them. Maybe their people would wait, believing that the three northerners had found shelter with Ho's band, until it was too late. Without Nuy, Bonnie and Tonio probably could not survive, might not have even lasted this long, and perhaps trying to survive was futile anyway.

Their lives belonged to her now.

Something flickered at the corner of her eye. Nuy crouched down, then peered over the grass at the plain to the northeast. At first she could hardly glimpse the tiny black speck in the sea of yellow and green grass. She narrowed her eyes, and then knew what she was seeing.

A black horse was out there, perhaps the horse they had so recently lost, and a rider was on its back, someone with a long brown braid. Belen, she thought, and her heart pounded; he had always been good with the horses when her people had them. The horse and rider were so far away that if they kept moving north, they would soon be lost to her sight. It did not matter. Being able to see Belen and the horse at all was enough for her to feel threatened.

Now her people had a horse, at least for a time. That would make it easier for one of them to ride to her refuge if Ho grew curious or else decided that he was ready to welcome her back. He might send Belen for her. She wondered how long she dared to stay here.

She sat there, waiting until long after she could no longer see the horse and rider, and vowed to leave this region as soon as possible.

Before crossing the swamp, Nuy made sure that her weapon was secured inside her sack of fish. The stun guns were most likely the only reason she and her two companions were still alive, and now they had only one weapon left. Tonio's had failed many days ago, so now Nuy was carrying Bonnie's weapon. She had insisted that she did not need it, that they had enough game for now and that she did not need the weapon for gathering and drying fish, but Bonnie had forced it on her. If by any chance her people had returned to the area bordering the shore, she might need to protect herself.

Bonnie and Tonio would be helpless against any predators, not that either of them seemed to care about that. More and more often, their growing passivity so enraged her that she welcomed the chance to get away from them for a while, to hunt the game that she could bring down so easily with the weapon.

She had fed them for months with meat from deer, rabbits, and the fat flightless birds that could be found near the river. Before that, she had crossed the marsh to seek out a safe place for them, and had found a deep recess in a rocky ridge that could shelter all three of them. She had brought Bonnie and Tonio through the marsh as soon as Tonio was able to walk, and he had been so weak and so careless about where he placed his feet that she had almost lost him to a sinkhole. She had tended the two for days when their wastes ran from their backsides like watery mud, afraid that she might lose them both. She had guided Tonio down to the river so that he could work his withered and still healing leg in the warm water, and had shown Bonnie which reeds could be chewed on and eaten and which of the hard thick ones could be used for making spears and poles. She had forded the swamp, always in the hope that she might find that others of their people had come to the caves to look for them after all. She had cut up hides for the two to wear over the rags that remained of their garments, and all any of her efforts had done was to feed their helplessness.

She should have abandoned them long ago, and wondered why she should not do so now. With the weapon, she could take her chances on following the river north. The weapon would bring down enough game to feed her along the way, and if she found her way to her destination, she could tell the northerners that she had done all she could for their lost ones.

Green and grayish pads of matted fibers floated on the surface of the shallow brown water. The mud sucked at her as she waded through the mire. The odors of salt and a smell like that of manure made her nose wrinkle. All this trouble for two people who seemed to be growing ever weaker; once again she wished that she had never found them at all. Then she quieted her worries, thinking only of the thick mud pulling at her and the small craters in the mud that might be sinkholes.

At last she came to the sandstrewn hill on the other side of the marsh and climbed up through the grass, then sat down to rest in the warm sun. Her legs were caked with mud to the knees, but the mud would soon dry, and then she could brush it off. She sat there and thought of what Bonnie had said to her only a few days ago.

"I thought I knew them." She had been talking about her mate, her son, her friends, all of the people she had known. "I tell myself that they couldn't have forgotten us, that they wouldn't just have given up on us, and then at other times they seem so far away that I'm afraid I'm forgetting them. Maybe I never really knew them at all. Sometimes they hardly seem real." How weak Bonnie and Tonio were, even weaker than the adults among her own people, even more blind and deaf to the world around them.

"And sometimes you hardly seem real," Bonnie had gone on to say. "There's something odd about you, Nuy, something different."

The doubt in the woman's voice had put Nuy on edge, and then she recalled hearing the same words from her father's mouth long ago. "There's something strange about you, Nuy, you and the others," and she had known Ho was talking about Carin and Sarojin and Belen as well as herself. "I turn around and there you are, even though I was sure you were in front of me only a few seconds ago. You tell me rain's coming when there isn't a cloud in the sky, you warn me that a big cat's on the prowl nearby when there's no animal in sight, you read signs I can't see." She had felt the fear and suspicion welling up inside her father just before he had grabbed her wrist. "Sometimes you don't seem human, and I wonder if I should get rid of you before you taint us all." She had never been so afraid of her father as she had been when he uttered those words.

"I thought it was just that you were more accustomed to this region than we are," Bonnie went on, "more used to surviving with little, and maybe that was the reason you seem to pick up on certain things and we don't, but it's more than that. Sometimes, I almost think you can hear my thoughts," and Nuy had thrown up her hands and shaken her head in denial. "You're different."

Ho had said the same thing. "You're different. Sometimes I wonder that you can even be my daughter." Bonnie's words frightened her, but in a different way than Ho's had. Maybe Bonnie's people would never welcome her among them; maybe they, too, would see her as too much unlike themselves to live among them even for a short time. Maybe they would look at her the way her father and the others sometimes looked at her, Carin, Sarojin, and Belen.

"Hai," Nuy muttered to herself. Bonnie and Tonio had told her more than her father ever had about Ship, that great mind encased in a giant gourd-shaped vessel that had brought them to this world and then expelled them from itself. Sometimes Nuy had wondered if Ship, wherever it might be in the sky by now, could hear their thoughts. Now she told herself that such notions were foolishness, that if Ship could have picked up their thoughts, then it would have returned long ago and gathered them all to itself again.

And if Ship did return, would it welcome her, or only those

who had once lived inside itself? It was useless to dwell on something so unlikely to happen.

Nuy stood up, having made her decision. They would have to go north, whatever the risks. Even with the weapon, she knew that their chances weren't good, but they were not that much better here. They could not wait here in the hope that others would finally come searching for them.

Bonnie and Tonio had chosen to leave their people, and there might be more behind that choice than they had revealed to her. She could almost understand why their people, however much they might have worried about them, might have reasoned that they could not take more risks to look for them, that they could do no more for them. Perhaps that was yet another of the lessons that they had learned from Ship.

10

onnie stood near the opening of the recess, hand around
the spear Nuy had made for her, keeping watch as Nuy
climbed toward her. Bonnie's vigilance came as a surprise.
Nuy had expected to see her sitting inside with Tonio, staring
at the walls of the hollow with dead eyes, oblivious to any possible threat. The woman's appearance was different, too. Her
hair, which usually hung past her shoulders and often fell over
her eyes, was tied back with a thin strip of hide, and the rips in
her shirt and leg coverings had obviously been mended. Her
necklace of bright stones, which she had not worn since they
had crossed the marsh together, had been taken out of the
pack where she usually kept it and now hung around her neck.

Bonnie pointed the sharpened end of the spear away from
Nuy as she entered the recess. Inside, she found another surprise. Part of the flat dirt floor of their rocky shelter was now

covered with clean yellow grass instead of the filthy grass they had been sleeping on for some time. Tonio sat on the grass, sharpening the end of a thick hard reed into a spear. Clearly he had been watching her closely, since he was doing a good job of it. He had also trimmed his beard, cutting it closer to his face.

Nuy untied her small sack, took out the weapon, and set the fish on the ground, then handed the weapon to Bonnie.

"Thank you," Bonnie said. Her offering of thanks had become a habit, but there was more feeling in her voice than usual.

"I see we still have much meat left," Nuy said, glancing toward the back wall of the recess, where strips of dried deer meat and what was left of some roasted meat were stored. "But it's good to have the fish anyway." That was also part of their ritual, to behave as if the only reason Nuy had crossed the marsh was to find fish for them. She did not have to say that she had seen no signs of another human presence, no signs of her people or theirs. They would know from her silence that she had found no signs.

"We've been doing some thinking while you were gone," Bonnie said as she sat down next to Tonio. "There's something we have to ask you."

Nuy sat down across from them. "I've been thinking, too," she said.

"Let us say this first," Tonio said. An uneasy look came over his face, and Nuy knew that he was again feeling the dizziness and disorientation that had never entirely left him. "We've been able to survive here longer than I could have hoped for, and that wouldn't have been possible without your help."

Nuy bowed her head for a moment. "None of us would have lived if I hadn't had the use of your weapons."

Tonio smiled. "I'm not so sure about that. I think you might have found a way to survive without any help from us."

Nuy shrugged.

"Anyway, Bonnie and I have come to a decision. We must try to get back to our home, however poor our chances might be, and we want you to come with us."

Nuy was silent.

"You talked about coming with us before," Bonnie said, "and to be honest, I don't think we'd make it back without you. But whether you come with us or not, we have to leave here. I think we'll go mad if we stay here much longer."

"I have been thinking the same thing," Nuy said. "We have to leave, and I must go with you. But now I wonder if your people will welcome someone who led one of you to his death."

"You can't be blamed for that," Tonio said, "and you did everything you could for us."

Nuy said, "I also wonder what it'll be like to live among people who would let so many days pass without trying to find out what happened to three of their own. I know how it is with my people. As long as my father has turned from me, no one will look for me or welcome me back. Carin and Sarojin might do so, but they are only two and they can't stand against the rest. There are so few of them, and maybe that made it easier for the storms inside my father to sweep away their reason along with his own. But I don't know why your people wouldn't have come for you by now if they cared for you at all."

"Maybe they did send someone out," Bonnie said in a whisper. "They might have waited until the cold season passed, and then they would have had to decide who should go, but I have to believe that by now they would have sent somebody out to look for us. So here's what's been tormenting me these past days." She paused. "Even if they were sure we were dead, I think someone would have been out searching for us after all this time, so perhaps a few of them have already tried to look for us and failed. Maybe they ran into some accident and had to head back, or maybe they died along the way. That's another reason we have to go back. I don't want to think of others taking risks trying to find out what happened to us."

Ho might have struck at them, Nuy thought, if any of their people had come south to search for them. Ho had Chiang's weapon, along with his own, and perhaps his band still had the black horse. He feared and hated the northerners enough to attack them if he saw them in what he regarded as his territory.

She envisioned what he might do, almost as if she were picking up his distant thoughts. He would strike at any outsiders and take whatever they had; his fear of whatever illness Chiang might have been harboring had not kept him from taking the dead man's weapon. He might have even more weapons now.

"That's it, then," Nuy said. "We'll leave here in the morning, but we won't cross the marsh. It would be better if we didn't return to where I first found you. We'll be safer on this side of the river for a while. We can find a place to cross when we're farther to the north."

"Are you certain?" Bonnie asked.

"I am." She forced herself not to dwell on her own fears.

Leila rode north along the river. She had tried and failed to talk Trevor into riding back to Haidar's camp in her place. He was the best rider of all of them, she had argued, and the ride might distract him temporarily from his fears about his mother. But he had insisted on staying with the others. Whatever had happened to Bonnie, Trevor preferred to find out about it sooner rather than later. That had decided the matter, since Yukio, Edan, and Sofia were all poorer riders than Leila, as they readily admitted.

She had kept the chestnut mare to a walk, urging her into a

trot when there was a stretch of wide flat ground ahead. "Speed isn't that important," Trevor had told her. "Better to get there six days from now rather than not getting there at all." She had been riding for three days now, with little sleep, not stopping to rest until long after nightfall and then riding on before dawn. Being alone with the horse, being completely by herself as she rode through the empty grassland, had disturbed her more deeply than she had expected, and she had not wanted to sleep any longer than absolutely necessary. She was exhausted and every muscle in her legs and back throbbed, but she would reach Haidar's camp before sunset. Already she could see the tiny black wall that was the ridge near his base.

She longed to be among people again.

The distant silvery loop that marked the bend in the river near the base was clearly visible when she saw that something was very wrong in the encampment up ahead. She could see no tent, and no horses. She dug her heels into her horse's flanks, moving her into a trot.

Two small lumps, blue and brown, lay in the grass. That had to be Hannah's blue tunic, while the brown would belong to Haidar. Leila was still far from the camp when she finally realized what she was seeing.

Hannah and Haidar were lying out there in the grass, a few paces from the riverbank, unmoving, without blankets or the shelter of a tent. They had to be sleeping, resting in the late afternoon sun. Her inner voice kept repeating that insistently, even as she knew it could not be so. They were only sleeping, they were resting, they would suddenly wake up and get to their feet to greet her. Her legs tightened around the barrel of the horse, which sped into a gallop. Forcing herself to quell her impatience, Leila pulled at the reins, and the mare slowed to a trot once more.

"Haidar," Leila called out, although now she could see that

the man was lying on his back, arms out, with a long pole jutting from his chest. "Hannah." The back of her friend's blue tunic was covered with a large dark brown stain; her head was twisted to one side, and a broken off pole stuck out from her back. The two horses that had been left here were nowhere in sight.

As she rode toward them, Leila still kept expecting Haidar to move, Hannah to sit up and wave to her. She reined in the horse and threw herself from its back, coming to herself only long enough to keep a grip on the reins as she approached the two people who lay on the ground. Already she could tell that there was nothing she could do for them.

The horse whinnied before death. Leila's legs felt boneless. She sat down abruptly, still clinging to the reins and choking out short, sharp gasps. Two packs were in the grass, with long gashes in their sides. A large flat piece of cloth was what remained of the tent; the stakes had been pulled up, and the edges of the cloth looked as though someone had torn them. Small mounds of flour were scattered over the ground, along with other pieces of food, but it seemed that much of the food had been taken.

"Tala," she whispered, realizing that two of the four people who had been left here were missing. "Shannon." She looked up. A hunched-over figure was leaning against the ridge several paces away. "Tala," Leila whispered again, recognizing the girl.

Somehow she managed to stand up. She walked toward the ridge on trembling legs, leading her horse by the reins. Tala's head hung forward, her face hidden by her black hair.

"Tala," Leila called out as she approached.

The other girl looked up, shaking back her hair. She seemed unharmed, but her eyes gazed past Leila, as if she were unable to see her. Leila halted near her, afraid to touch her.

"Tala, what happened?"

Tala stared at her for a long time, then suddenly crumpled to the ground. Her hands fluttered, darting toward her face; she wrapped her arms tightly around herself. Leila quickly looped the horse's reins around a crag, tied them, and sat down next to her.

"You have to tell me," she said, still unable to absorb what had taken place. "What happened?"

"They're dead," Tala said in a toneless voice. "They killed them. Haidar was on watch, and Hannah and I were in the tent, sleeping. That was when they came, in the night." She fell silent for so long that Leila feared she might never speak again.

"They? Who came here?" But Leila knew who the killers had to be. "What happened to Shannon?"

"She left here four days ago." Tala's voice rose to a higher pitch. "With one of the horses, for the next base to the north. That was what she was supposed to do, wasn't it?"

"Tala." Leila slipped her arm around the other girl's shoulders. "You have to tell me everything now."

"We were asleep, and Haidar was on watch. I needed to shit so I got up. I was over by the ditch and Haidar suddenly called out, I don't remember what he said, but he was calling out some kind of greeting, and then I saw a bright streak shoot toward him and hit him, and then somebody else started shouting. I didn't recognize the voice. I stretched out on the ground and rolled toward the river, and all I could think of was just to lie there among the reeds, be as still and as quiet as I could be. Or maybe I was just too scared to move."

She shook off Leila's arm. "So I was lying there. I think Hannah screamed once, and then I saw another burst of light. I was half in and half out of the water, and it was cold in the water, but I didn't dare move, I just kept lying there, by then

I couldn't move at all. Somebody said, 'There's another one here, I know it, I can smell it,' and someone else said 'Be quiet.' It sounded like they were arguing, and then I must have blacked out for a while. I heard voices and some awful moaning and these sounds as if somebody was pounding at something, and then somebody said, 'Don't get too close to them.' I remember that, and then some muttering that sounded like another argument, and then nothing. A while later a voice said, 'Take the horse.' I think that's when they left. I kept lying there, half in and half out of the river, and the next thing I remember, it was morning."

Tala's lips looked dry and cracked. Leila reached for her canteen and held it to Tala's lips. "How long ago?" Leila asked as Tala drank. "When did all of this happen?"

Tala pushed the canteen away. "Just a day ago," she replied. "I think it was only one day ago, or a day and a half. No, it was almost two days, I think . . . it had to be two days . . ." Her voice trailed off.

"Did you see them at all?"

"I didn't dare move, I was afraid to look. Even when it was morning, I was afraid to move, to get up. I had to be sure they were gone, that they wouldn't see me and come back to get me, too."

"Tala, listen, this is important. Did you see where they went, what direction they took?"

Tala shook her head. "I don't know. I'm not even sure of how many of them there were. Maybe three, maybe four, I couldn't tell." She shuddered, then grabbed Leila's arm, digging her fingers into the flesh so hard that it hurt. "I didn't do anything to help," she cried. "I had my weapon, I could have fired it." She let go and gestured toward the weapon at her waist. "I didn't even try to fight, I was too frightened. I just kept lying there hoping they wouldn't come after me."

"You couldn't help it," Leila said. "I don't know if I would have been able to fight, either."

"I was too scared." Tala shook her head violently. "I'm a coward." She covered her face with her hands and wept as Leila held her, waiting for the sobbing to stop.

She had to assume that the people who had done this had not followed the river directly south, or she would have encountered them on her way here; she shivered at the thought. They might have headed north, to the next base, or they might be out there, somewhere on the eastern plain. They might have traveled east and then turned south; they would know this territory a lot better than she did. If they still lived near the sea, they might be on their way back to their settlement there.

Her mother might still be there, with Gervais, as helpless as Haidar and Hannah had been, and as unprepared for any attack.

Tala's sobs were subsiding. "Listen to me," Leila said. "You mustn't think about what happened, about what you did or didn't do. You couldn't have known anyone would do something like this. You have to believe that. I might have acted the same way in your place. What matters now is warning everybody else." The others might strike at the camp to the south before returning to their home. There was that possibility, too.

Tala wiped at her eyes with one sleeve. "Go on," she whispered, sounding a little more like herself.

"You said that Shannon left here four days ago. That means she's probably at the fourth camp now. She or somebody else will be riding back here in a while."

"Two or three days," Tala murmured. "She said she wouldn't stay there more than two or three days."

Would that camp to the north be attacked? Leila tried to believe that such an attack was unlikely, but how could she be

sure? She had no way of knowing what might happen. It occurred to her then that all of their caution and preparation had
been useless. If the others went north and struck at one camp
after another, she and everyone in the southernmost camp
would be completely cut off from the settlements.

No, she told herself. It was unlikely that the outsiders
would go north to attack the nearest camp there, no reason to
assume that they even knew that anyone was upriver and only
a few days away. They might be more likely to believe that
Haidar, Hannah, and Tala were on their own, as the three earlier explorers had been. They would go south. They might
have been traveling at some distance from the river, since she
had not seen any sign of strangers during her ride, but if they
still lived by the sea, they would eventually go there, and they
might find the last base along the way.

The others had killed Haidar and Hannah without hesita-
tion. She realized then that Bonnie, Chiang, and Tonio were
probably dead, too.

"Tala," she said, "we have to warn everybody. One of us has
to warn Shannon when she rides back here, and the other one
has to go south. I think everyone downriver is probably in
more danger than anyone to the north, which means I should
take this horse and start riding south as soon as possible. You'll
have to stay here alone."

Tala let out a faint wail and covered her eyes. "I don't know
if I can do that, thinking . . ."

"Please," Leila said, wanting to shake her. "There isn't anyone else except us to do this. You have to warn Shannon, and
you'd probably both be safer after that if you went back upriver to the next camp."

Tala heaved a sigh, then leaned back against the rock. "I
have a better idea," she said at last. "You ride south to warn
everybody there, and I'll start walking north, I can carry what

I need. I'll meet Shannon on the way and that'll save her from having to see any of this."

"No," Leila said. "You'd be safer here. You'd be going north all alone, without a horse, with no one to keep watch while you sleep."

"I'd be all alone here, and I don't think I could sleep now anyway. And you look awful. You don't look like you're in any shape to ride anywhere."

"I have to, Tala, I have to warn them." She tried to get up and suddenly felt how overwhelmingly exhausted she was. Unable to rise, she sagged against the rock and slid into darkness.

L eila awoke to the reddish light of sunset. She was lying at the base of the ridge, with a covering over herself. For a moment, she did not know where she was, and then remembered. The memories stunned her into wakefulness and filled her with despair and dread.

Tala had covered her with what was left of the tent. She threw off the covering and sat up. Tala was walking toward her, leading the horse.

"You shouldn't have let me sleep," Leila called out.

"I couldn't have stopped you from sleeping," Tala replied, "and your horse needed rest, too. Now she's had time to graze, and plenty of water to drink, so you can leave now. I think you might be safer riding at night."

She would have to keep moving, Leila thought, and rest as little as possible. Sleeping would only slow her down; sleeping would leave her too vulnerable. She got to her feet and clung to Tala for a moment, afraid to look toward the river. "We should do something for them," she murmured. "We can't just leave them lying out there."

"That's exactly what we have to do," Tala said as she handed the reins to Leila. "I've been thinking. We have to leave everything the way it is. What if they come back? You don't want them to see that somebody else was here."

Tala was right, even though the thought of leaving Haidar and Hannah lying there on the ground was almost too painful for her to accept. But the two of them were gone now, their bodies no more than shells. Leila poked at the cloth of the tent with her foot. "Then you'd better put this back where it was."

"I will, and then I'm going to start walking north. I think I'll be safer away from here, and eventually I'll meet up with Shannon. She doesn't have to see this. Hearing about it will be bad enough." Tala's eyes still stared at her blankly, but her voice was hard. "I have enough food to get by."

"So do I." She had almost nothing left, but she would not need much, not if she kept going and rested as little as possible.

"Good luck, Leila." Tala stood near the horse as Leila mounted, helping to boost her onto the mare's back. "Send a rider to us as soon as you can."

Leila pressed her knees against the horse's flanks. Tala knelt and was folding up the tent as she rode away.

Deep blue clouds veiled the sky at dusk. By nightfall, the clouds had grown so thick that Nuy could no longer see the rising first moon or the stars. She had decided that it would be safer for her and her companions to travel at night, and not just because she did not want to risk discovery by her father. If there was any chance that people from the north were searching for Bonnie and Tonio, they might be as quick to lash out in anger and fear as Ho had been when she had brought Chiang to him. It might be better for her to hide and wait while her two companions went to greet them. The two might believe that their people would welcome her, but she had only their word on that.

Their pace was slower than she had expected. Tonio's leg might have mended, but he was still limping, still favoring the injured leg, and she wondered if he would ever truly recover its full use. They had forded the river only three days after leaving the marsh, at a place where the shallowness of the water and the closeness of the eastern bank had made for an easy crossing. Nuy would have preferred to cross farther north, but had discovered that Tonio and Bonnie could tell her little about what they had seen during their journey, about where the river narrowed and where it might be too deep and wide to cross, or the current too strong. They were poor observers, helpless without the device Tonio called their screen to recall much of what they had seen, their eyes seemingly as weak and their other senses as unperceptive as those of the adults among her own people.

She would have to hunt soon. They still had some of their meat left, but she did not want to wait until it was all eaten. She had hoped that they would be farther north by now, where it might be safer to build a fire.

Nuy halted. "We should stop for a while," she said. "I can hardly see where to put one foot in front of another." She squatted and sat on her heels while the dark forms of her companions sank to the ground. It came to her then that she could not be that far from the place where she had first seen Bonnie and Tonio. She had seen the cliff that loomed over the river against the sky, a black pillar in the distance, before the clouds had begun to thicken. She thought of how much had changed for her since she had hidden there.

"Is a storm coming?" Bonnie asked, sounding worried.

Nuy looked up at the sky as she sniffed the air, which smelled of grass and reeds and water and mud. The wind was picking up a little, but she could not smell even a trace of salt on the air, as she would have at this distance from the sea if a storm were approaching from the south.

"Those aren't storm clouds," she replied. "It might rain later on, but even that's not likely."

They sat in silence for a while, and then Tonio said, "It's good that we left the place you found for us, Nuy, but I don't know if I'm strong enough to make it all the way back."

Nuy shook her head. "You think too far ahead," she said. "Don't think further ahead than the next day. Then, when that day comes, think only of the one after that. String enough days together like that, and you'll find yourself back at your settlement."

"I don't know if I can do it. You and Bonnie would have a better chance if you went on by yourselves."

"You said that when I first found you," Nuy said, "and here you are, so don't say it again."

"I was just about to tell him the same thing," Bonnie said.

"You chances would be better if—" he began.

"We're sticking together." Bonnie interrupted.

Nuy stared into the darkness. A distant light flickered for an instant. At first she thought that her eyes might be deceiving her, and then she glimpsed the tiny speck of light once more. A fire, she thought; someone else was up ahead, perhaps her father and his people. She did not dare to hope that people from the north might be there.

"Keep still," Nuy said in a low voice. "I think I saw a fire up-river just now." She heard Bonnie suck in her breath. "If my father is there, we're in danger."

"Our people," Bonnie whispered. "It might be our people. They might have come looking for us after all."

"Perhaps," Nuy hissed, "but if so, they're in danger, too, sitting there as they are. If I can see their fire, so can others."

"What should we do?" Tonio said softly.

She thought for a moment. "I want both of you to creep toward the river and into the water, then hide among the reeds," she said at last. "They're thick enough to conceal you, but keep still, and with only your heads above the water. I'll find out who made that fire and then come back for you."

"I don't like it," Tonio whispered.

"Listen to me. If that fire was made by my people, my father might be ready to welcome me again. I'll do everything I can to keep him from spotting me, but if he does, it's likely to go better for me with him than it would for either of you. There's a chance he'll take me back. He'd kill you." She untied the sack from her back that held meat and thrust it at Tonio. Another thought came to her. "I'm leaving my weapon with you." She pulled her stun gun from the belt of her loincloth and pressed it into Bonnie's hands. "You may need it, and if my father sees it, he'll know that someone else gave it to me, that more of your people might have come south."

"Now I really don't like this," Tonio said.

She knew what he meant. If anything happened to her, he and Bonnie would have to fend for themselves.

"I'm going," she said. "If I'm not back by morning, keep yourselves hidden. If I'm not back by evening, you'll have to decide what to do by yourselves." She could do no more for them. Knowing that made her ache with weariness and despair.

She crept away from the river, moving east and then north. The darkness that concealed her was also making it nearly impossible to see what lay in front of her. Her other senses would have to guide her.

She moved through the grass slowly, keeping low, feeling her way with her bare feet and sniffing the air and stopping from time to time to listen. Once she heard a distant sound like that of a human voice, but maybe it was only the wind, which was picking up. Good, she thought; the wind would mask the sound of her movements.

She came to a gentle slope in the ground. She kept moving until the gentle incline had grown into a steep hill and she could sense the presence of someone not far away. She would spy on whoever was camped by the river from above, from the side of the cliff. The ground underfoot was growing harder, the grass more sparse, telling her that she was nearing the cliff. The night was so dark that she was almost upon the wall of rock before she saw it looming above her.

She had climbed this face before, and this side of the cliff was not as steep as the side that overlooked the river. She climbed slowly, feeling for the handholds in the rock that she remembered, halting every so often to rest. Her shoulders and arms ached by the time she was near the top.

Someone was there, just above her on top of the cliff. She heard a soft sound then, a sound between a breath and a gasp, and flattened herself against the rock, willing herself to keep still. Someone was keeping watch from up here.

Her eyes were adjusting to the darkness. She looked up and saw the hazy faint light of one of the moons through the clouds; the darkness might not conceal her for too much longer. She could smell something now, something familiar; the odors of dust and sweat mingled with a faint scent of reeds.

Nuy held her breath, pulled herself slowly up to the edge of the rocky surface, and peered over the top.

Two people were there, sitting near the opposite edge of the cliff, their backs to her. The small human shapes were barely visible. Her body tensed painfully as her fingers clawed rock. The two were as naked as she was, and one of them held a spear.

Belen and Carin, she thought, and yet they seemed unaware of her presence. Her heart beat so hard inside her that she was sure the two must hear it. Nuy pulled into herself, afraid to breathe, knowing that the slightest movement might give her away.

"Go to sleep," Belen's voice said, and Nuy stiffened. He had said the same words to her many times in the same contemptuous way. Go to sleep. Fetch the water. Get me some meat. Be quiet even if I hurt you when I do it. She had been unable to fight against him, knowing that he would read her intentions in her face or smell them on her body before she could act. He always seemed able to sense her rage against him even before her anger broke into her own thoughts. The only way she had been able to escape him was to go off by herself until loneliness and the need for others like herself finally drove her back to her people.

"I don't know if I can sleep." That was Carin, and Nuy heard a quaver in her voice. Perhaps Belen was doing the same things to Carin that he had once done to her. Nuy's rage caught like a stone in her throat, but she calmed herself, afraid that Belen would smell her anger.

"Go to sleep." She saw Belen raise his arm then, and the other shadowy shape shrank back.

They might be up here to keep watch while her father and the rest of the band stayed below, but somehow she did not think so. Her father would have no reason to send someone up here to keep watch to the east, the west, or the south. A fire would keep any predators away, and anyone coming downriver would be in sight long before he came to the camp. So the people at the base of the cliff had to be more people from the north.

Nuy pulled herself up slowly until the shelf of the rocky surface met her belly, then lay there with her feet poking over the edge. If Belen and Carin were here, then where were the rest of her father's people? Until she found out, she could not risk making her way back down the cliff and going back to fetch Bonnie and Tonio. She might reunite them with their people only to see them attacked by her father. Whatever weapons those camped below might have, Ho would have the advantage if he could surprise them.

One of the dark forms slumped toward the surface. Carin, it seemed, was obeying Belen and going to sleep.

"I wish he hadn't—" Carin's soft voice trailed off.

"I wish he hadn't, either," Belen said, "but if he was going to do it, he should have made sure he got all of them. I told him there was a third one there, I could feel it, I could smell it, but he wouldn't listen."

"Maybe you were wrong. I didn't sense anyone else there."

"I wasn't wrong, and maybe you were too far back." In spite of his words, Belen sounded uncertain. Maybe his senses were failing him. That would account for why he had not picked up on her presence.

"Will he—" Carin paused.

"Will he what?" Belen responded.

"Will he do the same thing to them he did to those others?" There was fear in her voice.

"Maybe he will, maybe he won't. He and Owen didn't leave me much to do except poke them with my spear and make sure they were dead."

Carin said, "I wish Ho hadn't killed them."

Who had her father killed? Other members of his own band? No, that was impossible. Nuy lay there, unable to move as her thoughts raced.

"He had no choice," Belen said.

"He did." Nuy was surprised at the tone of defiance in Carin's voice. "Ho can say all he wants to about those people bringing death with them, but I don't believe it and I don't think you do, either. We're the ones who bring death, not the people from the north."

"You shouldn't say that," Belen murmured, and now Nuy heard the fear inside him.

"I wouldn't say it to Ho. I can't do anything about what he thinks or does anyway. But I can say it to you. Those people were no real danger to him, and I think you know that as well as I do. They didn't have to die. It was horrible, what he did. The one Nuy was bringing to us didn't have to die, either."

Carin was talking about strangers, not her own people. Ho had attacked and killed more people from the north.

"He shouldn't have sent Nuy away," Carin went on. "We should have gone looking for her ourselves and brought her back with us. He couldn't have refused to welcome her back, and maybe she could have kept him from—"

"Be quiet."

"It's almost like she's here," Carin said. "Don't you feel it?"

"She's dead, she has to be dead. She couldn't still be alive, she would have come back to us if she were, or found some way to let you and me and Sarojin know she was still alive."

"Then maybe it's her ghost, haunting us."

"Shut up," Belen whispered.

Carin had sensed her presence after all. Nuy forced herself to keep still. Carin and Belen's senses had not failed them; all that was shielding Nuy from discovery now was that they believed her to be dead.

"Maybe she could have stopped her father from killing them," Carin said.

"And maybe they're better off dead. Without what we took from them, they wouldn't have lasted that long anyway. You saw how feeble a fight they put up, why, it was no fight at all."

Confused as she was, Nuy was beginning to put together what must have happened. A group of northerners had come downriver, perhaps looking for Bonnie and Tonio, and her father had killed them. Now she did not know what to do.

"Killing the people down there might not be so easy," Carin said. "For one thing, there are more of them."

Nuy tensed. Then those camped down below at the base of the cliff were indeed Bonnie's and Tonio's people, not her own.

"We've got two more of their weapons," Belen replied, "and if they're as meek and unprepared as the other ones were, we won't have any trouble with them."

"So you mean to go to Ho and tell him more of those people have come here?"

"Of course. What did you expect? He didn't leave us here just to watch them for a while and then do nothing."

"He'll come here and try to kill them, too," Carin said, and then she suddenly sat up. "What's the point of that? Are you going to let Ho tell you what to do forever?" She did not sound like herself, or all that intimidated by Belen. Nuy realized then that she had made a mistake by leaving the stun weapon with Bonnie and Tonio. By now, she could have immobilized both of them.

"What would you do instead?" Belen asked.

"I'd go down there and take the chance that they wouldn't harm us. The other ones weren't ready to fight, were they? These strangers probably aren't, either. So what I'd do is go down there and find out why they came here and eat some of their food while I was talking to them, and maybe I could even convince them to give us one of their weapons."

"And what good would that do?"

"Think about it," Carin said. "You'd be more than a match for Ho with one of those weapons. He wouldn't have the advantage anymore, and you'd know when his guard is down, when he'd be most vulnerable. You could be our leader."

Belen drew in his breath. "The others might be willing to follow me after that," he said, "but Owen wouldn't."

"With the weapon," Carin said, "you could get rid of Owen, too."

This was what Carin had come to, Nuy thought, plotting

murder with Belen, planning for the death of Nuy's father, and Belen was listening to her, and yet there was some justice and rightness in her words.

"And then," Carin continued, "you'd lead and we could trade with the northerners the way we once did. Maybe we could even live among them. Life would go a lot easier for us after that."

"You're forgetting one thing," Belen said. "Two of the northerners are dead. Sooner or later the others will find out about that. They might not want to trade with us afterwards. They might even decide to come after us."

Carin was silent for a few moments. "We can say that it was only Ho and Owen who did it," she said at last. "It was their idea, after all, and they were the ones who did the killing. We could say whatever we like, and no one in our band would say anything else."

Was this the Carin she had known? Nuy asked herself. Something had changed her. Maybe it was being with Belen; perhaps it was because Nuy had not been with her to look out for her and Sarojin. She could even understand why Carin would wish for Ho's death. Nuy thought of all the times she had longed for the father she dimly recalled from her childhood, the one who would tell her stories and show her kindness, if only intermittently. Now it seemed that her longing for that past father who no longer existed was only a way of hiding her own desire to be rid of the man he was now.

"We could wait until morning," Carin went on, "and then we can make our way down there and talk to them. They've got food, Belen, more food than we've had in a long time. And they've got those weapons. All you need is one of them and—"

"No," he said in a raspy voice, "it's too risky. They might not give us anything, they might want nothing to do with us. I say we leave at dawn and report to Ho and let him decide what to do, and if he decides to attack, we can take everything, including all of their weapons. It won't be just Ho and Owen holding on to all of the stunners after that and deciding who gets one, I'll make sure I get one of my own. And then we can start thinking about how to put Ho out of the way."

Carin said nothing to that, but Nuy could see her reluctance to give in to him in her rigid back and hunched shoulders.

"You know that makes more sense," he went on. "It might be better to lead them into a trap, too, instead of attacking. Maybe I'll suggest that to Ho."

The sky was growing lighter. Nuy could now make out the braid hanging down Belen's back. She would have to move now, try to disable Belen and hope that Carin would either come to her aid or at least stay out of it.

She raised herself on her arms, preparing to sneak up on Belen, and then he said, "Somebody's here, behind us." He jumped to his feet, spun around before she could get to her feet, covered the space between them before she could take another breath, then leaped at her. Her arms flew up, catching him as he fell on her. She tried to pinch the hard muscular flesh under one of his arms; he knocked her hand away. She could see his face now, looking pale in the dim light of the larger moon.

"Nuy," he said, "so you are alive, you're not a ghost." She wondered how she had given herself away; he might have heard her move, or smelled her in the air. He grabbed her braid, yanking her head back painfully. "Thought you were dead, I was sure you were dead. What are you doing here, Nuy?" She tried to think of what to say. "Think Ho's ready to take you back? Maybe he will, maybe he won't. He's so crazy now nobody knows what he'll do." He let go of her braid and pinned her, pressing her shoulders hard against the rock. She brought up one leg; her knee caught him in the back. He let out a moan and let go of her for a moment.

"Carin," Nuy gasped, "help me."

Belen grabbed at her legs. She rolled away from him; her hands clutched air. The realization that she was near the edge of the cliff came to her an instant before a kick caught her in the ribs and sent her over the side.

She was falling. She was about to scream when a flat surface slammed against her, knocking the air out of her. She lay there against the rock, afraid to move and unable to breathe. There was a buzzing sound in her ears. She swallowed hard and the buzzing grew more muted. She managed to take a breath.

"You killed her," Carin's voice said faintly from somewhere above her.

"She was trying to kill me," Belen replied, but he sounded uncertain.

"You killed her," Carin repeated.

"I didn't hear a scream, not even a whimper. What did she do, hold her breath all the way down?"

"She was alive," Carin said. "She stayed alive all this time by herself, and now—"

"Shut up, Carin." Nuy heard a sound that might have been a slap. "She was bringing a stranger to us the last time we saw her. Maybe she went north and found more of them, or maybe they found her, and it was the northerners who kept her alive. First there were the ones Ho killed and now there's another group of them down below. Maybe they helped her out. Maybe she even led them back here."

"What are we going to do?"

"Somebody might come looking for her. We'd better start downriver now, before morning comes."

Nuy listened as the two descended the cliffside, afraid that a foot or hand might discover her on the ledge. She thought that she could hear them panting for breath and held her own, willing herself to be as still as if she were lifeless and knowing that the slightest sound would give her away. She lay there until they were far below her, but did not move. The fall might have injured her; she would not know how badly she was hurt until she tried to scale the cliff. She would have to lie here and will herself to heal.

Had Carin been trying to help her? She had not sensed the same feelings of anger toward her from Carin as she had picked up from Belen. Her breathing was more painful now, even with taking only short, sharp gulps of air. The clouds were clearing, and the second moon would overtake the first before long. She lay there, waiting for dawn.

12

*L*eila's fears stabbed into her again. The darkness of the night, the sound of a rising wind that might keep her from hearing the approach of danger—everything in her world seemed a threat to her now. She thought of all the times she had lain in her bed at night, safe inside her dome, and wondered that she had ever wanted to leave her settlement.

She had grown careless. So far, she had been lucky, moving mostly at night and resting for only brief moments during the day, often sleeping on the back of her horse with her hand on her weapon. She relieved herself as infrequently as possible and only in spots behind a boulder or near a slope, where she felt more concealed. She started at the slightest sound and had fired her weapon twice, once when she heard what sounded like footfalls along the riverbank and again when she saw a form loom up from the grass that had looked human for a moment. The human form had turned out to be an odd formation of rocks suddenly revealed when a gust of wind had disturbed the grass; the sound of feet, she had decided, was only the blood pounding in her ears.

Someone might be tracking her. She wondered if the others could do that, follow her at a distance, invisible to her, waiting for a chance to strike.

Her horse was moving at a walk, no longer panting. She had stopped earlier to let the mare drink from the river and to rub down the horse's glistening coat with a spare tunic. She had kept her at a walk ever since, even after the night sky had cleared enough for the moons to light her way. As fearful as she was of what she might find at the base to the south, afraid that she might arrive only to find that she had come too late to warn her companions, she would be far less able to help them if she ran her horse into the ground.

She struggled to stay alert. Her mother and Gervais should be back at that encampment by now. She hung on to that thought. There had been a moment of terror for her not long ago, a thought so painful that she had started from a sleep that she had not realized she had fallen into, nearly sliding from the back of her horse. Zoheret and Gervais had gone to the place near the sea where they had expected to find the others. Maybe they had encountered some of those people there, ones who had stayed behind and had not been involved in the murder of Hannah and Haidar. Or perhaps Gervais and her mother had found no one there and had left, only to be attacked on their way north. Zoheret and Gervais might be dead by now. That possibility had stabbed at her in one sharp moment of panic before she had willed herself to suppress the thought.

They were alive. They had to be alive. She recalled all the times she and Trevor had plotted together, of how they had lured Sofia and Yukio and Edan into their plans for this expedition. Now they had lost two people, and might lose even more. There were so few of them as it was, so few people trying to live on this world. It would be a long time before that fact became unimportant enough to banish Yusef's fears.

The moons were sinking toward the western horizon when she glimpsed a spark of light to the south. She was suddenly furious with her friends and with Kagami for allowing such a visible sign of their presence. Her anger burned out abruptly, chilling her with fear when she realized that the murderers might already have reached that camp.

She reached for her weapon and pulled it from her belt. It would be dark enough for a little while longer to hide her as she approached. She would get near enough to find out who was there, and if enemies were camped around the fire, she would leave the horse and find a way to sneak up on them and a safe place from where she could fire at them. She would worry about what to do with her enemies after they were disabled and helpless.

Her enemies. That was how she thought of the others now.

She rode on. Against the purple of the sky, she soon made out the jutting finger of the cliff that overlooked the campsite. A voice called out, a voice she knew, carried to her along the river.

"Stop there," Yukio's voice commanded.

She could not see him, but he could not be more than twenty paces away. Her friends had been on guard after all. A wave of relief rushed through her.

"Stop there," Yukio repeated, "or I'll shoot."

Had they been attacked after all? Were they now afraid of being attacked again? Leila was suddenly shocked at how careless she had been; someone other than Yukio might have been hiding in the grass.

"Yukio," she called out, "it's Leila." She pulled at the reins and heard the grass whisper as he ran toward her. "You're all right."

"For now, anyway," he said as he came up to her.

"What are you doing out here?" she asked.

"It was my turn to keep watch. Thought I heard something earlier tonight, a voice. Woke up Edan so he could guard the camp while I took a look around. Climbed part of the way up the cliff to get a better view, and when the clouds started to clear, I saw what looked like a horse and rider to the north. Thought it was you, but I had to make sure before you got any closer."

She would have to tell him what had happened. If she told him now, she would have to repeat it all later for the others. "Yukio—" she began.

"I've got something to tell you," he interrupted. "Zoheret and Gervais haven't returned yet. They should have been back by now."

"No," she whispered.

"You know what your mother told us. We'll have to decide what to do."

She swung her leg over the horse and jumped to the ground. "Take this," she said, handing the reins to him.

They walked together in silence, with Yukio leading the horse, knowing that they would have to remain on guard until they were with the others. Talking would only distract them, and she still could not escape the feeling that the sound of their voices might be overheard by their enemies. She would have to wait until she was among them all to tell her story.

Somehow Leila managed to finish her account of what had happened without trembling, without having to stop too often to compose herself, without having her voice break or her emotions overcome her entirely. The sun was up by then, a reddish-orange light in a pale green sky that promised a cloudless day.

Yukio was still pacing, as he had been while Leila was speaking, looking to the north and then south. Their fire had died a while ago. Kagami stared into the embers. Sofia had drawn up her legs and had wrapped her arms around them, resting her chin on her knees; her dark eyes were as blank as Kagami's. Trevor's head was bowed, so she could not see his face, but could imagine what he was thinking. Hannah, who had shared his dome, had been like a sister to him. Any hope he had held out for finding his mother was now dead.

Edan was the first to speak. "Zoheret told us to break camp if she and Gervais weren't back by now," he said.

Trevor shook his head. "But she didn't expect anything like this to happen," he said. "I don't see how we can leave, not now."

"We lost an encampment," Edan said, "so it'll take us longer to reach our next base now."

Trevor leaned forward. "And along the way, we might get attacked by the same ones who killed Hannah and Haidar, who probably killed my mother as well."

"Then we'd better be ready to fight," Edan replied, "even if it means doing the same thing to them that—"

"Stop it," Kagami said. Sofia was watching the woman, as if waiting for Kagami to tell them what to do. "I'd hoped that none of you would ever have to go through something like this."

Trevor was thinking of his mother, Edan was talking vengeance, Sofia wanted guidance, and Kagami sounded bewildered and lost. "They attacked upriver, days away from the sea," Leila said, still struggling to keep her grief and fear from overwhelming her. "That could mean they're not living near the sea now, which means my mother and Gervais might not have run into them at all. They might have had an accident, we don't know what kind of trouble they might have had. Those people aren't the only thing we have to worry about."

"But you know what she told us." Edan got to his feet. "We were to leave if they weren't back here by now. Look, if one of them were injured, the other would have ridden back by now to get help. If both of them were still able to ride, they would have come back. You know why your mother gave us that order. She didn't want us to risk losing more people by coming after her."

"So you think she's dead."

"I'm saying that she and Gervais must have run into something they couldn't handle."

Leila stood up. "Then maybe they need our help."

Edan caught her by the arms. "You know what she told us."

"I know."

"You both have a point," Trevor interrupted. "We know what Zoheret told us to do, but things have changed since then. She didn't know one of our bases would be attacked, that two people would . . ." He paused. "Maybe we'd all better decide on what to do together."

All of them looked as exhausted as Leila felt. She was fairly sure that she could count on Trevor to support her, but the others would believe that they were now more concerned about their mothers than anything else and that this was clouding their judgment.

She took a breath, then said, "I have to keep looking for Zoheret and Gervais until I find them or at least find out what happened to them. Maybe I can learn something about what might have happened to Trevor's mother and the others, too. I hope all of you will stay with me, but I can't stop you from leaving. You also can't stop me from staying here by myself."

She had said the words. Now she would have to abide by them. Her fears rose up once more, threatening to choke her, and she wanted to call back her words.

"You won't be alone, Leila," Trevor said. "I'll stay with you."

"That's crazy," Edan objected. "Breaking up the group will only put us all in even more danger. We should stick together now."

"Stop there," Yukio said suddenly in a sharp, loud tone. He was staring up at the cliffside, his right arm raised high with his weapon in his hand. "Don't move."

Leila looked up to where he was pointing. A small brown-skinned creature perched on a rocky ledge high above them. Its arms were up, palms out. How long had it been watching them? Again she found herself shocked by their carelessness.

"Hai," the creature called out in a high, piercing voice, and Leila saw it for what it was: a child, one of the outsiders, an enemy.

"Shoot it," Edan said softly.

"If I shoot," Yukio said, "she might fall off the ledge. That'd kill her for sure." His sharper eyes had apparently seen that the child was a female.

"What difference does it make?" Edan said. "She has to be one of them."

"Hai," the child shouted again before crumpling onto the ledge.

Kagami rose to her feet. "She's hurt."

"She may need our help," Leila said. The child was alone, and it did not look as though she was armed. Maybe she had run away from her people. She wondered if she dared to trust her more compassionate feelings.

Trevor said, "I'll climb up and get her. Sofia, get me a rope." Sofia got up and ducked inside the tent, where their packs were kept. "Yukio, keep aiming at her."

"Shoot her now," Edan said. He glanced at Yukio, then put a hand on his own weapon. "If we shoot her now, we can be sure she's out. We can carry her down after that with no trouble."

"No," Kagami said. "If she's seriously injured, the shock of being hit might kill her."

"I'm going up," Trevor said. "Edan, follow me and keep me covered. Shoot her if she gives us any trouble."

Sofia came up and handed Trevor the rope. He looped it over one shoulder and moved quickly toward the cliffside. Edan shook his head, but followed him.

Leila craned her neck, watching them as they climbed, wedging their feet into crevices in the rock and pulling themselves up by the arms. As Trevor neared the ledge where the child lay, Edan continued to climb higher, then braced his feet against an outcropping just above them as he removed his weapon from his belt and aimed it at the stranger.

Trevor hauled himself onto the ledge and crawled toward the child. "She's breathing," he called out, "but she isn't moving."

"She's got a knife," Edan shouted down to him. Trevor took something from the stranger, tucked it under his belt, then slipped the coil of rope from his shoulder. In a few more moments, the rope secured, he descended the cliff while hanging onto the rope, with the small body flung over one shoulder; a long black braid hung down from the child's head. She looked so small, Leila thought, and so frail.

Yukio remained cautious, keeping his weapon aimed at the stranger until Trevor had reached the ground. Leila stepped forward and reached for the child as Edan made his way down the cliffside.

The child lay inside the tent, sleeping. She had roused herself for an instant to mutter a few words, "my people," "two of you," "help me," and then had closed her eyes once more. She had awakened again to drink some water after Kagami brought it to her, then had gone back to sleep.

Kagami was still inside the tent with the child, having sent everyone else outside. The healer had frowned after scanning the girl, but had assured Leila that the child seemed uninjured, with no broken bones or any sign of serious injury despite the bruises and other marks on her small body. The muscles of the thin body were hard, and the shoulders broad for a child of that size, while the soles of her wide bare feet with their splayed toes were so thick with callouses that Leila suspected she had never worn shoes. Her only clothing was a loincloth; Kagami had removed the long leather cord that held a leather skin filled with a little water. Except for the slight swelling of tiny breasts, the girl's chest was flat, and the brown skin tight across the visible ridges of her ribs. To Leila, her face was the child's most surprising feature. Her thick black lashes, curved mouth, and gentle expression could almost be called beautiful.

Kagami came outside only long enough to fetch a screen. Leila was about to ask her what she was doing when Kagami disappeared into the tent again.

By early afternoon, Yukio and Sofia had scaled the cliff in order to get a better look at what was below. Yukio shouted down that they had found no one else up there and that they would be able to see anybody approaching at a distance as long as it was light. He and Sofia would remain on watch, and would stay up there that night to watch over the camp. Leila realized then that she should have thought of putting somebody on watch at the top of the cliff as soon as Zoheret and Gervais had left the camp. She was struck once again by their negligence, at how vulnerable they had left themselves.

She was sitting with Trevor and Edan near the tent, sharing a small portion of dried fruit and worrying about how much longer their food would last, when Kagami lifted the flap and crept outside, clutching her scanner and screen to her chest. The healer sat down, her back to the tent, and gazed at each one of them in turn with a bewildered expression on her face.

"What's wrong?" Leila asked.

"I'm not sure how to explain this to you," Kagami said. "That girl has to be the child of people in Ho's group, I heard her whisper his name and some of the others', but otherwise I'd almost think—" She was silent for a few moments. "—that she's not quite human."

Leila stiffened in surprise. "Not human?" Trevor said. "But how—"

"Let me put it as simply as possible," Kagami said. "She carries a few unfamiliar genes that I've never seen before in any of our records. The DNA base sequence of other genes appears to have been altered. Because of that, I'm not even sure how to interpret some of my other readings. She seems malnourished but otherwise in reasonably good health, but I can't be certain—"

"She has to be one of the others," Edan said. "You said that Ship made sure that there were no signs of intelligent life here before sending you down."

"Oh, she's one of Ho's group, I'm certain of that. If she's a mutation of some kind, perhaps exposure to something in her environment that isn't present in our settlement affected her or her parents. In any case, however human she looks, it seems that she carries a few alien genes as well. It's almost as if—"

"Hai," a voice said. Kagami turned her head. Leila started; she had been so focused on Kagami that she had not heard or seen the stranger crawl out of the tent. Edan and Trevor seemed equally surprised.

The child slowly stood up. Her hand moved toward her waist; her eyes widened.

"Don't try anything," Edan said. "We took your knife, and I'll shoot if I have to. I suppose you have a name."

"My name is Nuy," the girl replied.

"What are you doing here?" Leila asked.

"We know you're alone," Edan added, "since we haven't found anyone else."

"I came to see who was here," the girl said.

"Spying for your people. That's what you were doing, isn't it?" Kagami put a hand on Edan's shoulder, as if to restrain him.

"I came to make sure no one was here who would harm me." The look in her dark almond-shaped eyes was more fiery than fearful. "My people cast me out some time ago. I've been hiding from them ever since —"

"You're lying," Edan said.

"Let her speak," Trevor objected.

"I've been hiding from my people for many strings of days now, ever since I found two of your people. They told me they had come south to see what was here, to find out what had become of my father's people." The girl lifted a hand, made a fist, then let her arm fall.

Trevor gaped at her. Edan suddenly looked uncertain.

"I kept them both safe," the girl who called herself Nuy continued. "I kept them hidden, and I found food for them. We were heading upriver when I saw that someone was camped here. They're waiting for me now, I told them I would come back for them if I found out it was safe for them to come here."

"It's a trick," Edan said, but he sounded more unsure of himself.

"I can show you it's no trick," Nuy replied. "I'll fetch them and bring them back here. That is, if you're willing to welcome them."

"Of course we'll welcome them." Kagami clasped her hands together. "I never thought—"

"How do we know you're not planning to come back here with more of your people instead?" Edan said.

Nuy shrugged. "Come with me if you doubt me."

"And walk right into a trap."

"You must listen to me," Nuy said. "The two I found waited many days, hoping that others from the north would come to search for them. I did what I could for them over the past months, and at last we saw that we would have to go north to their home, however long and hard the journey was and however bad our chances were. Let me bring them here, and after that, my advice is to leave this place. If you stay here, you're in danger."

Edan seemed about to speak. Trevor lifted a hand before he could. "Three of our people did come south over a year ago," Trevor said. "Are you telling us—"

"I found them," Nuy interrupted. "I'm sorry to tell you that one of them is dead, the man called Chiang." Leila held her breath for a few moments. "But I kept the others safe, the ones named Bonnie and Tonio."

Trevor grew pale. "Bonnie?" he croaked.

"Bonnie and Tonio," Nuy said. "For a time, they were bitter and unhappy that no one had come to look for them. Later, they saw that they could not rely on anyone else, although I did what I could for them. And then it came to them that they would have to try to return to their home, because otherwise more of their people might endanger themselves if they came south to search for them. Now will you listen to me?"

Trevor jumped up. "She's alive." He grabbed Leila's hands and pulled her to her feet. "My mother's alive." He let go of her and put a hand on Edan's shoulder. "She has to be telling the truth—she knows their names, why they came here. My mother's still alive."

"It could still be a trap." Edan jerked away from Trevor. "Just because she knows their names—"

"Hey!" a distant voice called out from overhead.

Leila looked up. Yukio and Sofia were standing at the edge of the cliff. Yukio waved an arm over his head as Sofia began to climb down the side, hanging on to the rope that the two had carried up with them.

"They must have seen something," Trevor murmured. Edan continued to watch Nuy with narrowed eyes, his hand still on his weapon. Nuy held up her hands, palms out, then took a step toward Leila and Kagami.

"You at least seem willing to listen to me," Nuy said, lifting her head. Small as the girl was, Leila felt intimidated by the intensity of her gaze. "I should bring Tonio and Bonnie here, and then you'd all be wise to leave here as soon as you can. My father will try to kill you . . ."

"Your father?" Trevor said.

"My father is Ho. My father is mad."

Leila thought of Hannah and Haidar lying in the grass, of Tala's helpless terror.

"There's something else I have to tell you," Nuy said. Her voice was not as strong now, and she seemed more uncertain as she turned toward Leila. "Two of my people were up there last night, spying on you." She thrust out one arm and pointed toward the top of the cliff. "They—"

Edan glared at Leila. "It's a trick. They'll wait until night, and then they'll attack. How can we be sure of anything she says?"

Sofia was nearly at the base of the cliffside. She let go of the rope, dropped to the ground, and hurried toward them. "Yukio spotted somebody to the south of us," she said quickly. "Two people—they're moving toward us from the south, along the riverbank, but they're staying low in the grass, as if they're trying to keep themselves hidden."

Edan pulled out his weapon. "So they're not even waiting for night."

"What do they look like?" Nuy asked.

"My eyes aren't as good as Yukio's," Sofia replied, "but one has dark hair and a beard, I think, and the other has brown hair, and they're wearing—"

"Bonnie and Tonio," Nuy whispered. She darted away, running so swiftly across the mossy ground around the campsite that she was in the grass before Edan took aim.

Leila stepped in front of him and grabbed his wrist. "No point in shooting now," she muttered.

"You don't know—"

She let go of him. "I'm going after her. I could use somebody to cover me." Leila motioned to Trevor, then took off after Nuy through the tall yellow and pale green grass.

Away from the campsite, the grass was almost as high as her chest; soon she could not see Nuy at all. She looked back and saw that Trevor was following her, trailed by Edan. She thrashed her way through the grass and soon spotted Nuy's black head in the distance, just above the field of grass.

The girl was calling out, but Leila could not hear what she was saying. Far down the river, near the bank, she could barely make out two human forms. Nuy ran toward the pair as they began to run toward her.

Leila slowed her pace. Trevor and Edan soon caught up to her. She squinted and cupped a hand over her eyes, seeing two people in what looked like brown shirts. The larger one had dark hair; the smaller one wore something around her neck that might have been a necklace. She did not dare to hope.

"It's Bonnie," Trevor said, and then he was running after Nuy. Edan was about to go after him; Leila caught him by the sleeve.

"Let him have a few moments with her," she said.

Edan let out his breath. "Looks like I might have been wrong about that girl."

"Anybody can make a mistake," Leila said.

"Still, you heard what Kagami said about her. We don't even know—" He sighed.

In the distance, the two lost explorers were already embracing Nuy. Leila's eyes stung; she held back her tears. If Bonnie and Tonio could survive, it meant that there was more of a chance for Zoheret and Gervais. She hung on to that hope.

13

Nuy sat on one of the flat rocks near the riverbank, watching as Bonnie hugged her son, the one called Trevor, yet again. Tonio sat near the woman named Kagami, asking her once more for additional details about his mate and children.

Nuy should have been pleased and happy. Instead, she felt removed from the joy and relief now enveloping these people. Sitting in the midst of this group, seeing Bonnie and Tonio reunited with those who had thought them lost, she had not expected to feel so alone.

"Not quite human." She had heard the woman Kagami say those words outside the tent, and then other words she didn't understand. "Sometimes you hardly seem like my daughter." Those had been her father's words.

By the river, Bonnie and Tonio had thrown their arms around her, embracing her with a fierce affection she had not known they possessed. "You shouldn't have come here," she had told them. "You should have stayed hidden. I would have come for you, I wanted you safe."

"We were a lot more worried about your safety," Tonio said. "Last night, while we were still hiding in the reeds, we heard something on the bank, and then a voice. Couldn't hear what the person was saying, but I didn't recognize the voice, and then another person spoke. We kept as still as we could. I was afraid to breathe."

Carin and Belen, Nuy thought. Maybe the two had been so distracted by talking that they hadn't picked up on the presence of two others so close by. She had been right to warn Bonnie and Tonio to stay among the reeds; perhaps the smells of the plants and the mud had also masked their odors.

"We couldn't hear most of what they were saying," Bonnie said, "only a few words about what they were going to tell Ho."

"They were talking of going downriver," Tonio added, "so I guessed that the people camped upriver had to be some of our own people. We waited until daybreak, thinking that you'd soon come back for us, and then when you didn't, we started to worry. That's when we decided we'd better look for you—I was afraid you might have had some bad luck, an accident of some kind."

It had made her happy, hearing them admit that they had come to care enough about her to go after her, knowing that they weren't clinging to her only out of concern for themselves. Then Leila and Trevor and Edan had caught up with her, and that moment had passed.

Now she was alone again, feeling small and overwhelmed by all these larger people, a couple of whom were nearly as tall as Owen and Gerd and Zareb. But as big and muscular and strong as they looked, they seemed to have their own weaknesses. She had heard enough from them now to know that all of them, except for the woman Kagami, were close to her own age, and that had surprised her, because they all seemed as blind and deaf to certain sights and sounds as the adults among her own people. Her assumption that aging might account for such lacks was apparently mistaken.

Not human. Different. Alien. Nuy wanted to close her mind to such words. Carin, Sarojin, and Belen were like her; did they also carry tiny alien things inside themselves? Was that why their senses were sharper than those of the adults around them, why the illnesses Ho feared had never affected them?

She had no time to dwell on such questions. They were still in danger from her father's people. The one called Yukio seemed aware of that possibility, since he had come down from his perch atop the cliff only long enough to greet Bonnie and Tonio before climbing up again to keep watch from the ledge where they had found Nuy. Now Leila was looking about herself, turning her head one way and then the other, remaining vigilant.

Leila had spoken up for her before. I think I can trust her, Nuy thought, but wondered how much she could trust any of the others. Perhaps Trevor could be trusted, if only because Nuy had restored his mother to him. She could not tell about the others but still sensed wariness and distrust inside them.

Kagami had performed a mysterious action, first with Bonnie and then with Tonio, that she called a scan, in which she had passed a wand resembling a weapon over each of them. After that, Kagami had sat with her flat screen for a few moments with a frown on her face. Nuy recalled that the woman had done a similar thing to her before going outside and murmuring to her companions about the strangenesses she had found in Nuy's body.

Not human. Maybe, in spite of what Tonio and Bonnie had told her, these people would not want her among them.

Bonnie and Tonio had each spoken in turn, telling the others about how Nuy had found them, what she had told them about the death of Chiang, and of how she had kept them alive. She was relieved that they had spoken, since it saved her from having to tell the long tale herself. They were talking now of how Nuy had insisted that they hide themselves while she went to see who was camped in this place.

She would have to interrupt this happy reunion soon; the late afternoon sun had already dropped behind the cliff. They would be safer far from here, far from any place where her father might be able to strike at them.

". . . and then we heard voices while we were hiding," Bonnie was saying, "and even though we couldn't hear most of what they said, we heard enough to know that they were two members of Ho's band."

Leila glanced at Nuy. "Two of them were spying on us last night, from the cliff. Nuy told us that earlier."

All of them were looking at her now. "I found them last night," Nuy said, "on top of the cliff. I gave myself away somehow. One of them was struggling with me when I fell over the side, but I didn't fall all the way down. Fortunately, they don't know that, they think I'm dead, so my father won't know that I was able to warn you." She spread her arms, palms out. "Listen to me. You must leave this place and return to your own, you're not safe from my father if you stay."

"We know," Leila said. "He attacked another camp of ours north of here. Two people are dead and the third would be if he had found her. She's on her way to another camp of ours farther to the north, and I rode back here."

That explained part of what she had overheard last night. "My father has gone south," Nuy said. "I heard enough last night to know that much, and what Bonnie and Tonio overheard confirms it. He would be most likely to go to our old caves near the sea, so you should go north while you can, while you can stay well ahead of him." A sudden longing for her old life near the sea came over her. Perhaps she should return to her father and hope that he would take her back, and then maybe she could find a way to quiet the storms inside him.

The color had gone out of Leila's olive-skinned face. She gazed at Nuy with glassy dark eyes. "We can't go north," she said.

"You must," Nuy insisted.

"You don't understand," Leila said. "We can't leave because two of our people went downriver a few days ago to explore the region near the sea. They were supposed to be back here by now, and they're not, and now you say that your people may be there. It was my mother who went downriver with Gervais, one of our men, so I have to worry that your father might have found them. We can't abandon them now."

The young woman named Sofia looked uneasy at that statement. Nuy could tell from her expression and her posture that she was thinking that abandoning this place and heading north was exactly what they should do. Perhaps she was afraid to say so to Leila. It was becoming clear to Nuy that the others, even the older woman, were deferring to Leila, if not following her as unquestioningly as Nuy's people had obeyed Ho.

"If my father has found her," Nuy said, "she may already be dead."

Leila's face flushed with anger. "She would have fought. If there's any chance—" She took a breath. "I can't leave here until I know."

"Are you ready to fight?" Nuy asked.

"Oh, we can fight," Trevor replied.

"I meant are all of you willing to fight," Nuy said, "because anyone who isn't may endanger the rest of you who are."

Edan heaved a sigh. With his big shoulders and strong-featured face, he looked like a fighter; even his voice was commanding. He seemed the one most able to challenge Leila for leadership. But she also sensed a wall around him, and saw coldness in his amber eyes. She did not pick up any of the quieter strength that she sensed in his companion Trevor.

"You say that two of your people were killed upriver," Nuy said. "What did my father take from them?"

"A horse," Leila replied, "and two of our weapons." She gestured toward the one at her waist. "It looked like he took most of what was left of the food, too." She shook her head. "Why, Nuy? Why did he do it? If he needed food, we would have given it to him."

Nuy considered how to answer that question. "At first," she began, "it was because he thought you had brought us death. Some years ago, when I was a child, two of our people returned from the north. Soon they and others were burning with fever, struggling to breathe, coughing up slime. Some lived, and others died, but there were so few of us to begin with that—" Nuy closed her eyes for a moment. "A great storm had already driven us away from the sea not long before, and then the fever came, and after that my father wanted no more trade with your people. He talked of your having sent death to us, and only I and three others escaped the illness altogether."

Kagami was staring at her intently. "Ten years ago," the woman murmured, "almost all of our children came down with a kind of pneumonia, a fever and illness of the lungs, but all of them recovered."

"I remember," Leila said. She kept her eyes on Nuy. "I was still recovering when two of your people came to trade with us, a thin dark woman and a man with a yellow beard."

"Katti and Owen," Nuy whispered.

Leila leaned forward. "Do you think—"

"I would have to examine your people," Kagami interrupted, "run some tests—maybe we developed some sort of immunity to that particular disease that your people didn't have. I suspected at the time that the illness might be the result of some mutating virus we'd picked up from our animals, but since the symptoms were relatively mild and everyone eventually recovered, I didn't pursue it. If I had known how it affected your group—" She looked down for a moment. "And yet you say that you didn't succumb to the illness. Maybe—"

"All this talk of that is useless." Nuy folded her arms. "However it came about, Ho blamed you for the deaths. That's why he kills. At least that's why he killed Chiang, but maybe by now he's found other reasons to want you dead. Even before the fever swept over us, even before the great storm came, he sometimes raged against your people, so maybe it's Home that has driven him mad. It no longer matters why he wants to kill you, it only matters that he does."

"What are we going to do?" Sofia asked, and Nuy heard the fear in her voice.

"I told you before," Nuy said. "You should leave here and go north. Leave now, and you can keep ahead of my father even if he decides to come after you. I doubt he would follow you all the way to your settlement."

Leila said, "I won't go north until I find out what happened to Zoheret and Gervais." She looked around at the others, as if appealing to them for support.

Those two may be dead, Nuy thought, but did not say the words aloud. If they had gone to the caves near the sea, her father might have come upon them while they were there or waylaid them on their way back to this camp. If the two northerners had not kept themselves hidden, if they had been ambushed by Ho, they were surely dead by now. To look for

them was probably futile; she wondered how she could convince Leila of that.

"I won't go north," Leila said again, "not until I know, one
way or another."

"And what will you do?" Nuy asked.

"I told you," Leila said, even though she had said nothing
yet of any plans; her words were no more than insistence. "We
have to look for them."

"And how will you look for them? How will you search
while guarding yourselves from my father? What will you do if
you find them dead?"

"How can we answer that?" Tonio said. "All I know is that
I'm not about to abandon two friends who were willing to
search for me."

Bonnie nodded. "Neither am I."

Leila reached out with one hand. "Help us, Nuy. You know
this land, and your people. I know this may be asking too much
of you, and you owe us nothing, but our chances would be a
lot better with you to guide us."

"Your chances would be even better if you went upriver."
Nuy stared at Leila until she looked away. "You know what you
are asking me to do. You're asking me to help you in hunting
my own father. Whatever he's done to me and to others, I have
to ask myself if I can do that." She took a breath. "When Ho
knows you're here, and the two who were watching you last
night will be telling him all about you by tomorrow night, he'll
come after you, and there are only two paths you can follow
after that. You can leave this region, or you can hunt him down
and kill him. That's the only way this can end."

Leila lifted her head. "Those can't be our only choices," she
said, looking directly at Nuy, "but I agree that we can't stay
here."

"I can lead you south," Nuy said, "but I don't know if I can strike out at my people unless I must to defend myself."

"What about Tonio and Bonnie?" Kagami asked gently.

"What about us?" Bonnie asked.

"Tonio, your scan shows a broken leg that's imperfectly healed as well as evidence of a severe concussion. You're going to need all of your strength just to get home. And both of you are very malnourished. What you need more than anything right now is more food and rest."

Bonnie sniffed. "No chance, Kagami."

"If we're going after my mother and Gervais," Leila said, "there's no point in bringing along anyone who isn't up to what might lie ahead." She was silent for a moment. "Nuy, how many people are with your father?"

"There are only three left who are close to my age," Nuy replied, "Carin, Sarojin, and Belen. I think Sarojin might be unwilling to fight you, but we can't count on that. Of the others, Owen will do whatever Ho wants, and so will Daniella and Katti most of the time. Gerd and Zareb are too thick-headed to be anything but fearless and loyal. Eyela and Ashur might give up peacefully if they think things are going against them, but I wouldn't count on that, either."

"Only eleven people," Trevor said. "I thought there would be more."

Nuy said, "Any one of them could give all of you much trouble, but it's Carin and Belen and Sarojin you should worry about most. Your senses aren't as sharp as theirs, I could see that right away." She might as well get that out in the open. "They would be able to sense your presence even before you saw any sign of them."

Edan scowled. "What do you mean?"

"They're like me." Nuy swallowed. "When we were little, we could come up from behind the adults even before they knew we were there, we could see things they couldn't, hear sounds their ears couldn't pick up, feel when bad weather was coming, sense what someone might say or do before he spoke or acted. I don't know if Sarojin or Carin would fight you, but they might give you away to the others."

Kagami's eyes widened; the woman looked as though she was trying to grab hold of something that was eluding her. "There are three more like you?" she asked.

"Yes." Nuy averted her eyes. "Once I thought it was only that we were younger, and that the senses of people grew much duller as they aged, but now I don't know. My father sometimes told me that I seemed unlike him, that I—" Her throat tightened. "I heard you say it, too, outside the shelter, that I seemed not quite human."

"And you say there are three others like you," Kagami said. "I wonder—"

"Whatever I am, we should be talking of what to do now."

"We have two horses," Edan said. "That has to be an advantage."

Nuy glanced at the animals, which were tied to a rope strung between two stakes. "If you're determined to search downriver, your greatest advantage may be stealth. My father won't be expecting you to go south—he'll be planning on finding you here, waiting for your two comrades. As soon as Belen and Carin tell him what they saw here, my guess is that he'll start moving north to this place, because he'll be thinking that you won't be expecting an attack. Going after him with your horses will only make it easier for him to know that you're on the move. Believe me, Belen would see you long before you spotted him."

Leila was very still, as if conserving all the strength in her body for what was to come. "Is there a chance he might decide not to attack us here?" she asked.

Nuy shrugged. "Do you want to take that chance?"

"Maybe we should stay here and get ready to fight," Sofia said. "If he isn't expecting us to fight, that might be enough of a surprise for him."

"That would mean giving up on any hope for Zoheret and Gervais," Leila said.

"We don't know for sure that anything's happened to them." Sofia waved an arm at the ridge behind her. "If we move to the top of the ridge, we'd see him coming. We could shoot at him from up there."

"Where you'd be cut off from water," Nuy said. Again she had picked up the fear behind Sofia's words. "My father wouldn't get close enough to let you shoot him. All he'd have to do is stay out of range and wait you out."

"If we're going to do anything," Leila said, "we'd better decide now. The longer we wait, the worse our chances get no matter what we do."

Nuy had said what she had to say. She waited for the others to speak. "I'm with Leila," Trevor said at last. "We should go south and find out what happened to her mother and Gervais."

"I agree," Edan said. He might be afraid, Nuy thought as she picked up the quaver in his voice, even as fearful as Sofia, but he would never admit it. She liked him a bit more for that.

"Those two horses will be useful for one thing," Leila said then. "Bonnie and Tonio can ride back to the next camp upriver, and they'd better start now, because it'll take them at least eight days to get there."

"No," Bonnie said, shaking her head. "Our place is with the rest of you."

"You're not strong enough to fight, if it comes to that," Leila responded. "You heard what Kagami said. With the horses, you might make it to the next base, but it isn't just that. There

is something you can do to help. Somebody has to tell everyone upriver what's happened here."

"And someone should go with you." Kagami leaned toward
Bonnie. "You might need someone to look after you."

"Wait," Tonio objected. "Don't you think we—"

"You've gone through enough," Kagami interrupted, "and
it'll be a while before you recover your strength. You won't
help the rest of us if you're unable to keep up with us."

"I agree," Leila said. "Sofia, would you be willing to go with
them? It's either you or Kagami, and if . . . when we find Zoheret and Gervais, they might need a healer."

Leila, Nuy thought, had heard the terror in Sofia's voice,
too. "Why me?" Sofia asked.

"I'll be honest," Leila said. "Trevor and Edan are both better
shots than you, and we'll need Yukio's sharp eyes." Nuy was
grateful that Leila had not been too honest.

"I'll go," Sofia replied, sounding resigned but also relieved.

"And if you're able to do it, bury Haidar and Hannah on the
way." Leila paused. "We should do that much for them."

Bonnie bowed her head. Nuy saw the sorrow in her face.
"There is something else you can do," Nuy said. "Give me your
weapon. I may need it, and Sofia has one of her own." Bonnie
handed the stun gun to her without speaking.

"What should we tell everybody in the next camp?" Sofia
asked.

"Just tell them everything that's happened up to now," Leila
said. "After that, they'll have to decide what to do for themselves."

"They might send more people after you," Sofia said, sounding more hopeful. "We could organize another group to come
back here as quickly as possible."

"That's up to them," Leila said, but Nuy heard no hope in

the young woman's voice. Leila was clearly aware of the dangers that faced them. With only six of them left, they would be outnumbered by Ho's band. Whatever anyone upriver decided to do would make no difference to them; any help they might send would arrive too late. They would have to fight this battle alone.

14

Nuy crept through the thick reeds, then stopped to listen. There was the sound of a cry in the distance. She hunkered down and held her breath. The high-pitched, almost musical cry sounded again. The sound might have been that of a big cat, or perhaps the whinny of a horse. She did not think it was human.

The moons had set. Above her, the sky was the deep dark blue-green of early dawn. Nuy sat there, looking east across the river at the grassy plain and the bright rose-colored light of the rising sun as the others settled around her. They had crossed the river to the western bank just before nightfall, because Nuy had advised them that they might be safer on this side of the river.

Now she worried that she might be wrong about that. The closer her father came to the place where he would expect to find the northerners, the more likely he was to move at night, to keep his band more easily concealed. Perhaps he would also think of sneaking up on them along this side of the river.

Leila leaned toward her and seemed about to speak. Nuy shook her head and put a finger to her lips. Leila opened her pack and gave Nuy a small handful of nuts, then passed the food around to the others. They had brought food with them, enough, Nuy estimated, for a few days at most, even if her companions ate as little as she did. Bonnie, Tonio, and Sofia had taken most of what was left of the food and supplies with them; they would have more need of things that would only weigh Leila and her comrades down. It was also likely that any confrontation with Ho would come before their food ran out, if Nuy's guesses about what he might do were correct. She would not dwell on what might happen after that.

Nuy chewed on the nuts. The others were silent as they ate. They had managed some sleep while Nuy, Yukio, and Trevor took turns keeping watch, but all of them looked exhausted. Their clothing was still damp from sweat and river water, and their foot coverings were cracked and worn under the mud. Edan took off his boots, wrung out the dirty cloth coverings he wore under them, then put them on again. The rest of them had all been doing that almost every time they stopped to rest, pulling off their boots and examining their feet as if surprised to find that they still had them.

Belen and Carin were likely to rejoin Ho and the rest of the band by nightfall at the latest, when he would learn of the northerners camped upriver. It had seemed so clear to Nuy earlier that her father would decide after that to attack. Now all of her imaginings seemed suspect. Just because Belen and Carin had been talking about an attack didn't mean that Ho was planning one, and if he had, he might have changed his mind. She was assuming that he had gone back to their former home near the sea, but he might be somewhere else entirely, perhaps a lot closer than she realized. He might be lying in wait, plotting an ambush, expecting more people to come looking for Leila's mother and her friend. He might be anywhere.

No, she thought; she still had the advantage. Her father believed her to be dead. He would not expect her to be guiding these people to him. Belen and Carin believed that she had fallen to her death; they would never guess that she was guiding these people south.

Nuy stood up. The others rose to their feet, slumping with weariness. She peered over the tops of the reeds and gazed at the grassland to the south, a monotonous flat landscape broken only by the long gray ribbon of the river, the brown and black stalks of the reeds and plants along the banks. patches of green shrubbery, and two distant fingers of rock pointing at the sky.

Then she saw a tiny dark speck move along the southern horizon.

She quickly motioned to the others to be still. The speck slowly swelled into a larger spot as it continued in their direction. A horse was heading their way.

"It's a horse," Yukio muttered behind her after a few moments had passed. She looked back at him. "But I don't see a rider."

"Neither do I," Nuy said; she had already seen that no one was riding the horse.

The animal was galloping through the grassland to the southeast of them, along the other side of the river. They watched in silence as the horse slowed its pace, then sped into a gallop again.

At last it slowed to a trot and then to a walk. The horse had a black mane, a chestnut coat, and did not seem skittish enough to be a wild creature.

"I know that horse." Trevor stepped to Nuy's side. "Zoheret

was riding her when she left us." Leila was standing just behind Trevor, and Nuy knew from the stricken look on her face that the same thought had come to the young woman.

"You're sure," Nuy whispered.

"I'm sure," Trevor said softly.

Leila shook her head, then covered her face. Kagami put an arm around Leila; the older woman's eyes glistened. It came to Nuy then that Leila's mother had to be dead. She could see it now, the woman riding toward Ho, perhaps calling out a greeting, and then her father raising his weapon and bringing her down in the same way he had killed Chiang. Zoheret's companion was probably dead, too.

"This horse must have run away right after he shot her," Nuy murmured. "That's how he might have done it, shot her with a stun gun first, maybe while she was on horseback, and after that he would have made sure she was dead, he could have used his spear then, so he wouldn't have to get too close to her. The horse must have panicked and run away." There was no way that she could keep the harshness out of her words. She wanted them to be harsh. Maybe then Leila would understand that there was little to be won now in fighting Ho. If they retreated, they might still be able to save themselves.

"There's no bridle," Trevor said, "and no rope, either."

Nuy shrugged. "What are you talking about?"

"If Zoheret was riding this horse," he replied, "she would have been using a bridle, and if she wasn't, she would have put a rope on her horse and secured her before doing anything else."

Leila grabbed Trevor's arm. "Do you think—"

"This means nothing," Nuy said. "She might have been surprised before she could get a rope around its neck."

"Maybe," Trevor said, "but I doubt it. Gervais and she would have made sure they were in a safe place before removing a bridle from a horse."

"Zoheret might be alive," Leila said.

"Maybe, maybe not," Nuy said. "All we really know is that this horse got away from her somehow."

"That's more than we knew a few moments ago." Leila gazed steadily at Nuy. "You said that you would help us. We have to go on. We still need your help."

"I said that I'd help you." Nuy looked down. "I won't go back on my promise now."

The horse stood across the river near an outcropping of rock, drinking from the water, as they passed on the opposite side. Trevor and Nuy had been arguing over what to do about the horse, with Trevor reluctant to leave the animal behind, while Nuy kept insisting that the horse would only be more trouble and was of no use to them now.

Throughout the night, Leila had been brooding on what Kagami had discovered about Nuy. A dream had come to her, one in which Nuy could look into her mind and enter her thoughts. Nuy had compelled Leila to follow her across the grassy plain, refusing to leave her behind even when she begged to lie down and rest. Leila was powerless to resist her in the dream, bound to Nuy by mental tethers, forced to wander through the high grass while knowing that she would never see the settlements again. The sharp pain of that thought had been enough to wake her, and she had slept only uneasily after that.

In the daylight, Nuy looked as human as any of them, and the idea that she could read thoughts seemed absurd. Nuy had spoken of others being blind or deaf, which might mean only that her senses were far more acute than Leila's. But Kagami had uncovered genetic material in Nuy that was unrecognizable to her scanner. Something had altered Nuy's DNA, and the girl had admitted that there were others like herself, which indicated that she might not be just a random mutation.

Nothing like that had shown up in anyone in the settlements; if it had, everyone would have known, and what to do about such mutations would have been fodder for a public meeting. So they had managed to avoid whatever had affected Nuy's people, at least so far.

Maybe the longer they lived on Home, the more they would change. Perhaps the only reason children like Nuy had not been born to anyone in the settlements was because, unlike Ho's group, they kept close to their transplanted environment while drawing on the stored genetic material brought down from Ship for many of their children.

It was pointless to dwell on such thoughts, especially now, with more immediate worries to face, but there it was. What they discovered out here might only convince others that leaving their settlements might mean eventually losing their humanity, becoming something else.

The horse lifted its head and whinnied. Leila halted and stared back at the horse; the others gathered around her. "I've been thinking," Leila began.

"About that horse?" Nuy snorted and rubbed at her nose. "You people care more about your animals than you do about yourselves."

"I'm thinking that maybe one or two of us should go ahead with you while the rest follow with the horse," Leila said. "The more of us there are in a group, the more easily we can be seen. We ought to find out more about what's ahead, and we might need that horse later." Zoheret or Gervais might be injured, unable to travel very far without a horse.

Nuy arched her brows and folded her arms across her bare chest. "I was thinking the same thing, that two or three of us should go on ahead and do some scouting."

"I don't like it," Edan said. "We should stick together."

"We won't have to go far," Nuy said. "By now, we can't be that far away from them. If they're where I think they are, we'll reach them sometime tomorrow, and if they've decided to come north, they'll be even closer than that. My father might have sent two or three ahead of him as scouts." She narrowed her dark eyes. "If we're lucky, we might be able to bring them down and find out a few things."

Leila did not want to think about exactly how Nuy planned to accomplish that.

"Who stays behind?" Yukio asked.

Leila thought quickly. "You and Trevor and Kagami," she replied. "Trevor, you can swim the river and get that horse and then all of you can follow us. Nuy and I can go ahead with Edan. If we need you, we'll wait for you, or one of us will run back for you."

Trevor said, "I don't like it."

"Just do it."

"Be careful," Kagami said.

"You, too." Leila touched Kagami's arm. "Especially you." She turned toward Nuy. "Let's go."

Nuy moved through the grass, with Leila and Edan just behind her.

By midmorning, the grass through which they were moving was only as high as Leila's knees, and Nuy had led her and Edan closer to the river again, where tall patches of reeds and scattered groves of gourd-bearing trees would provide more cover. Occasionally Nuy motioned them to a halt while she stood still and gazed into the distance, twitching her nose or cupping an ear. Whenever Leila was about to speak, Nuy signaled for silence. Edan said nothing, and the expression on his face was empty of emotion.

Not long after midday, they stopped and sat down in the shade of three trees amid scattered gourds to eat small pieces of dried fruit. Leila could feel how loose her frayed clothing had become on her. By now, she should have grown used to being hungry, but felt even hungrier after the meager meal than she had before eating.

"We can speak now," Nuy said, although Leila noticed that the girl was keeping her voice low. "Things will get more dangerous for us from this point on, and one person would be less visible than three. I should go ahead while you two wait here."

Leila was about to protest. Nuy shook her head at her. "I know this land better than you," Nuy continued, "and if I find no sign of my father's band by late afternoon, I'll return to you by nightfall."

Leila opened her mouth again, but Nuy suddenly stiffened and put a hand to her lips. Leila held her breath for several moments. She could hear it now, a sound that might be the faint thunder of a distant storm.

They dropped into the grass and flattened themselves against the ground. In a little while, far to the south, Leila could glimpse what looked like a gray horse, galloping swiftly in their direction on this side of the river. Gervais had been riding a gray horse, and now she could see that there was a rider on the horse's back. But the rider was too small to be Gervais, and even at this distance, she could see that the rider was almost naked.

Edan already had his weapon out. He propped himself up on his elbows and took aim. Nuy's hand snaked out and grabbed his wrist.

"No!" Nuy whispered.

"Why not?" Edan whispered back. Leila was reaching for her own weapon when Nuy suddenly chopped at Edan's arm with one hand. His weapon fell to the ground. Nuy seized his weapon, then jumped to her feet.

The horse kept coming toward them, the rider clinging to the horse's mane. He seemed to be a boy, with a long black braid like Nuy's. Nuy suddenly ran out from under the trees. Leila aimed her weapon first at Nuy, then at the rider coming toward them. Nuy shouted a word Leila did not understand. The horse swerved to one side and then reared, nearly throwing the rider.

"Nuy!" the rider called out. The horse reared again as the stranger clung to the mane. "You're alive!"

Nuy took aim. "I warn you," she shouted back. "I'll shoot you if I must." The horse danced under the boy. "Calm that horse, and then climb down, and be quick about it or I will shoot you."

Leila aimed her weapon at the stranger, although Nuy seemed to have him under control. The horse stopped dancing. The boy slipped off its back, landed lightly on his feet, and thrust his hands up as he turned to face Nuy.

"What's this all about?" Edan said angrily.

Nuy pulled her own weapon from her loincloth, then threw Edan's gun back to him; he caught it awkwardly with one hand. "This is Sarojin," she replied. "We can trust him, I think."

"You think?" Edan took a step toward her. "You mean you aren't sure?"

"You can trust me," the boy said, his eyes wide as he stared at Nuy. "If Ho catches me now, he'll kill me."

"Is he moving north?" Nuy asked.

The boy shook his head. "No. Not yet, anyway."

Leila could restrain herself no longer. "How did you get this horse?" she asked.

"Two people are trapped in one of the caves," the boy replied. "They sent the horse at us, right after their first horse charged us. I don't know what they thought they were doing, but I saw my chance when the second horse galloped toward us. I went after it as fast as I could and luckily nobody was able to hit me or the horse before I caught up with it. I jumped on its back and rode out of there as fast as I could."

"What do you mean by two people trapped in a cave?" Leila asked, feeling hope well up inside her.

"Two people from the north," the boy said. "They were riding upriver when we saw them. We cut them off and chased them south. Now they're trapped in one of the caves near the seashore, so Ho's going to wait them out. They tried to make a run for it, but Ho started shooting as soon as they were in range, and that forced them back. Night came, and then they sent the first of their horses at us, but whatever they were trying to do, it didn't work then or the second time, either. Somebody's always watching the cave now, so they can't get out. Don't know how much food they have, but they couldn't have been carrying that much water."

Zoheret and Gervais might have driven their horses away in desperation, hoping that at least one of the animals would find its way back to Leila and her group. Leila thought of what Trevor had said. By releasing their horses, Zoheret might have been trying to tell them that she and Gervais were still alive. She was letting them know that she needed their help.

"Can we believe anything he tells us?" Edan asked.

"Yes," Nuy whispered. "I can tell. Believe him."

The boy lowered his arms. "You have to believe me. All I was thinking when I ran after that horse was that I had to get away, no matter what happened to me."

"We know your people attacked some of ours," Leila said, "and killed two of them, and that you did it for no reason at all."

"I had no part in that," the boy said. "Ho left me with Zareb and Gerd and Katti and told us to go west and wait for him by the river while he and the others went north. I didn't know what he'd done until he and Owen met up with us again. He told us what he did and then he gave us some of the food he took from them and he said he'd killed some more of the ones who sent death to us but he was eating their food the whole time he was saying it."

Nuy said, "My father is mad."

"Mad or not, he was quick enough to go after those two people he's got trapped now, and if he had just been a little faster and Owen's aim had been a little better, he would have had them, too. He'll get them anyway when they run out of water."

"He won't get them," Leila said. "We'll see that they don't." She could grasp enough of what the boy was telling them to have a fairly clear idea of what had happened.

"I found Belen and Carin spying on these people." Nuy waved a hand at Leila and Edan. "I heard enough of what they said to know that Ho was thinking of attacking them, too."

"I didn't see Belen or my sister on my way here," the boy said, "but I'd crossed the river to this side and I was riding as fast as I could and keeping well to the west except when I had to water the horse." He paused. "The bond we once shared with Carin and Belen is broken."

Nuy grimaced. "I think I knew that already." Her eyes glistened; the look on her face was that of someone mourning a death. "Hai." Her voice was hoarse with sorrow.

Edan said, "I hope we can trust you."

"You can trust him," Nuy said. "We have no choice but to trust him. We should listen to more from him and then we'll have to think of how to save the two my father has trapped."

Sarojin spoke of what had happened since Nuy had been cast out. Nuy listened, interrupting Sarojin whenever she saw that Leila or Edan seemed confused, then asking him to explain something in more detail.

His tale was a grim one, as Nuy had supposed it might be.

Eyela, it turned out, had died some months back giving birth to a child, and then that child, born too early, had died, too. Not long after that, Ashur had left the band, going east to hunt, even though that region was more unfamiliar to them than the lands to the west and south, and he had never returned. Perhaps some accident had overtaken him, or maybe the death of his mate and child had made him more careless with his own life.

A month after they had all realized that they would probably never see Ashur again, Gerd had been kicked in the head by a horse Belen had captured. Since then, he had been useless for anything except tending the fire or doing whatever small chores Zareb found for him. By then, Belen had claimed Carin as a mate, and Carin hadn't seemed to mind that as much as Sarojin had thought his sister would. After that, Katti had retreated to the back of their cave and refused to eat or speak to anyone until Ho and Owen had beaten her nearly senseless, and now Katti did as she was told, but barely uttered a word. More recently, Belen had returned from hunting to tell them that he had seen strangers in the distance, by the river. That was when Ho had decided to attack them.

Nuy heard all this and it came to her that she was listening to the story as if all of the people in it, her people, were strangers to her. She had to hold herself apart from them now, or else her grief would overwhelm her. She would have to harden herself against mourning for what had been lost; she had to both pity and be pitiless. What the suffering of her people meant was that whatever battle lay ahead might be easier for Leila and her companions to win; Ho and his band were not as strong as they had once been. It was cause for both hope and hopelessness.

"We were sure that you were dead," Sarojin finished. "I thought you were lost long ago."

There was Sarojin, at least. She took his hand for a moment.

"Belen and Carin found out I wasn't dead," Nuy said, "and Belen and I fought. I fell over the side of a high cliff when he kicked me, but he didn't see that a ledge caught me, so now even he and Carin will believe I'm dead."

"But how did you—"

"I can tell my story another time." She glanced at Leila and Edan. Leila's face was a mixture of horror and sympathy. Edan's eyes were even colder than they had been before, but she sensed that he was pushing his feelings of anger and fear outside of himself, as she had.

"So Belen may think that he killed you," Sarojin said.

Nuy nodded. "I wonder if my father will be happy to hear of my death from Belen or if finding out that I survived for so long will only anger him even more."

"Belen will say nothing to your father." Sarojin leaned forward. "If he goes to him and says that he brought you death, I think Ho would kill him, and maybe Carin, too, for not stopping him. Belen will say nothing, and neither will my sister."

Nuy drew up her legs. "My father drove me out. He wanted me dead."

"For a while, those were his thoughts. He would curse the stranger you brought with you, the one he had to kill, and then he would curse you, too. He kept saying that you should have killed the man instead of bringing him to us, that you deserved to be punished for that, and that you had to stay away until he was sure that you couldn't carry death to us. Many days passed, and then he began to wonder why you hadn't even tried to return to us. After that, he would send out Owen and Daniella to search for you while they hunted, and I know they must have searched near this river and near our old grounds, but perhaps they didn't look that hard."

Nuy said, "I was careful, and I found a good place to hide." There was no need to tell him more than that.

"When Belen told Ho that he wanted to take Carin as a mate, Ho went into a rage, because he knew that what Belen was really saying was that you had to be dead. They fought, and after they had beaten each other bloody, Ho relented and told Belen that he could do as he liked." Sarojin's mouth twisted. "Carin told me that it would be wise of me not to object, but she didn't have to say it, I could see it." He cleared his throat. "Since then, Ho has mourned for the daughter he lost. I think if you went to him now, he would welcome you back."

Nuy tried to absorb what he was saying. Ho would welcome her back. For a moment, a day she had spent with her father by the sea, in the days before the great storm, came to her. They had gone to collect fish, and Ho had thought of bringing a few shells back so that Katti could make necklaces for them. They had sat there until dark, looking out at the vast blue-gray sea as the waves lapped against the yellow sand. That had been the first time Ho had told her about how their people had come down from the sky. He had told her that story in a soft, gentle voice that had risen to anger only when he had spoken of leaving with his band to come south. She remembered how content she had been then, up until the more familiar note of anger had crept into his voice. She wondered now if the storms inside him had finally destroyed the man who had been with her that day or if he might still somehow persist in the recesses of Ho's mind.

"I don't want to go back," she said, but that wasn't so. She wanted to go back and find everything as it had been, her father gentle towards her once more, those who were dead still alive, and her bond with Carin and Sarojin and Belen as strong as it had been when they were children.

"I can't go back," Sarojin said, "and when Ho comes after these people, he'll come after me as well. My only chance is to keep going north and stay ahead of him." He looked around at the others. "You should turn around now and head north and keep going. He won't think of coming after you until he knows that the two people he has trapped are dead."

"We can't turn back," Leila said. "My mother is one of those people. Her name is Zoheret."

"That was the name he used whenever he called out to her," Sarojin said. "I don't know what your mother did to him, but he kept saying that she had taken what should have been his, but that it wasn't enough for her, that she had wanted him dead after that."

"My mother wanted nothing like that," Leila said. "All she wanted was to find out what had happened to your people and offer them help if they needed it."

Nuy lifted a hand, knowing what she would have to do now. "I don't want to go to my father," she said, "but now I know that I must, and I'll have to go alone."

Leila's eyes grew wide. "But you can't," she said.

Edan said, "You told us we could trust you."

"Listen to me. I can take this horse and ride back and tell my father that I killed Sarojin along the way, and in the meantime, the rest of you can follow me. Let me see if I can find a way to convince my father to let your mother and her friend go, and if I can't, then you'll have to do whatever you can to save them yourselves."

"It's too dangerous," Leila said. "You told us yourself that your father is mad. I don't care what this boy says."

"I think he would take you back," Sarojin said, "but he might turn against you after that. How can you know what he'll do?"

"I must take that chance." Nuy stood up and took out her knife. "Sarojin, I won't hurt you, but bow your head now, and keep still." He frowned at her, but did as she asked. She reached for his long braid and swiftly cut it off at the base of his neck. "I may have to offer some proof that you're dead."

Sarojin fumbled at his neck. "I'm sorry," she said. She could imagine how he felt, being robbed so suddenly of the braid he had worn ever since they were all children. "It's only hair, Sarojin. You can grow another braid more easily than another life."

"Exactly what do you think you can accomplish?" Edan asked.

"I don't know," Nuy replied, "but if there is anything of the father I sometimes knew still alive inside him, I must reach him." Clutching the braid in her hand, she moved toward the horse.

15

The horse seemed worn out by her long run with Sarojin, but willing to allow Nuy to ride her as long as they kept to a slow pace. Nuy preferred a slow pace. She did not want the horse to throw her, and did not want any of her people to shoot at her before seeing who she was. Sarojin had told her exactly where her father was camped, near their old grounds, at the edge of the land that had once been their garden, below the cave where she had found Bonnie and Tonio.

The horse kept near the river, halting every so often to drink. Occasionally Nuy had to pull at the mane or dig her knees into the horse's flanks whenever her mount seemed about to turn back. When night came, she remained on the horse, falling into a light sleep and then waking to catch herself before she could slip to the ground. Occasionally the horse stopped to rest, to graze, or to drink from the river. The animal could do as it pleased as long as it continued to carry her south.

Belen and Carin would be in Ho's encampment by now. Nuy still had her stun gun but she would have to find a place to hide the weapon before she reached her father's encampment. There would then be nothing to link her to the northerners unless Belen or Carin spoke of their encounter with her. Maybe Belen would admit that he had seen her fall and done nothing to save her. But even that could work in her favor if it roused Ho's anger against Belen. The greatest danger to her was that Belen or Carin would hear the dishonesty in her words or glimpse it in her eyes. She wondered if she could mask the truth well enough to hide it from them.

She did not think about what she would do or say when she came within sight of Ho's camp. She would know what to do.

By the time the sun rose, the air had grown so still that Nuy wondered if a storm might break by the end of the day. A storm might drive Ho and his band to seek shelter elsewhere; that would give the two people trapped in the caves a chance to escape. There were no clouds in the sky, and she smelled no salt in the air, but the weather was more uncertain at this time of year, when the days were growing shorter. She sniffed at the air again and then knew that no storm would come that evening.

Her father might have sent one or two of the band to watch out for anyone approaching from the north. He might be thinking that the northerners would soon come looking for the two he was holding at bay.

She waited until her horse had stopped to graze, then swung one leg over her mount and jumped to the ground.

She ran through the grass, staying low, then looked back. The horse was following her, but slowly, at a distance. The encampment could not be far away. She did not care now if one of her father's people spotted the horse. The animal might serve as a distraction.

Soon she was able to see the small bulges of hills to the south. Remaining in a crouch, she peered cautiously over the top of the yellow grass. Across the river, about one hundred paces to the south, stood a small grove of boltrees, a good place for anyone keeping watch to conceal himself. She sniffed at the air and picked up the faint scent of smoke. Her father might have put out any campfire by now, but a fire had been burning nearby not long ago.

Nuy ducked down, barely able to glimpse the boltrees through the grass. Something moved under the trees, and for an instant she saw a head of thick reddish-brown hair before shadows cloaked the person once more. Zareb was the one keeping watch. She wondered if she dared risk revealing herself to him and asking him to take her to her father.

Zareb suddenly burst from the trees and ran toward the river. Nuy froze, then realized that he must have seen the horse. He plunged into the river and splashed through the water in her direction, arms wheeling, his long brown hair and graying beard a stark contrast to skin burned to a dark brown by the sun. He was not yet reaching for the stun gun that was tucked under his loincloth over his hip, next to his knife.

"Hai!" he shouted at the horse. His arms slapped against the water as he swam across the deeper waters of the river. Nuy waited until he neared the bank, found his footing, and stood up in water nearly as high as his waist. She pulled out her own weapon and jumped to her feet.

Zareb's hand darted toward his weapon. Nuy fired. The beam caught him in the chest. He toppled forward and fell into the water with a loud splash.

The horse whinnied behind her. Zareb floated on the water,

face down. Nuy stood there, hesitating, not knowing what to do. The only emotions Zareb had ever shown towards her as she had grown older were irritation, often accompanied by a slap, and indifference. Allowing him to die would keep him from endangering Sarojin, Leila, and Edan, and would also decrease the number of people they might have to fight later on. He was unconscious, so he would not suffer a painful death.

Zareb floated away from her toward the middle of the river; the current bore him downstream. Nuy ran toward the river and threw herself into the water, flailing about with her arms and legs as she swam toward him. The current was much stronger than she had expected, a fast-flowing stream of cold water below the surface that tugged at her legs.

She reached Zareb and grabbed him by the hair, then managed to loop one arm around him. The weight of him threatened to pull her under. She struggled to turn him onto his back so that his face would be out of the water, but felt herself sinking again.

The water closed over her. She let go of him and pushed herself up with her arms, coughing up water as she gulped air. Zareb was being pulled downstream again. She swam with the current toward him and seized him by the shoulder, kicking furiously with her legs, and was pulled under the water once more.

Nuy struggled to the surface. Her hand struck Zareb's head; she grasped his hair tightly, then hooked an arm around his neck. Propelling herself with one arm and kicking hard with her legs, she kept swimming, pulling Zareb with her, until they drifted into a patch of reeds.

They were in shallower water now, where the current was not as strong. She let her legs sink until she felt mud against her feet.

She stood up. The water was still nearly up to her neck. She hauled Zareb through the reeds. When the water was only as high as her waist, she grabbed him under the arms and pulled him out of the water and onto the bank before collapsing next to him.

She lay there, gasping for breath, then forced herself to sit up. They were on the eastern side of the river now, several paces down from the boltrees where Zareb had been keeping watch. On the opposite bank, the horse lapped at the water, ignoring Nuy.

Zareb lay on his stomach, his head turned toward her. He did not seem to be breathing. Nuy crawled to him and pounded on his back, trying to pump the water from his lungs while sensing that this was useless, that there was nothing she could do for him now. She had known that when she was still in the water, trying to drag him onto land, even if she had refused to admit it to herself. She had shot him and then waited too long to rescue him because a part of her had wanted him dead.

At last she gave up on her futile efforts to revive him and sat there, gazing across the river at the horse. The animal lifted her head, snorted, then trotted away from the river toward the western plain of grass. She could not wait here much longer; she had lost time as it was.

An idea came to her. She leaned over Zareb and took his knife and his stun gun from him, then pulled out her own weapon and lay it at his side. Leila and her companions would see the body easily from the other bank, and she was guessing that they would swim across to investigate. There would be a stun gun for Sarojin to use. She did not yet know what she would tell her father about Zareb when she reached his camp, but she would think of something.

She had killed a man. That she had not planned to do it

changed nothing. Zareb was dead and his death was to her advantage. She got up and walked south, aching and sorrowing.

*T*he wind blowing from the south was dying down, but it had carried the faint odor of burned meat to Nuy before she glimpsed her father's camp. Ho's band was exactly where Sarojin had told her they would be, north of the hills that marked the caves, at the end of the patch of ground where Ho's people had once grown their crops. She had remained alert, keeping low in the grass, stopping from time to time to conceal herself behind boltrees or amid the reeds to observe what lay ahead.

Three horses were tied to what looked like long strips of leather knotted together and strung between two poles. Five people sat around the flat rocks of a fireplace, although the fire was either banked or else had gone out. In the distance, below the nearest hill, she glimpsed a head of pale yellow hair and another head with brown hair poking above the yellow grass. That had to be Owen and Belen. Ho had apparently sent them to keep watch near the hill, probably just out of range of the weapons the two trapped people presumably possessed.

This meeting might go more easily for her than she had expected. The only people sitting with her father were Katti and Daniella, the now simpleminded Gerd, and Carin.

Her hand closed around her stun gun. She did not want to approach her father without the weapon, even though there was little chance of using it, but she would have to explain how she had acquired the gun. The story she had made up to tell her father now seemed completely unconvincing to her. Carin would be there to sense the deceit in Nuy's tale.

Nuy took a deep breath. If he shot at her, she was far enough away that he was likely to miss her. Still in a crouch, she took a step forward, inhaled again, then stood up straight.

"Hai!" she screamed. "Hai!" She rose up on the balls of her feet, ready to run if her father aimed his weapon at her.

Ho turned his head, then slowly got to his feet. Daniella was shaking her head; Carin seemed frozen.

"Nuy!" That was Katti's voice.

Nuy waited. Her father stood there, arms hanging at his sides, even though the small cylindrical shape of his weapon was visible against his right hip. He was not going to shoot her; she was sure of that now.

She walked toward them. Ho's eyes widened as she approached; he lowered them for a moment, and she knew that he had noticed her weapon.

"Zareb was careless," she shouted. "He let Sarojin—Sarojin, of all people—run him down with his horse. Sarojin didn't get away with it, though. The two of them fought and now they're both dead."

"Really," Daniella murmured.

"Here's the proof." Nuy gestured at the braid hanging next to her waterskin, then put her hand on her weapon. "Since Zareb didn't need this weapon anymore, I took it from him." If she was lucky, her father would accept that as the truth and ask her nothing more.

Gerd grinned at her. Carin was looking at her with an expression that might have been either horror or bewilderment. Even Ho seemed frightened of her; his right hand was twitching, as if he could not control it.

Katti waved her hands at Nuy. "It's a sign," she said. Her blue eyes were empty and her face wore an odd, almost ecstatic expression that Nuy had never seen on her before. Katti wrapped her arms around herself. "It's a sign."

"I didn't think you'd be so resourceful," Daniella said, "that you'd be able to survive for so long."

"She's my daughter," Ho said. He took a step toward Nuy.

"Maybe it's good that I drove you out, so that you could show us exactly how resourceful you are. I shouldn't have doubted that you were, I should have known that you'd return to us."

Ho raised an arm. Nuy instinctively shrank back. He drew her to him and held her for a moment. "Nuy," he said, in the gentle voice he had sometimes used with her long ago.

"Sarojin," Carin whispered. Her face had grown harder. "I would know it if he were dead, I would feel it." Nuy forced herself to look toward Carin. The slight twist in Carin's mouth and the coldness in her eyes revealed her disbelief, but Nuy sensed that Carin would not push at her for the truth, at least not yet.

Ho released Nuy. "Odd that he didn't keep running," Carin went on. "Odd that he would have turned back and gone after Zareb. That isn't like Sarojin."

Katti held up her right hand, palm out. "Don't say his name so soon after his passing."

Ho said, "He deserved whatever he got for running down Zareb." Daniella nodded. He turned to Carin. "Since my daughter is Belen's mate, I don't know where that leaves you after he takes her back."

Carin winced. Nuy threw Sarojin's braid to the ground. Carin bent to pick it up and clutched the braid to her chest. Tears trickled from her eyes, but Nuy could see that she was forcing herself to weep. She doesn't believe me, Nuy thought, and wondered if that was because Carin could not believe that her brother was dead or because she could so readily read Nuy's deceit.

"Nuy certainly is resourceful," Daniella said to Ho, "to survive so long, with only a knife and no companions and no help. Hard to believe that she could."

Ho shot Daniella an angry look. "She's among us again,

isn't she?" He raised a hand, as if to strike her; Daniella shrank back.

Carin, still forcing her tears to flow, continued to gaze at Nuy. Gerd, who was still smiling, stared past Nuy. Katti plucked at the necklace of shells around her neck.

Nuy glanced at the hills to the south. "Owen and Belen haven't come to greet me," she said.

"That's because they're keeping watch," Ho said. "We've got two of the others trapped in a cave, two of the ones who brought death to us, and I'm not about to let them get away."

"They can't get out to find water," Daniella said. She narrowed her small eyes as she looked at Nuy. "Ho's going to wait them out. They'll either have to leave that cave or eventually die of thirst."

"I thought I could wait them out," Ho said, "but I'm getting a bit impatient with that. Now I'm thinking we should leave this place, let them believe that we've given up on them and moved on. But we'll be ready for them. We'll sneak up on them from another direction and be ready to pounce on them as soon as they leave their refuge."

"Do you think they'll be fooled by that?" Daniella asked.

"They'll be getting more desperate," Ho said. "They'll let themselves hope and believe that we're gone because they'll need to get to water. That'll be their choice, taking a chance on trying to escape or dying for sure if they stay there." He slapped Nuy's shoulder; his fingers dug painfully into her upper arm. "You've come back just in time to see me have my revenge, and this won't be the end of it. After that, we'll take care of another encampment Belen told me about, one only a couple of days away. And after that—" Ho let go of her "After that—"

Daniella was still gazing suspiciously at Nuy. "Only a couple of days away," she said softly. "I could almost think—" Daniella sat down next to Gerd.

Daniella doesn't believe me, Nuy thought. Carin knew that she was lying. She had to hope that neither of them would give voice to their doubts.

"Daniella," Ho said, "go fetch Belen and tell him that his mate's returned to him. You can keep watch with Owen for a while."

"Let me go to Belen," Nuy said quickly. "He's my mate, after all."

Ho shrugged, then nodded.

Nuy hurried away from her father, her heart pounding. Daniella might be afraid to say anything about whatever doubts she was harboring, but it would be easier to speak of them to Belen and Owen. Carin might keep silent in the hope of protecting her brother, or she might mention her suspicions to Belen, who might sense them inside her anyway. The suspicions of all three would only grow if they could nurture them together.

The ground was softer against her feet as she crossed the land where they had once had their garden; only short tufts of yellow grass now grew here. She was still many paces away from Owen and Belen when Owen rose and turned toward her, a stun gun already in his hands. She reached for her own weapon and aimed it at him.

The blond man seemed to be saying something to Belen. "Ho has welcomed me back," she shouted to them at the top of her lungs. "I ask my mate Belen to welcome me, too."

Belen did not turn around, but his back stiffened with shock. Owen kept his weapon aimed at her. "Where did you get a stun gun?" he asked as she approached.

"This is Zareb's weapon," she replied. "My father will tell you the story." She felt unprepared to utter her falsehoods to

Belen, who was refusing to look at her. "Go back and rest for a while. I can keep watch with Belen."

Owen scratched at his long yellow beard. "Did Ho tell you who we've got trapped up there?" he asked.

"He told me."

"I'm getting tired of waiting for them," Owen said. "They haven't so much as poked a finger out of that cave." He showed her his teeth. "Ho was hoping you'd come back," he said. "Thought he was deluding himself, but here you are, and looking better than you did when he drove you away. Didn't think it was possible." He strode away, leaving her alone with Belen.

"I see that you didn't say anything to my father," Nuy said softly.

"You should be dead, Nuy," he said without facing her. "I saw you fall. How did you do it?"

"A ledge caught me when I fell."

"You've been awfully lucky. You should have been dead a long time ago."

"Ho still considers you my mate," Nuy said.

"I liked Carin a lot better as a mate than you," Belen said.

"Keep her as your mate, then. I'll leave you free to stay with her if that's what you want."

"It doesn't matter what you want or what I want. All that matters is what Ho wants. How did you do it, Nuy? How did you stay alive all that time by yourself?"

"I was used to being alone for days at a time before. Being alone for longer than that wasn't so different."

"For months? For over a year? You must have had some help."

Nuy forced herself to stare back at him. "I was resourceful, I have some advantages. I needed no help." She could see that he still did not believe her, but he would keep his doubts to himself, at least for now. "You didn't tell Ho about what happened with us."

"No, I didn't tell him. Carin told me I'd better not."

"She gave you good advice."

"Why did Zareb give you his weapon?"

"He didn't. I took it away from him after he died. That was Sarojin's doing, he ran him down on the horse he was riding. Sarojin's dead, too." She had spoken in as flat a voice as she could muster. She pressed her lips together, knowing that to say more than that would only rouse more of his suspicions.

Belen sighed, and she smelled some sorrow on his breath. He lifted his head and looked toward the cave. "I wish they'd come out," he said, "so we could get this over with."

"They can't last that much longer," Nuy said.

"We don't know how much water they had with them when we chased them there."

"Probably not much more than for a day or two. Why would they have carried any more than that? They would have assumed that they could get more any time from the river."

Belen glanced at her from the sides of his eyes. She had already said too much to him.

They sat together, not speaking. The air was so still that, for a few moments, Nuy could hear the distant sound of waves rolling toward the shore. She thought of getting up and walking on until she came to the sea. She could stay there and forget all about her father and Leila and the others and Zareb, the man she had killed. She could walk into the sea and let it carry her away from shore. The longing for that kind of oblivion was suddenly so strong inside her that it made her catch her breath.

Belen grabbed her arm, as if to restrain her. At last he said, "Why did you come back to us after all that time?"

"I was lonely."

"Why did you assume Ho wouldn't just chase you away again? How did you know that he wouldn't kill you?"

He was asking her too many questions. "I didn't," she said, "but I was ready to run away again if it looked like he might try." She glanced back at her father's camp. Daniella was walking toward them across the empty field.

"Belen," Daniella called out, "Ho wants you back at his side." She squinted at Nuy. "You, too."

Belen stood up. "So he wants you to keep watch here."

"Nobody's going to keep watch here," Daniella replied. "We're all going to wait back there for a while. Ho wants to see what they'll do then."

Nuy got to her feet and followed the others back to her father's encampment.

Evening came with no sign from the two people trapped inside the cave. The wind had picked up during the day and was now blowing hard from the north, rising occasionally to a wail, as it often did when the days began to grow shorter. Nuy had seen dark clouds in the southern sky that afternoon, but the clouds had dispersed; the northern wind would keep any storm at bay for that night.

Ho and Owen led the horses to the river and stood with the animals as they drank, their backs to the camp. They were talking, but in voices too low for even Nuy to pick up their words. The two men led the horses back and tied them up again.

Owen sat down near the flat rocks of the fireplace and whispered something to Daniella, who nodded. Ho cupped a hand over his eyes and gazed north. He seemed to be sniffing at the air, and for a moment, Nuy was afraid that he might have picked up the scent of someone approaching at a distance. It was foolish of her to think such a thing; she would smell anyone before her father did.

At last Ho wandered back to them, sat down, dug inside one of the packs and passed around handfuls of nuts and dried fruit. The packs were nearly flat, indicating that most of the food had been eaten.

Nuy ate her food, thinking of the people her father had killed to get it. Coming here had been useless, and the longer she stayed, the more suspicious all of them would become of her. Belen and Daniella had their doubts, even if they wouldn't say so in front of Ho, and Carin had fallen into a tense silence, watching Nuy as if preparing to leap at her and force the truth from her.

"Who's going to keep watch tonight?" Owen asked.

"Belen," Ho replied, "and Daniella." Ho looked toward Belen. "You can take turns getting some rest. I'll keep an eye on the cave, and I won't need any sleep tonight."

Nuy knew that she would get no sleep at all. Leila and her companions could not be far away now, and their best chance might be to attack at night, when they could more easily conceal themselves. But then they would not be able to see their targets as easily.

Worrying about the possibility that an attack might go wrong was not the only concern threatening to deprive her of rest. Belen and Daniella might have a few moments while keeping watch in which they could discuss their suspicions about her.

"Nuy," Ho said, breaking into her thoughts, "give me your stun gun." She tensed. "Now."

"But why—" she began.

"Now."

She did not dare to defy him. She reached for her weapon and handed it to him; he passed it on to Daniella. Belen and Daniella took up their posts, Daniella facing northeast while Belen watched the northwest, in case an attack came from across the river. The others stretched out around her, but Nuy was sure that, except for Gerd, the rest of the band would sleep as lightly as she would.

Nuy stood up. "Where are you going?" her father asked.

"To piss," she replied. She needed time by herself to think. She moved down the gentle slope, away from the river, to where a small trench had been dug.

Carin was following her. Nuy pulled down her loincloth and squatted, keeping an eye on Carin. The other girl suddenly squatted next to her, but did not remove her loincloth.

"Why did you come back?" Carin said in a voice so low that Nuy could barely hear her.

"I had nowhere else to go," Nuy whispered back.

"You were behind us, on the cliff. How long were you listening to us?"

"I didn't—"

"You did. Your ears are as sharp as mine. Maybe you came back to look out for your father." Carin grabbed her wrist. "Why did you say that my brother's dead?"

"Because he is."

"I feel your lie." Carin's grip tightened. "Admit it. I would have smelled death on his braid. He's alive, admit it."

Nuy said nothing. There was no point in denying it; Carin would not believe her.

"Now Ho will force Belen to take you back as his mate," Carin said.

"I don't want that," Nuy replied. "If you want him—"

"It doesn't matter whether I want him or not. I need him now, I need him for our child."

Carin stood up. Nuy adjusted her loincloth and quickly got to her feet. "You want to have a child with Belen?" Nuy murmured.

"I'm already carrying a child. I'm pregnant, I know it, I can feel it. It's more than you managed to do when you were his mate. It's my child I care about now, having someone to look out for us."

"Have you said anything to Belen?"

Carin shook her head. "But he'll know soon, he'll find it out for himself, he'll be able to sense it soon. Ho can't take him away from me now." She hurried up the hill to the others before Nuy could respond.

Nuy lay on the soft bare ground near the fireplace, her vigilance at war with her exhaustion. Near her, Katti's breathing was the even sound of a woman asleep. Overhead, through the thickening clouds of the night sky, she made out the small patch of light that was the rising first moon; she had fallen asleep in spite of herself.

Belen rose to his feet, then turned north. Leila and Edan and the others might be closer than Nuy realized, but without her weapon, there was little she could do to aid them in any assault. She had hoped to stun one or two of her father's people, who would not have been expecting her to shoot at them while the band was under attack.

"Hai!" Belen shouted. A beam of light cut through the darkness and Nuy knew that the attack had come.

Gerd was on his feet, roaring as a beam hit him in his broad chest. Carin let out a scream. Another beam shot past Nuy. Katti was still lying near her, curled up into a ball, whimpering.

Someone grabbed Nuy by the wrists and pulled her to her feet. A hand was suddenly clapped over her mouth. She struggled, trying to kick. Her feet left the ground as she was flung over a strong shoulder. The hand fell from her mouth; she opened her mouth to scream.

"Shut up, just shut up." That was her father's voice, and his thin but muscular arms were carrying her as he ran. They were near the horses; Nuy could smell them. Carin screamed again. Ho flung Nuy onto a horse's back and then leaped onto the animal behind her.

He was running away. Mad as he might be, she had never believed him to be a coward. She fought to breathe as the horse under her moved into a gallop. Ho knew that he had lost and was abandoning his people, the few who were left, instead of fighting at their side.

The horse was moving too swiftly. Pain shot through her chest as she bounced against the horse. She could hear other horses now. "Almost out of range," a voice called out near her; that was Owen. Nuy twisted her head. In the moonlight, she could barely make out the small form of Daniella on the third horse, her long hair streaming behind her.

They galloped on. Ho panted as his horse's hooves pounded against the ground. She could hear nothing except the steady thunder of the hooves, her father's gasps for breath, and her own heart thumping inside her.

Her father had been ready for this, she realized. He had guessed that he might be attacked and might be outnumbered. By now the two people he had trapped inside the cave had probably joined the fight, if the battle was not already over. He had been ready to flee with the two whom he trusted most. He had taken Nuy's weapon from her so that she would be unable to fight. She wondered if he had done so in order to protect her or because he had grown suspicious of her.

The wind was rising. They rode on. "Nuy," her father sighed. She kept silent. "Nuy." She did not speak. He had to be riding toward the caves to the east, where he could rest and plan what to do next. What would he do? Could he be so certain that none of the northerners would ever come after him? And why had he brought her with him?

He had driven her away before. He could turn against her again.

The horse was slowing. She held her breath and forced herself to stay limp. The horse was cantering now, not jostling and bruising her nearly as much. If Ho was slowing their pace, it had to mean that no one was pursuing them.

"What now?" Daniella asked.

"Hah!" Ho exclaimed. He slumped over her. Nuy felt his breath on her back as he exhaled. "Let me think."

"What are we going to do with her?" Owen said.

"Be quiet," Ho said.

"She brought them down on us," Daniella said. "It had to be Nuy, she had to be the one—"

"Shut up," Ho said.

"You know I'm right, you have to—"

"Shut up, Daniella." Ho's voice was higher as he sat up again. "She's my daughter, I'll decide what's to be done about her."

She could expect no mercy from him. As that thought came to her, Nuy felt her right arm take a swing at him. She struck him in the chest. As he slipped from the horse, she swung her right leg over the horse's back and grabbed its mane, twisting her hands into the horsehair. The horse reared, nearly throwing her.

A burst missed her; Owen's weapon was in his hand. His hair looked white in the moonlight. He fired and missed her again. Nuy dug her heels into the horse's flanks. The animal wheeled around, nearly throwing her again, then began to gallop through the tall grass. She heard the high whine of the weapon once more.

The horse collapsed under her. She flew over its head and landed flat on her back. She lay there, stunned, then forced herself to draw a painful breath.

Her father was screaming at Owen, howling words she did not know. Nuy stumbled to her feet and ran, knowing that she had no chance, that she could not outrun Owen's horse. The grass slapped against her chest and abdomen as she raced west. She kept expecting a beam to hit her, and wondered if she would hear the weapon before she was hit or if everything would just suddenly go black, as it had when Ho had shot at Chiang and then at her.

She glanced back. Owen was reaching for Ho, pulling him up onto his own horse. Nuy took a deep breath and kept running.

16

The girl who sat next to the body was even smaller than Nuy. Sarojin stood next to her. Leila bent to pick up the stun gun that lay at the dead boy's side. The girl twisted a long braid of hair in her hands, looked up at Leila with her large black eyes, then handed the braid to Sarojin.

"It's yours," the girl said, her voice breaking. "Take it."

Sarojin fingered the hair, as if not knowing what to do with it. Leila kept her weapon trained on the girl, as she had throughout Kagami's scan. There was nothing they could do for the boy, but that had been obvious as soon as they found him.

"I'm sorry, Carin," Sarojin said. "I didn't know, I couldn't tell, if I only could have—"

"Stop it." The girl's voice was thick, and her fine-boned face had the stunned and empty look of someone still recovering from being hit by a beam. "He would have killed you, I saw that much. I can't—" She covered her face, then let her arms fall. "You know what Belen was like towards me much of the time, I have to think of that, but all I can remember now are the few times he was kind."

Sarojin turned toward Leila. "I thought—I didn't know—"

"You had to defend yourself," Leila said. The dead boy had been screaming in a way that terrified her, and Sarojin had fired at him and had kept shooting even after he was down. That was all she could recall from the confusion of the fighting. In the moonlight, their targets had been hard to see.

"It was a stun gun," Sarojin said. "I didn't think it could—"

"It can happen," Leila said. "Not often, but it can. It wasn't your fault."

Sarojin shuddered, then lifted his head. "I have to tell myself that it's better this way, that he would have done the same or worse to you without thinking."

The dead boy almost seemed to be smiling. Sarojin reached for the girl and helped her to her feet. "She's my sister," he whispered, but Leila had already guessed that. "Her name is Carin."

"At least I have my brother." A harder look came over the girl's face. "I knew he wasn't dead, whatever Nuy told us."

"What happened to Nuy?" Leila asked. "Why isn't she here?"

Carin shook her head. "I don't know." She let go of her brother's arm. "Maybe she's with Ho."

The battle had ended quickly. Leila and Edan had led the assault, with Sarojin right behind them. Before Yukio and Kagami had even had a chance to fire their weapons, Zoheret and Gervais had left their cave to race toward the encampment. Trevor had ridden in on one of the horses while leading the other, ready to set one horse loose as a distraction while he fired on Ho's band from horseback, only to find that the battle was already over. It had hardly been a battle at all.

Except that one person was dead and Nuy was missing, Leila reminded herself.

Sarojin moved closer to her. "It isn't like Ho to run away like that," he murmured.

"Who was with him?" Zoheret called out as she walked toward them, Edan at her side.

"It would have to be Owen and Daniella," Sarojin replied. Zoheret grimaced. "And it looks like Nuy went with them, but I doubt she went willingly."

To the east, the sky was lightening to a dark gray. Yukio paced near the fireplace, keeping watch. Kagami had scanned Katti and the big man called Gerd while Edan hastily told Zoheret and Gervais what had happened during the past few days. Leila slipped her arm around her mother's waist, reassuring herself again that she was alive, but could not help noticing the troubled look in Zoheret's eyes. She would be thinking of those they had lost. Leila had seen the shock on Zoheret's face when she heard about the deaths of Haidar and Hannah.

"It looked like they were riding east," Carin said. "They must be headed for our caves."

"What caves?" Zoheret said.

"The caves where we were living. It would take about two days to get there from here. I can't think of anyplace else they would have gone."

"We should get going," Kagami said as she came up to them.

"I agree," Edan added.

"What about Nuy?" Leila said.

"What about her?" Zoheret said.

"Shouldn't we go after her?" Everyone was silent. "She helped us," Leila continued, "she kept Bonnie and Tonio alive, she risked her life for them and for us. We can't just abandon her."

"We wouldn't be of much help to her right now," Zoheret

said. "We have very little food left, and it'll take us at least eight days to get to our closest base. Once we get there, we can consider what to do for Ho's daughter, but—"

"We owe her more than that," Leila interrupted. "We don't know what might be happening to her now."

"I didn't say—" Zoheret began. Leila noticed then how limply her mother's left arm was hanging at her side. The fingers of her left hand were curled into a fist; she was probably in pain. Her prosthetic arm might finally fail her.

"How do we know Ho isn't using Nuy to lead us into a trap?" Edan said.

"That sounds like something he might try," Sarojin said.

Edan sighed. "Then that's all the more reason not to go after her right now."

Leila could not let that cruelly practical remark pass. She was about to speak when Yukio shouted, "Somebody's coming this way!"

Leila looked east and saw the head and torso of a small human figure stumbling through the plain of grass.

"It's Nuy!" Yukio said.

Leila raced down the small hillside and into the grass, Sarojin at her heels. Nuy staggered toward them, arms out. Leila ran to her and caught the other girl as she fell.

Working on their knees and using the edges of the fireplace's flat stones, Yukio, Edan, and Trevor dug a shallow grave for the dead boy, whose name was Belen. Katti had wailed when his name was uttered, had said something about bad luck, and then wept over the body as it was covered with dirt. Carin leaned against her brother and stared at the grave with a tight-lipped expression.

Leila sat with Nuy, giving her sips of water from her canteen whenever the other girl raised her head. Nuy lay on the ground, a pack under her head. Leila could see that Nuy was fighting to stay awake and felt her own exhaustion. She longed to lie down and sleep and wake up to find the walls of her old room around her.

"She needs rest," Zoheret said, "and so do you. So do we all, or we'll be no good for anything." She looked around at the others. "I'll keep watch for a while with Gervais, and the rest of you should get some sleep. After that, the two of us will sleep while a couple of you keep watch, and then we'll all head back."

No one spoke. Perhaps, Leila thought, everyone else was also too tired to argue with Zoheret. Her mother had said nothing about food, but all of them already knew that they would probably not eat anything more today or even tomorrow; there had been almost no food left in the packs Ho had abandoned in his flight. Zoheret had not mentioned that they would also have to keep an eye on Katti, Carin, and Gerd while watching out for Ho and his two comrades. Katti and Gerd seemed harmless enough now, but there was no way to know what they might do if Ho decided to attack. Carin had to be guarded for another reason; the girl was pregnant, as Kagami had discovered after a scan.

Kagami had already found out that Sarojin had the same unfamiliar genetic markers as Nuy. Her scan of Carin had shown that she carried the same genes, as did the fetus inside her. Nuy had said that they were all like her, Carin and Sarojin and the dead boy called Belen.

Leila was about to lift her canteen to Nuy's lips once more, then saw that her eyes were closed; Nuy was asleep.

By midafternoon, they were on the move. Nuy was astride one of the horses, with Sarojin leading the animal. Zoheret had decided that they would take turns riding the two horses, depending on who was weakest and most in need of rest. Carin rode the other horse, which was being led by Trevor. The dead boy was the father of Carin's child; Sarojin had mentioned that Belen had been Carin's mate.

They traveled largely in silence, speaking to one another only when they needed to stop to get more water or to relieve themselves. By evening, Nuy had dismounted from her horse to allow Katti to ride, but Carin remained on horseback, with Edan now leading her mount.

When the first moon was rising, they stopped in a grove of gourd-bearing trees to rest for the night. Zoheret and Gervais said nothing about sharing a meal, and no one asked for any food. Leila felt alert enough to volunteer to keep watch for part of the night with Trevor. She noticed that Edan, who had kept close to Carin for most of the day, had stretched out next to the girl. He seemed to be growing more protective of her. Perhaps he pitied her, or maybe her odd beauty and seeming helplessness drew him.

Trevor, silent as he was while they kept watch, was a comforting presence. They would all get home safely; she refused to doubt that. Their journey would not be an easy one, but the worst had to be over. Clearly Ho had fled because he had realized that he lacked the means to fight them, so he was not likely to attack them now.

But Leila's thoughts were still troubled by worries over what might happen when they got back. Katti and Gerd had chosen to leave the settlements; would they now be welcomed back? Would they be accepted, or would they instead be held accountable for whatever cruel acts they might have committed in the past? Carin had lost the father of her child; would she be shown compassion because of that, or feared because of what her child might be when it was born? Would Sarojin find a place for himself? Would Nuy be welcomed with gratitude for what she had done, or scorned because of what she was?

Leila got up, paced along the riverbank to loosen her muscles, then noticed that Kagami was awake and sitting up. She went to the healer and said softly, "Go back to sleep. We'll wake you when it's your turn to keep watch."

"I don't think I can go back to sleep," Kagami whispered. "Too much to think about."

Leila continued to scan the horizon. "I know."

"Ho killed two of our people," Kagami said in a low voice, "and I can guess what Zoheret will say when we're back, that we can't let that pass, that he and Owen and Daniella will have to be hunted down and punished. But I'm more worried about . . ." She paused. "Those three young ones. Nuy and the other two."

Leila squatted, still keeping watch. "I've been thinking about them, too."

"The embryo inside Carin is carrying the same strange genes as she and Nuy and Sarojin do, so it's clear that they aren't simply mutants who can't breed. I've also seen nothing to indicate that they wouldn't be able to interbreed with us."

Leila sighed. "You're talking about them as if they're—"

"As if they're something other than human," Kagami finished. "Ship was programmed to set us down on a world with no intelligent life, one that would become a new home for our species. Perhaps it didn't occur to Ship or its designers that we might eventually be transformed ourselves."

"What do you mean?"

"I'm only speculating," Kagami murmured. "I don't know enough yet even to make an informed guess about what may be happening, and I certainly don't know enough to form a hypothesis. But what I've been imagining for a while now is the possibility of some kind of microbial life—a kind of virus, if you like—that's capable of entering us and altering our DNA, a native symbiote that's adapting to us and in the process adapting the human genome to Home. We've seen no signs of anything like that in ourselves, but there's no reason to think the same traits I found in Nuy and those other two young people couldn't appear in our descendants if they leave the settlements, and maybe even if they stay there. We may only have delayed it a generation or two. Or it's possible that if we remain in the Earthlike environment we've created around our settlements, we can avoid such genetic changes." Kagami shook her head. "I'm not being all that coherent."

Leila was silent. The wind was blowing from the northeast, cooling her face. A strange glow had appeared on the eastern horizon, even though dawn was still three or four hours away. She was about to tell Kagami that they should wake Yukio to take his turn on watch when she heard a series of small but sharp squeaks.

Nuy suddenly sat up. The squeaks sounded again. Leila turned toward the other girl. "Do you hear that?" she asked.

Nuy nodded. "That's what woke me."

"What is it?"

"Rits." Nuy quickly got to her feet.

"Do they often make that sound?"

"They almost never make that sound," Nuy replied. "The last time I remember hearing them squeak like that was before the great storm." The glow to the east was swelling in size, and now Leila could see the tiny black forms of wild horses fleeing from the light. The squeaking sounds grew louder; the two horses whinnied and tugged at the ropes that bound them. A mass of small creatures with silvery fur burst from the grass and scurried toward the riverbank, then hurled themselves into the water.

The others were waking. Edan sat up. Zoheret was already on her feet. "What is it?" Zoheret asked.

"Fire," Nuy replied. The two horses neighed and pawed at the ground. Leila could already make out the flames. "It's spreading, and the wind is blowing it our way."

Several wolves ran out of the grass, halted for a moment, then threw themselves into the river. Another glow had appeared in the east. A big cat flew out from the grass bordering the bank, landed lightly on its feet, and fled south.

Something else was out on the plain, moving ahead of the flames. Leila narrowed her eyes; it looked like someone on horseback, someone carrying a burning torch. The fiery torch flew from the rider's hand and landed in the grass.

"My father!" Nuy called out. "He's setting the plain ablaze!"

Another patch of grass burst into flame. The glow behind the rider was turning into a fiery wall. Leila thought that she could hear the man laughing, but she had to be imagining that; he was too far away for her to have heard him.

"What'll we do?" Carin cried. She grabbed Nuy's arm. "What'll we do?" The distant horse reared up on its hind legs. The rider tumbled from its back and vanished into the grass. Carin screamed.

"Stop it," Nuy shouted, then pulled away and slapped the girl in the face. Carin stumbled back. The wall of fire was swelling rapidly, and now Leila could smell the smoke.

"Into the river," Nuy continued, "and let the current carry you south, and then we'll have to get to the other side and keep moving south."

"Can the river stop the fire from spreading?" Leila asked.

Nuy opened her arms. "I don't know."

Upriver, three deer leaped out from the grass onto the bank and into a patch of reeds. Trevor ran to the horses and freed them from their bonds; they would have to fend for themselves. The two horses neighed and trotted east, then opened up into a gallop as they turned south.

"Come on!" Gervais cried. Sarojin threw himself into the water, followed by Nuy and Yukio. Katti still sat on the bank; Leila heard what sounded like a whimper. Gerd reached down for her, pulled her up by one big arm, then picked her up and threw her into the water.

Leila plunged into the river and felt a current of colder water around her legs. She pushed into deeper water and felt the weight of her footwear and clothing pulling her down. Behind her, on the bank, Trevor and Zoheret were pulling off their boots; Leila saw that her mother was using only her right hand. Zoheret awkwardly stripped off her trousers, then leaped from the bank. Edan was already stripped to his tunic; he jumped into the river behind Carin.

Leila swam for shallower water, pulled at her own boots, and finally managed to get them off her feet. Downriver, blossoms of splashing water appeared around Yukio; his head disappeared under the black surface. She shed her pants, then swam after him.

Yukio bobbed up. Leila reached his side. "Get rid of your boots," she said. "Your pants, too." He flailed around with his arms. She looped an arm around him, trying to keep him afloat as he struggled with his boots.

"I'm all right," he gasped. "Got them off." He was pulling at the waistband of his trousers. She let him go and swam toward the center of the river, then looked back. Yukio's arms were straight as he swam, hitting the water like windmills, but at least he was staying afloat. Other heads bobbed behind his, their faces pale in the light of the fire. The wall of fire was closer now, the smoke growing thick enough to make her choke. Leila coughed to clear her lungs, kicked her legs, and swam with the current downriver.

The current embraced her, bearing her swiftly down the black waters of the river. Nuy kept herself afloat, moving her legs and arms as little as possible, conserving her strength. Sarojin was ahead of her, keeping to the center of the river.

Her father was dead. Nuy tried to summon some grief for Ho, but could not. He had made his own death; she had seen him fall from the horse he was riding into the flames. She suspected that Owen and Daniella had most likely been consumed by the fire earlier, perhaps after helping Ho to start the fire and set the grass ablaze. They had always been loyal to Ho, and if they had objected, he would have gone ahead and set the fires anyway and made certain that neither of them could stop him. It was clear that all three had planned to desert the rest of their band if they were attacked. Ho might even have realized that Nuy had returned to him only to betray him.

It came to her then that, by going to his camp, she had set her father on a path he might otherwise not have taken. He might have set these fires to punish the daughter who had turned against him. She had hoped to find some kindness and rationality alive inside him. His inner fires had long since burned all of that away.

She looked back. A glimpse of the number of heads bobbing above the water told her that everyone was in the river. The boltrees under which they had been resting were burning now, their twisting black branches covered by blossoms of fire; even at this distance, she could hear their gourds popping. Something howled far overhead, perhaps a rising wind. A burning branch flew out from one of the boltrees and fell into the river.

Nuy propelled herself forward, kicking hard with her feet. The current kept threatening to pull her under. The water seemed to be growing warmer. She willed herself to keep swimming, riding the current.

The water swept over her, pulling her down. She swam on through the darkness, listening to the oddly soothing sound of water flowing past her, then broke the surface again.

She turned on her back and floated for a moment. The wall of fire pursued them along the eastern bank. The flames seemed to be reaching for her, demanding to be fed. She noticed a small patch of light to her left. The light flared into a ball of flame and she realized with dismay that the fire had jumped the river.

The wind shrieked overhead. Nuy dived below the surface, feeling safer in the darkness, where she could not hear the crying wind or smell the burning grass. Ho would have burned all of Home if he could. She wondered just how great the fire could become and how much it would devour.

Leila ached with pain; her calves were cramping. She felt as though she had swallowed most of the river, yet her arms and legs went on pumping and kicking, keeping her head above water as the current propelled her downstream. Fire burned on either side of her, lighting up the river; dark clouds of smoke roiled overhead.

She fought for breath, certain that the water was growing warmer. She wondered how long such a fire could burn, how much oxygen it would use up to feed itself, whether the river that she hoped would save them could also boil them alive.

Her strength was nearly gone. She floated for a while, curling her toes to ease the cramps in her legs, paddling with her arms just enough to keep her head above water and allowing the current to carry her. Strands of burning grass blew past her and hit the water with a sharp hiss.

Leila closed her eyes and drifted downriver, then felt an arm slip around her. Someone was trying to hold her up. She opened her eyes and looked into Nuy's face.

"Leila." The flames made patterns of yellow and white light on Nuy's forehead. "We have to keep going."

It's no use, she wanted to reply, but there wasn't enough breath left in her to say the words. It would be easier to sink into the cooler dark waters below her, to find rest on the muddy bottom of the river.

"Leila!" Nuy still held her up. "Come on!"

"I can't."

Leila felt herself being turned onto her back, and then Nuy's arm was around her again, cupping her under the chin. Above her, dark smoke was streaming to the north. For a moment, she saw a bit of pale green sky before the black smoke veiled it once more.

"Don't you see?" Nuy said. "Can't you feel it? The wind's shifting." Leila tried to shake her head, but Nuy's arm restrained her. "It's blowing from the south now, it's shifted. It's not pushing the fire toward us now, it's pushing it away."

Leila felt her strength returning, and wondered that she had any strength left. She reached up and removed Nuy's arm from herself, then let her legs drift downward. "It's all right," she said, treading water. "I can make it." She still could not feel the wind, but above her, more of the green morning sky had appeared in the south.

The storm swept in from the south, a storm with heavy rain and enough of a wind to halt the fire and herd the flames back toward the north. Nuy pushed through reeds and climbed onto the western bank as the storm broke over her. A fork of lightning flashed above the dying fires to the north. Nuy flattened herself against the ground, hoping that no lightning struck near her. Others were stumbling out of the water to lie along the bank, curling up and making themselves as small as possible as needles of rain pelted them.

Thunder rumbled above, growing more muted as the wind shifted again. The rain fell more slowly, then became a soft and gentle shower. Nuy drifted into a light sleep, dreaming of the shelter of a cave as the thunder died.

She woke to the clear green sky of late afternoon and the pain of strained muscles in her neck and legs. She sat up and rubbed at her sore shoulders. Zoheret was lying next to Leila, her eyes closed, while Leila slowly sat up. Farther up the bank, Edan was stretched out next to Carin.

Yukio was on his feet, one hand cupped above his eyes, his back to her as he looked northeast. Far to the north, two sinuous plumes of smoke rose toward the sky, all that seemed to be left of the conflagration. A wide ribbon of what looked like black ashes ran north along the western bank. The plain that stretched to the northeast was a barren black wasteland.

Others were stirring, sitting up and stretching their arms. Trevor gasped as he looked across the river at the desolate plain. No one spoke. Ho, Nuy thought, would have rejoiced to see the lifeless land he had made.

Zoheret woke and lifted her head, then propped herself up on one elbow. "What now?" Leila asked.

Zoheret sighed. "We have no food," she replied. She sat up slowly, then waved an arm at the thin cloth coverings on her feet. Nuy saw again how the woman's thicker left arm hung lifelessly from her shoulder. "We've got our socks but no boots. The nearest camp is days away, and that's assuming that we can actually make it there with no footgear and no supplies and that the people there aren't already heading back to the settlements."

"They wouldn't come to look for you?" Sarojin asked. "They'd just abandon you?"

"That was what they were supposed to be doing by now," Zoheret said, "going back to the camps we made farther upriver and then on to our settlement. Under the circumstances, it would have been the most practical course of action, so as not to risk even more lives."

"My father won't threaten them anymore," Nuy said. "They don't have to worry about him now."

Gervais stood up. "They don't know that," he said, "and they've also got two people in a weakened physical condition to care for and take home."

Nuy studied the people around her. Defeat was in their faces, a look as empty as the land around them.

"Zoheret! Kagami!" Edan was calling to them. "It's Carin—something's wrong."

The two women stood up and hurried to him. Nuy followed them and then saw the blood on the inside of Carin's thighs.

Kagami knelt next to her. "She's miscarrying." She slipped an arm around Carin. "It's all right, I'm here."

"Can you do anything for her?" Edan asked.

"I can't stop this, I have none of my tools now." Kagami stripped off Carin's loincloth. "Leave me with her. I'll do what I can. There's nothing any of you can do to help."

Nuy led the others away. Carin was being brave about it, not screaming, not making a sound. Perhaps she should mourn the child who would be lost, another one like them.

Zoheret sat down and everyone else settled around her. She said, "We have to decide what to do."

"Bonnie and Tonio survived," Leila said, "thanks to Nuy. Maybe we could stay in this region until—"

Nuy said, "We must go north."

"We have no boots," Trevor said. "We wouldn't get very far."

"We can walk on softer ground, in the mud along the river,"

Nuy said. "We'll have water, and when we get to a place untouched by the fire, we should find game. By heading north, you'll be following the trail of your people, and the closer you get to them, the better your chances will be."

"Our chances won't be that good in any case," Edan muttered.

"Go north," Nuy said, "or head south and live in the caves you found there, but I can tell you that it wouldn't be easy for you. Bonnie and Tonio had some food left, and their foot coverings, and enough to keep us alive until I could find more food for them, and if we hadn't found you when we did, I don't think they would have lasted too much longer."

"The caves are a lot closer," Zoheret said. "We could get to them more easily."

"Yes," Nuy said, "and then you would have to hope that we would always have good hunting and could find more food, because the fish we could find there wouldn't be enough to feed you. You would have to hope that you have no accidents, that no one is seriously injured, that no illness troubles you and that another great storm doesn't come. I've had more than my share of good fortune already. I wonder if we can count on that much luck."

"I suppose you'd decide to head north no matter what the rest of us wanted," Edan said. "That would mean less of a chance for us, of course, without you to help us."

Nuy shook her head. "I won't abandon you, whatever you decide."

Edan leaned forward. "A long journey might kill Carin."

Nuy held out a hand to him. Edan shrank back. "We can find a way to carry her," she replied.

"Nuy is right," Trevor said. "We have to try to get home."

Zoheret nodded.

No one was objecting. Nuy knew then that they were all ready to endure the long journey.

*L*eila and the others gathered enough of the thick reeds along the riverbank to make a litter for Carin, tying it together with strips torn from the edges of tunics. Carin's pregnancy was no more than three months along, Kagami had said, and maybe that accounted for the calm way in which the girl had taken her loss.

Or maybe, Leila thought, Carin was thinking that if she survived this journey, she would be more easily able to start a new life with that last bond to her old life severed. Edan had hovered over her while Kagami tended her, and now the front poles of Carin's litter rested on his broad shoulders. Gerd was behind him, holding up the back of the litter.

They had started out at dawn, after one night of rest, moving north along the western bank of the river. The desolation of the burned-out plain to the east reminded Leila of what her uncle Yusef had said before they had set out on their expedition. Perhaps he would not have been surprised by the sight of the plain. He had believed that they were doomed to fail, sooner or later; setting fire to the grasslands might only hasten what he saw as an inevitable outcome.

Their pace was slowed by their lack of any footwear. Nuy's thickly calloused feet might find their path easy going, but Leila had to tread carefully, afraid of twisting an ankle or knee if the softer and muddier ground near the river gave way. Walking on the harder and rockier ground farther up the bank inflamed her heels and tendons too much for her to keep up her pace there for long. During the day, they seemed to spend as much time resting and bathing their damaged feet in the river as they did on the move.

On the third day, Nuy abruptly halted, gazed across the

river for a bit, then dived into the water and swam across, returning with the small burned carcass of a bird. There was
enough for each of them to have three or four small bites of
meat. Leila devoured her share and sucked the marrow from
the small bones, relishing every bite.

On the fourth night of the journey, Leila and Trevor kept
watch together during the last part of the night. They might
not have to fear human enemies now, but they still had to look
out for any dangerous animals, although it seemed that all of
Home's creatures, even the rits, had abandoned the scorched
plain. The wind had changed again during the night, blowing
from the north, and Leila felt a chill in the air, a reminder that
colder weather would be returning to the region around their
settlements.

The sky was growing lighter in the east when Trevor said in
a low voice, "I have to ask you something."

She was sitting with her back to him. Leila turned for a moment, but he was looking away from her. "Go ahead," she replied.

"What do you think our chances are?"

"Not very good."

"I'd call that an understatement. We don't have any chance,
not really. Look how long it's taken us to get this far. And
everybody in the nearest camp would have seen some sign of
the fire, would have known how big it had to be. They'll tell
themselves that we couldn't have escaped it and that they were
supposed to start back for the settlements and that it would be
stupid to wait there for us. At least one of them will guess that
Ho's band might have deliberately set the fire and that they'd
be risking more lives if Ho tried the same tactic on them. So
even if we get that far, we won't find anybody there, or at the
camp after that, because they'll all be heading back. And we
won't catch up with them." Trevor's voice sounded oddly calm
as he spoke, as if he were at peace with having no hope.

"Are you sorry about it?" she asked. "I mean, are you sorry we did what we did, coming here?"

"I don't know. That'd be a lot easier to answer if I were home now, lying in my room knowing that everything turned out all right. Or to put it another way, it'd be much easier to believe it was all for nothing if we hadn't found Bonnie and Tonio."

"And Nuy."

Trevor cleared his throat. "And Nuy. But I think you're as brave as she is in your own way."

"No, I'm not." She was afraid now, afraid of dying and of losing all that was left of her life. She was beginning to feel what the darkness inside Yusef must be like.

"And then I remember that Hannah and Haidar are dead, and I don't know what to think. Zoheret—"

He seemed about to ask her something else. She waited.

"I'll say this." His voice was lower and harsher. "Better for us to keep going than to give up and just wait for the end."

"Then you actually think there is still a chance."

"Most of the time I'm too tired to think about whether there is or not. That's why it's better to keep going, it keeps me too tired to think and reason clearly about our actual chances. Right now, reason isn't really our friend. It says lie down and quietly die."

To her surprise, Leila felt herself smiling at that. Reason was not brave enough.

By the sixth day, Kagami and Katti were using two thick reeds as walking sticks. Leila could see the look of pain on Kagami's face, but she had insisted that she was able to walk as long as she could ease the pressure on her strained right ankle. If Katti were suffering, she showed no sign of it. She had said nothing during the journey, and wore her usual placid expression, as if the sight of the burned plain brought her peace.

Patches of yellow could now be seen on the burned plain.

Far to the north, waves of green and yellow grass lapped at the edges of the blackened land.

On the seventh day, in late morning, Leila spotted the distant finger of the cliff where they had set up their last camp. At the rate they were going, they would not reach the bank opposite that site before tomorrow.

"Stop," Kagami said, "I have to rest." Leila turned around, worried about the tightness in Kagami's voice; she would not be asking to rest now unless she was in great pain.

Gerd and Edan set down the litter that held Carin. The girl stood up slowly, her legs shaking slightly. Nuy watched Carin with narrowed eyes. There were hollows in Carin's face, and her legs were little more than sticks; she looked even weaker than she had right after losing her child.

"I'm able to walk now," Carin said, holding out a hand to Kagami. "You can use the litter."

"Are you sure?" Kagami asked.

"So maybe I'll start bleeding again. I can stand it. You need this litter more than I do."

Kagami limped over to the litter in silence, offered her reed to Carin, and stretched out. Her face was sallow and pale. Leila swallowed hard as Gerd and Edan lifted the litter to their shoulders.

They stopped at dusk to rest. Leila lay with a hand over the hollow between her hips and thought of all the foods she had eaten only reluctantly in her settlement, the carrot and leek soup that had not appealed to her as much as potatoes and leeks, the shreds of chicken that she had happily given to Scrapper because there would be a much more delicious piece of pork for supper, the goat cheese and bread that she had grown tired of eating for her midday meal. She would have relished the raw meat of a rit by now, if any rits could be bothered to return to the river and the blackened plain around it.

Leila slept that night amid dreams of roasted chicken and bean soup and cups of milk and fruit juice, and awoke again to the shock of the cool morning air and the hollowed out feeling inside her. She tried to sit up and felt shooting pains in her hips and knees and wondered if this would be the morning when she would finally admit that she could not go on, that all her strength was gone, when she would lie down and never get up again.

She forced herself to sit up. Her socks had been walked into shreds. She tore them from her feet.

"Don't." That was Zoheret's voice. Leila leaned against her mother, feeling the bones under Zoheret's tunic.

"I can't," Leila said.

"Yes, you can."

Yukio was struggling to stand up. Edan stood up and pulled Yukio to his feet. "Look there," Yukio said, pointing north.

"What is it?" Zoheret asked.

Yukio lifted an arm and pointed. "People, on horseback."

Leila felt Zoheret stiffen against her. She managed to get to her knees, hanging on to Zoheret's right shoulder.

In the northeast, on the other side of the river, three indistinct dark shapes were moving south, partly obscured by dark clouds of dust. A vise tightened around Leila's throat. Ho and his comrades had survived the fire and were coming after them.

"It's Sofia," Yukio called out, "and Shannon, and Tala. They're coming for us."

Leila sagged against her mother. Zoheret gently lowered her to the ground. "They didn't obey me," Zoheret was saying, "they didn't do what I told them to do. Good for them." She collapsed next to Leila. "Good for them." Leila grabbed her mother's right hand and gripped it tightly.

Part Four

Nuy and Yusef were out on the lake again, in one of the boats, Yusef at the oars, Nuy seated in the stern. Yusef had been going down to the lake often that spring, every time he had a free moment, to work on the boats, and Nuy was always one of those who went there to help him. Now all of the rowboats had rudders as well as oars, and Yusef was working on designs for a sailboat.

Leila knew that they would need more boats to ferry supplies south to the first of their bases. Trevor was at that base now, where the long river branched off from the lake, along with Sofia, Shannon, Yukio, and Sarojin, setting up more tents and scouting out sites for a dock. By summer, at least two more bases to the south of the first would be established, and by next year, at least a couple of the tents at the first camp would be replaced by more permanent dwellings.

She sat down at the base of the hill. It had taken five public meetings and several smaller gatherings to convince the boards to offer enough resources to establish those camps. Some of the settlers would never be at peace with that decision. Some would choose to stay here, hanging on to everything they had brought to this world, preserving it for their descendents. Even if they succeeded in retaining what Aleksandr now referred to as their "true humanity," that might only mean that they would become a divergent strain of humanity, an older strain growing, with each generation, ever more alien to Home and to the descendants of those who had left the settlements. That division between the settlements and those outside, even if it did not result in violence, might become unbridgeable in time.

Ship had sent them here to live as human beings in an Earthlike environment, Aleksandr had declared at one of the meetings, and he was not about to abandon Ship's mission. He would do what he could to ensure that any descendants of his would be able to greet Ship, if Ship ever returned, as truly human people. In the cause of true humanity and the preservation of the human genome, Aleksandr had even turned his back on his son Edan.

The grass of the pastureland was thicker and greener than usual for late spring. To the southeast, a few horses grazed, watched over by Katti, Gerd, and three settlers on horseback. Strange, Leila thought, that she had ever worried over how those two survivors of Ho's band would get along here. Katti and Gerd now shared a room in Edan's dome and ate with everyone else at the halls. They did as they were told when there was work to be done and kept to themselves the rest of the time. If they weren't entirely accepted by some, they were tolerated by almost everybody. There was nothing left inside the placid Gerd and the silent, withdrawn Katti to hate.

It was time that she left this place, Leila told herself, and joined Trevor and the others. She missed Trevor much more than she had anticipated, and recalled the look of disappointment on his face when she had told him that she could not go south with him, not yet. She would not leave without Nuy, although she had not said so outright to Trevor, but Nuy showed no sign of wanting to go.

Zoheret had insisted that Nuy live in their dome, and Nuy still shared a room with Leila and Rosa. During the cold season, she had spent most of her time at the library, learning what she could from Lillka. Nuy could read some records now, and had mastered most of the lessons taught to the youngest children. Leila admired her for her persistence, which seemed nearly the equal of her courage, yet she still did not really know Nuy in the way that she knew her parents, her sister, or her closest comrades.

Nuy never spoke of her father, her earlier life, or of anything that had happened before she had come here, as if she were as oblivious of the past as Katti and Gerd. There were times when Nuy retreated into herself and became as silent and distant as Katti, although such moods never lasted for more than a day or two. Somehow Leila had known that those were not times to prod Nuy or to ask her what was troubling her. Nuy, with her senses as sharp as they were, would be only too aware of the hostility of some of the settlers. She would know that there were those who fervently believed that she had no place here, and yet she refused to go south, where she would have been welcomed.

"Leila!"

She looked up to see Edan and Carin descending the hill. "We were waiting for you," Edan continued; he had a small pack strapped to his back. "Finally decided to look for you. What happened?"

Leila remembered then that she had promised to meet them at their dome after her shift in one of the kitchens. She shook her head. "I forgot. Sorry about that." She was not lying, but felt as though admitting only to forgetfulness was in fact a lie. She was well past the hurt and dismay she had felt, and then quickly concealed, when the two had announced some months back that they wanted to make a pledge to each other, but it was still easier for her to avoid their dwelling. Carin and Edan had been sharing a dome in the eastern settlement for two months now, and Leila had not yet visited them there.

It was time that she put such feelings aside. Edan might have begun by pitying Carin, but his feelings for her had grown; Leila had seen that even before he had mentioned wanting her as a mate. "Carin understands me," he had told her once. "I never have to apologize to her, or make excuses, it's almost as if she knows what I'm thinking or feeling before I do."

She adjusted the straps of her own pack. Edan had agreed to come with her to help Nuy and Yusef patch and sand and refinish two of the boats, and had talked Carin into coming with them. They would stay by the lake for a couple of days, pitching their tents and rewarding themselves for their labors with some of the new wine Luis had made from greenhouse grapes. Edan had saved a bottle from the party Zoheret and Manuel had given to mark his pledge to Carin, since his own parents had not offered the two such a celebration. In the end, his mother Maire had come to the party, but Aleksandr had stayed away.

He might never speak to his son again. Leila promised herself to visit Edan and Carin in their dome as soon as they returned.

"We'd better get going," Edan said, "if we're going to get there before dusk." Carin looked up at him and smiled. Short as she was, she looked rounder under her tunic and pants; she had cut off her long braid and now wore her dark brown hair in short curls. Leila felt a small pang of envy and regret, but only a slight pang this time.

Edan seemed happy with Carin, even with all that he had given up for her. He would have been with Trevor and the others if not for Carin. "She needs me here," Edan had explained to Trevor and Leila not long after his and Carin's ceremony. "She needs more rest, she's still recovering from all that happened. We'll join you eventually, it'll just take some time." Looking out for Katti and Gerd was one of Carin's excuses, and another was her bond with Nuy. She could not leave Nuy alone among those who were suspicious or fearful of them both, and in the meantime, she would try to show that such suspicions were unfounded. Carin might not be as diligent a student as Nuy; she avoided the library, and Leila was certain that she was incapable even of spelling or reading her own name. But she did her share of work in the kitchens and with the animals, and if she resented the way some talked about her, she gave no sign of it.

The three walked toward the lake in silence. At last Edan said, "I thought you'd be at the base by now, with the others."

"Zoheret wanted to discuss some plans with me before I left," Leila said. That was partly true. Zoheret might have tried to take up her old position as leader of her settlement, but instead had asked to be appointed as the member of the council in charge of plans for the encampments. She would never be leader again; Aleksandr, who had finally given in and allowed those plans to proceed, would see to that. "And she still needs me around to help her." Zoheret had lost enough mobility in her left arm to make certain tasks harder for her, but Rosa was old enough to help with most of the work, and Zoheret would have been very annoyed at anyone's thinking that she had more than a minor disability.

Carin's eyes widened slightly; she looked as if she did not believe Leila's excuse, as if she knew that Nuy was keeping them both here. Nuy held them all, she and Carin and Edan, and Nuy did not want to leave because of Yusef.

After she had come to the settlements, it had seemed natural for Nuy to spend time with Yusef, as she had with several of the adults. Nuy had made it clear that she wanted to learn everything she could from the most skilled people among them. Lillka and Luis had become mentors to her, but others had shied away from her, and by midwinter, Nuy had been spending more time with Yusef than with almost anyone else.

No one in Leila's household had thought anything of that. Yusef had been coming to Zoheret's dome more often, to share a meal or to talk, and all of them had grown closer to a man who clearly needed to be around people who might ease his unhappiness. By then, it was common knowledge that his mate Gisela was living in their son's dome, and that the severing of their bond was probably permanent.

But some of the talk about Nuy and Yusef had turned uglier that spring. Leila knew that only because she had overheard Rina and another woman gossiping in the library a month ago, in voices loud enough to be heard from outside the doorway.

Yusef had turned to Nuy even before Gisela had walked out on him, so the creature had obviously precipitated the break. Nuy had lured him on. She wasn't like the rest of them, she and the other two young ones from Ho's band; better if they had never been brought here, if they had vanished along with Ho and all the others.

The two had fallen silent as soon as Leila entered the library.

They would not have dared to say such things to her face. They certainly wouldn't have spewed such poison in front of

Zoheret. Leila wondered what other kinds of stories were going around.

She knew that such stories could not be true, if for no other reason than Yusef and Nuy were rarely alone or out of sight of others. Yusef was still too hurt and bewildered by the failure of his bond with Gisela to turn to someone else, and he would hardly have taken advantage of a girl still new to the settlements and adapting to their ways. Most of the settlers had to know that, or at least be unwilling to speculate about what might be going on between Nuy and Yusef, but a few thoughtless words from a few careless people might be enough to raise doubts in other minds, especially those who already resented Nuy for what she was.

Leila knew that she should leave this place, even if Nuy remained here. Maybe that was all that would calm the fears of the settlers, seeing all of those who were willing to embrace this world abandon the settlements for the encampments. Some people would go on here as they had, but eventually their children might grow curious about what lay beyond these hills.

But she could not go, not yet. Nuy had saved her and others from much worse than evil words. The least she could do now was be Nuy's protector here.

Yusef was silent as he rowed the boat toward shore. Nuy sat in the stern, wishing that she could pull the oars as strongly and with as even a stroke as he did. Yusef had said little to her while they were out on the water, but she was used to his long silences. It had taken her this long to understand what had drawn her to him, why she feared losing him more than almost anyone else she knew.

The darkness inside him, the despair and the anger that he

had sometimes shown to her, that she could sense even when he was silent and impassive, had reminded her of the storms inside her father. She had found herself mourning for Ho much more in Yusef's presence than she ever had during the long journey north to the settlements. Yusef might be as tormented as her father had been, and yet there was still kindness in him, and gentleness, and a need to do whatever he could do to be of use to his people even when he believed that their lives had no purpose. Hearing what had become of most of Nuy's people and seeing how some had reacted to her presence had only confirmed Yusef in his bleak vision, but he was teaching her what he knew, and designing a boat to carry people and supplies to their first camp.

In Yusef, she saw the kind of father she might have had if Ho could have found a way to see past the fires inside him. She had grown able to read his thoughts and feelings in his simplest gestures, the way he held himself, by the expression in his dark eyes; she had learned what words or actions might lessen his despair for a little while. She might have done the same for her father, whose burnt body, never found, haunted her sleep.

The cloth of her pale brown tunic was making her shoulders itch. Nuy scratched herself, then tugged at her long sleeves. She had grown more used to wearing tunics and pants, but had given up her shoes almost two months ago, as soon as it was warm enough to go barefoot outside without treading on droplets of ice. She would shed her trousers, too, if the weather grew much warmer; all that had kept her from doing so already was knowing that she would feel even more disapproval and enmity from those who were wary of her. Sometimes she could almost feel that they were stealing the air around her, drawing most of it into their own lungs before she had a chance to take a breath. She suddenly wanted to see the plains where she had once wandered, to sit among the reeds along the riverbank, to rest in one of the caves near the sea and sniff at the salty air and listen to the waves.

"Leila should be here soon," Nuy said.

Yusef grunted.

"She'll want to know if I'll go south with her. She'll be asking me that question even if she doesn't say a word."

"Then go."

She would have to go, whether he came with her or not. She had sensed Leila's longing to leave, and Carin might soon be with child, a child that was likely to be like one of them if the healer woman Kagami was correct in her assumptions. Nuy had made a story for herself, pieced together from bits of what Kagami had told her and what she had found out for herself in the library. Strands of Home, pieces of its spirit, had entered the bodies of those who had come here so that they could more easily live in their new world and see it clearly in all its beauty and terror. In time, those who were once strangers to Home would be as much a part of this world as the cells of Nuy's body were part of her.

Nuy sighed, longing for the sea. The only reason Leila and Carin stayed here was because of Nuy; they didn't have to say so for her to feel it.

"I can't go and leave you here." Nuy took a breath, knowing what she would have to say to Yusef. "I want you to come with us."

He stopped rowing. "I can't leave. I have plans to draw up here."

"You can bring a screen and work on your designs there."

"I have other work to do."

"And others can do that work for a bit. Or do you think that you're so needed, so valuable and so special that no one else can take your place here even for a little while?"

He leaned back, still gripping the oars, his face tense with pride. "There are other reasons for me to stay here, but you should go. I know that's what you want to do. There's no sense in your having to put up with people who treat you—"

"I'm not like them, so I can understand why they feel the way they do. They're afraid, that's most of what it is. And now you're thinking that if I go, and leave you here, then people will finally stop talking about us."

Yusef sat up. His bearded face was pale. "You know about that, all that ugly talk?"

Nuy shrugged. "How could I not know? Your own son is a healer, you know what he and Kagami found in me and in Carin and Sarojin. I can hear beyond your range, so picking up a few whispers isn't that hard. When I first heard a woman talking about us, I thought of confronting her and telling her the truth, but then it came to me that anyone who would say such things without knowing what was true wouldn't listen to the truth anyway, and might even see the truth as a lie. So I said nothing."

"You might have told me that you knew."

"What good would that have done?" she asked. "You would only have thought of avoiding me after that, to keep them from talking, and I still have so much to learn from you."

Yusef smiled. She warmed to his smile, maybe because he so rarely showed happiness. "You're probably right about that."

"Come with me and Leila," she said.

"That might only make people gossip even more."

"We'll be too far away even for me to overhear it."

His smile faded. "It won't matter in the long run, whether we stay here or leave."

Nuy nodded. "You've said that often enough. There's no purpose to what we do, this isn't our world, and we'll never truly be a part of Home. If you believe that, you may as well come with me, because it won't matter anyway, and at least I won't have to listen to all that ugly talk."

Yusef shook his head and resumed rowing. "You send my own words against me like a warrior!"

Nuy said, "My place is with those people making that camp in the south. And after that we'll have another camp, and another, and settlements up and down the river, and there will be some like me and others like your people, living together. Maybe then you'll see that Home can embrace us after all."

"I won't live long enough to see it."

"You will see the beginnings. Come with us, Yusef."

"Will you go if I don't come with you?"

"No."

"Then you've forced me into it. I'll have to go with you, or know that you're giving up what you want because of me, and I really couldn't endure that." He smiled again, and she answered him with a victorious smile of her own.

They would go south. She would lead Yusef to where her people had lived, when the grass had returned to the plains her father had burned, and find ways to live closer to Home without being swept away by the storms that had struck down her father. She contented herself with that hope and with this father beside her.

Epilogue

*M*y doubts are always with me.

Ahead lay a cold and gaseous world of methane and ammonia and bright colorful bands. Ship fell into orbit around it, trailing the small icy mass of a satellite. There were no homes for humankind in this system.

Search.

"Ship," said Zoheret's voice. "You promised to return." Her face rode the darkness, her cheeks hollower, the skin around her eyes and lips thin-lined, not as Ship remembered her, but as she might look after many years had passed.

"I have my mission," Ship said.

"Yes," Zoheret said, "but there are many ways to carry it out. You have to change, or else make more mistakes." Those were not Zoheret's words, but Ship's own thoughts in her voice.

"I have told myself that," it said, "and yet the promise I made to you works to overwhelm my task."

"To help seed other worlds," Zoheret continued, "go back and find out what's happened on the one you've already seeded."

"But it may delay my mission."

"You promised to return."

"You must learn not to depend on me," Ship said.

"And by now we've succeeded in making a life for ourselves, or we haven't, and nothing you can do will change that."

"Yes. Despite my doubts, I didn't turn back, and now I know that too much time has passed for me ever to speak to you again."

Zoheret faded. Ship fell through the darkness, sensing loss. Altering its mission had occurred to Ship before; it had even considered sheltering a permanent human community inside itself. Would returning to see what its children had built change its mission or suggest new ways of completing it?

Ship whipped around the planet. Decision came as Ship's engines threw it free of the giant.